I0674624

The Believers

In the Crucible Nauvoo

Written by Alfred Woollacott III

My Four Legged Stool

First Myfourleggedstool Publishers Edition, September 2017

P O Box 2911 Oak Bluffs, Massachusetts 02557

Copyright 2017 © Alfred Woollacott III

All rights reserved, including the rights to reproduce this book or portions thereof in any form whatsoever.

For information address Myfourleggedstool Publishers

P O Box 2911 Oak Bluffs, Massachusetts 02557

Attn: Alfred Woollacott, III

This book is fiction, riveted to historical times and the lives of some believers. Any references to historical events, real people, or real locales are used fictitiously. Other names, characters, places, and incidents may have occurred and how they are presented are products of the author's imagination, and any resemblance to actual events or locales or persons, living or dead, is entirely coincidental.

Cover design by jennyq@historicaleditorial.com

ISBN: 978-0-9904423-5-6

Acknowledgements

The challenges presented in writing *The Believers* would have been insurmountable if not for my childhood upbringing. As a pre-teen, I often attended gatherings at my grandparents' Woollacott where I would inevitably tease my cousin. When the commotion grew too much, Grandmother would sit me in her breakfast nook and ask probing questions. More than once she said, "We have six generations of Methodist ministers in our family," and with only a pause she would add, "and have you thought what you might want to do when you grow up?"

My parents, even after partying late on Saturday night, would arouse us and take us to Sunday school. I had twelve years of it (with summers off) at Christ Episcopal Church in Fitchburg, Massachusetts; perfect attendance in the eleventh grade. Church-going in general has waned since the fifties and early sixties, and I am no exception. Yet when I do attend, I am reminded of what I heard, felt, and sang in my youth, and of course, those who were seated near me at the time. Without those who are now in a better place instilling within me an early Christian foundation, this endeavor would have been impossible.

My research is considerable as shown in the Appendix. The Monadnock Center for History and Culture, the on-line resources at FamilySearch.org, and in particular, the resources available from the George Washington Taggart Family Organization were invaluable.

Carol Cornwall Madsen's "In Their Own Words – Women and the Story of Nauvoo" gave me insight on these remarkable women, like Naamah, like Aunt Susan, and what they endured.

But reading is one dimensional, so I visited Nauvoo to allow my other senses to experience what Naamah and the Taggarts bore witness to. The Temple on a promontory captured me immediately and was always visible while I was there. And the Mississippi, as it did to Easterners like Naamah and the Taggarts, told me I was in a different place. Walking among the current day faithful, many families, and many from the West, I felt like an outsider, a researcher observing and not as immersed as they seemed to be. The re-enactors dressed in period clothing, Joseph Smith, Emma, and others, gave life to what I had read. The missionaries in Lands and Records helped me to pinpoint where my ancestors lived and where some were buried.

I journeyed to Carthage via automobile while trying to imagine Joseph's last horseback ride in June 1844. There, a woman on mission, perhaps twenty years old, led our small group through the two story jail. At each stop she struggled, tearing at times, as she described the events of 27 June 1844. The room where Joseph and Hyrum were last alive was dim, cooler than the outside, and eerie. As the missionary spoke, some snuffed back their tears, and as I glanced around, many eyes had become welled. As we left, I said to the missionary, "You must be exhausted by the end of day." She nodded "yes" and added that her strength came from having the Prophet so near to her. My visit confirmed what I knew – Joseph Smith continues to have a profound effect on many in this modern day.

As in my first book, *The Immigrant*, Rick Herrick did an early read, offering insightful comments as always. A less than glowing Kirkus Review told me I was not done, and significant rewrites ensued. A final read from Merle Lincoln, a Vineyarder and erstwhile editor, shaped the manuscript further. Jennifer Quinlan, "Jenny Q", turned my vague cover concept into an eye-catching image consistent with the book's theme. Alex Beam, an accomplished journalist and author of *American Crucifixion*, offered marketing suggestions and provided other referrals. Helen Schatvet Ullmann, who tutored me in my earlier genealogical writing, gave me an inscribed "Book of Mormon" that deepened my understanding. I thank the readers of *The Immigrant* who asked, "Is the second book ready yet?" Your questions and kind remarks about *The Immigrant* spurred me and encouraged me out of my occasional doldrums.

Last yet most important, to my wife of forty-four years who still wonders how someone retired seems busier than ever, I deeply appreciate your loving patience.

Another from My Four Legged Stool

My first book, *The Immigrant – One from My Four Legged Stool*, posited the following:

"We have unique four legged stools, each leg extending from our grandparents who contributed to our being. At conception, our biology stems from our forebears, the history that preceded us. Our environment, first from within the womb then without, people, and events often beyond our control, further shape us. If history repeats, did our forebears experience what we are experiencing? If so, will we react as they did? And if our biological bonds forget, will random energy pulses trigger a memory cord?"

John Law, *The Immigrant's* protagonist, is part of my stool leg stemming down through my maternal grandmother. Naamah Kendall Jenkins (Carter) (Twiss) Young, my great, great, grand aunt, and the Taggart family, my three-greats aunt and uncle and first cousins a few generations removed, descend from him, too. John, a pioneer thrust into a foreign land involuntarily, persevered against religious intolerance, hostile forces, and bigotry, fortified by belief in a supreme being. Naamah and the Taggarts encountered challenges akin to John Law. Did their faith and drops of John's Scottish blood helped them to persevere?

 *My Four Legged Stool*

The Believers contains historical characters and actual events, some widely known, and has been meticulously researched, even though it is fiction. If you desire just the facts, an Appendix has been provided. But to bring the facts to life, continue reading.

Chapter One

12 August 1827

Jarmany Hill Cemetery, Sharon, New Hampshire

Reuben Law's hike up the steep rise had tired his aged body, but he had a purpose. He rested beneath overhanging birch limbs, enjoying the shade, while surveying the ill-maintained cemetery. His coarsely woven wool suit and vest clung to his body, and the blue cravat wrapped around a dampened, extended white collar was knotted askew. Unsuitable clothing for August, but worn every Sunday morning, regardless.

He sighed and moved from the shadows through the stone wall's opening. He stepped carefully among the gravestones to avoid the ground where his friends had been laid to rest. Sunshine cooked his suit, and he removed a handkerchief to wipe his brow. A stone at the cemetery's far western edge occupied his attention. He dawdled, still unready to move toward it. He refolded his handkerchief and tried several times to slide it into his vest pocket before crumpling it and cramming it in.

Ahead, a lichen sprinkled stone intrigued Reuben. He thought as he gimped toward it. *How long has it been?* He scratched the moss to reveal two sevens and stepped back to read the inscription:

"SPAFFORD Mary, wife of Abijah d. Sep. 9, 1802, in her 67 yr. Abijah d. Oct. 19, 1811 in his 77 yr."

"Goodness, ole Abijah has been dead sixteen years." He shook his head. "And he was my age when he died." His eyes darted between the two death dates. *Nine years without his Mary.* He snorted and thought, *Abijah was dead, too, but didn't know it.*

He shuffled west and paused at the thick stone with spiked florets and wheat heads carved into the upper portion. "Billings Carter" in raised letters laid below on a smooth arch, and farther down was etched "DIED Dec. 5 1825 E. 34 yrs". Logs had broken free at a saw mill where Billings worked, rolled over him, and pinned him in icy water. He was rescued, but died soon thereafter leaving Reuben's daughter Elizabeth a widow and six children fatherless. Their ages ranged from ten to a newborn. Naamah, a middle child, was halfway through her fifth year on earth when her young father was abruptly snatched from her. Devastated at first, the accident turned her precocious about the promise of life eternal as proclaimed by preachers of Peterborough. "Father's in heaven now, saving a special place for us," she often observed.

Reuben smiled now recalling Naamah's oft-spoken words. Whenever she said them, he would kiss the top of her head and say, "Just like Jesus tells us." He didn't believe those words at the time since he was as dead as Abijah had been after his wife's passing. To him, Heaven was a crutch for the living, and when you're dead, a crutch is worthless.

He glanced west, shook his head, and wandered east, trying to ignore six small stones he knew too well. But he couldn't, and soon was standing with arms hanging, gazing at markers for the children of his son James.

The first stone, aligned next to the others and barely above ground, was inscribed "J. L. 1811-1812" and marked where James Law, the firstborn and first child to die, was buried. "J. L. 1815-1817" was inscribed on the next stone. "James, too," said Reuben. "I remember the night you died - on my birthday. You and young Reuben were so sick."

He stepped to a third stone with "R. L. 1817-1818" on it. "My namesake, and I was so proud. But you never had a chance." He thought of his firstborn son, also named Reuben, and their estrangement over the years. *I was too hard on the lad,* he thought. *One's always hard on his eldest, his namesake.*

He recalled his mistakes in rearing his son, regretting each, until his eyes welled. With blurry eyes, he glanced at the stones for Lyman, age two, Betsy, age one and a half, and Alice, age eight. He brushed his tears and looked skyward. *Lord, why do you bless us with them only to snatch them away?*

He had asked that question often and never received an answer. He used to wonder if the sulphur smell from his son's well was the cause. But the stench occurred only in summer, and the children had not died in summer. Yet doubts persisted. He sighed. "Ah Reuben, get away from this misery."

He moved west while thinking of James's wife, now eight months pregnant for the ninth time. An impending grandchild should bring joy, but he feared this unborn child would meet an early death, too. James and his wife seemed optimistic, which Reuben sensed was contrived to conceal the dread in their souls. He slowed to a shuffle as he reached his purpose for coming.

He sat on the stone wall and leaned against the birch tree. He fidgeted for comfort, which came quickly as muscles never forget the familiar. The rectangular slate stone for his wife, Allis, lay in front of him. His eyes drifted to "died 5 Feb. 1821."

"Been a while," he said as he massaged his arthritic hand. "But you're always in my thoughts." He inhaled, and twittering birds broke an unnerving silence. His eyelids grew heavy as he listened, and when the chirping ceased, he refocused on the stone.

"Did you know ole Abijah was my age when he died? You'd say how sad and lonely he became after Mary died. Remember?" He glanced at the ground. "Our children said the same about me." He chuckled as he scanned the cemetery. "Susanna would say, 'You be as grouchy as ole Abijah.' "

He eased from the tree to arch his back. "You know I'm friendly with your cousin's widow, Ruth. Wasn't much at first, just pleasantries after church, but then, well . . ." He rubbed his hand while pondering what to say. "The children say Ruth is good for me. I reckon they're right." He raised his head and saw "Allis, wife of Reuben" on the stone. He grimaced and said, "I'm thinking of asking Ruthy to marry me."

"Ruthy? You've become quite familiar, Reuben."

That thought came in Allis's voice. He closed his eyes to block "Allis, wife of Reuben" from them and tugged his lapel. "We're just friends. We need each other. Help each other." He eased off the stone wall and gimped to Allis's gravestone. He placed his hand on it to steady himself. "Allis, I never wanted another wife. When we said 'til death do us part years ago, I didn't know what it meant. You left, but I wasn't ready. I died with you." He lowered his head. "I was Abijah, alone, miserable, and dead."

He stepped back and stared. "You're my first wife, my only wife. Not 'til death do us part, but forever. You understand, don't you?"

"For eternity, Reuben. I do understand." Reuben smiled as Allis's response remained in his thoughts. *"I've been saving a seat for you next to me in heaven,"* came to mind in a voice similar to young Naamah's.

He cherished his inner peace until rustling leaves disturbed him. He looked east to the stone wall's opening and waited. His daughter Elizabeth marched out of the shadows with Naamah close behind and holding a flower bouquet.

They continued until Elizabeth spotted Reuben. "So this is where you wandered to. I asked Ruthy, and she said you left abruptly. " Elizabeth glanced at Allis's stone. "Talking with Mother?"

Reuben shook his head. "Needed a spot of air, and I thought of this peaceful place."

"Jarmany Hill, peaceful? I thought you hated this damn place."

Naamah broke from her mother's side and rushed to Reuben. She clung to his leg and placed her head on his hip. By habit, she would cling until he patted her head, just as her father used to do. She cherished the protective strength an older man gave. Reuben's woolen jacket was coarse and lacked the smell of sawdust that had marked her father's clothing. His leg, while sturdy, wasn't as strong as her father's had been. When Reuben stroked her head, she looked up, smiled, and dashed to her father's grave.

Reuben and Elizabeth ambled toward Naamah. "Yesterday, Billings would have been thirty-six," said Elizabeth. She pointed to Naamah. "After services, she asked the preacher for the church flowers for his birthday. He's been gone less than two years. Seems like an eternity."

Naamah knelt, facing the ornate gravestone, and folded her hands. Her lips moved, but what she said was unheard. Naamah Kendall Jenkins Carter was born six and half years earlier and three weeks after an aunt, Naamah Kendall Jenkins, had died. Once she realized the legacy she carried, she had a unique bond with a person now in heaven. Her younger sister, Betsey, couldn't pronounce the three syllables, and 'Nay-a-mah' elided to 'A-amah', creating Amy as her nickname.

She brushed her knees as she arose. "Father thanked me for the flowers." She grinned and turned to Reuben. "Said he's saving a special spot for us. Just like Jesus says, huh Grandpa?" She beamed as Reuben smiled and patted her head.

Elizabeth smiled, too, barely masking her sadness.

"The widow Piper was wondering where you went," said Naamah. "I like her. Do you?"

Reuben didn't answer, content to enjoy the often smiling and at times, chattering Naamah. Her cheery disposition and smooth round face were similar to her father's, and unlike her mother's dour, long face with an immediately noticed hooked nose.

"Grandpa, are you going to marry the widow Piper?"

"Gracious Amy," said Elizabeth. "You shouldn't ask such questions."

"Perhaps someday, I reckon I might."

"You should marry her real soon."

"Amy enough," said her mother.

"It's all right Elizabeth," said Reuben as he slouched to be eye level with Naamah. "And why should I marry her real soon?"

"Cuz Mother says she makes you happy. I like it when you're happy."

Reuben straightened up and chuckled. "Then I better marry her real quick-like."

"Come along. You've pestered your grandfather long enough." Elizabeth turned to Reuben and said, "We'll leave you to your peaceful spot."

Naamah held her mother's hand as they headed away. When she looked over her shoulder at Reuben, his smile broadened. She paused and said, "When we're in heaven, will you sit next to Grandma Allis or the widow Piper?"

Elizabeth tugged on her daughter's hand, "These questions about heaven -- will you ever stop?"

"But Aunt Susan said that in heaven . . ."

"Enough."

Reuben turned to Allis's stone. He thought he had answers for whatever Allis would ask. But he couldn't answer Naamah's

innocent question. He stared, hoping to hear Allis's voice. He
mumbled, "Grandma Allis." He heard nothing and inferred the
silence meant Allis's disapproval.

He turned and responded to Naamah. "I will sit next to
Grandma Allis." But Naamah had vanished, and he doubted she
heard him. When he heard the rustling leaves from Naamah and her
mother moving down the hill, he considered shouting to her but
didn't. His answer was lost forever – or was it?

He pushed his palm across his balding pate. *It's not 'til death
do us part, it's for eternity.* He glanced at Billings's gravestone and
the flower bouquet. Images of his broken body pinned in frigid water
returned, more horrific than when it had occurred. His eyes shifted
and couldn't avoid the six barely visible gravestones that lay farther
away.

As he trudged to the path, thoughts of his impending
grandchild returned. He glanced skyward and scowled. *How soon
before we'll need a seventh stone, Lord?* He reached the opening and
turned back. The trees on the perimeter diffused the glare to a
mellow glow while birds twittered -- serenity if Reuben cared to see
or hear it.

Reuben turned from the brilliant hilltop and moved to the
shadowy darkness, leading to the depths below. "God, I hate this
damn place."

Chapter Two

Fall 1841

Peterborough, New Hampshire

"I'm late," said Naamah Kendall Jenkins Carter, "Amy", as she bustled along a side road. Petite and with a porcelain complexion, she appeared younger and more innocent than twenty. Although it had been fifteen years since her father's death, she often reflected on death's uncertainty and the hope of eternal life. At first, Reverend Elliott's words were nourishing, only to grow stale and unfulfilling later. She found her occasional discussions with Aunt Susan, Susanna Law Taggart, most rewarding. She smiled as she recalled telling her once, *"You're a better preacher than Reverend Elliot."*

Of recent, Aunt Susan had told her of a young prophet, Joseph Smith, who claimed none of the religions now on the earth were correct. Only he could restore the true church. She discussed with Aunt Susan the possibilities of the being reunited with her father in flesh for eternity and descriptions of God as a glorified human, which appealed to her in profound ways that she could not quite explain. She wanted more, but the established churches were less than enthusiastic over this Prophet and his missionary, Elder Maginn. *My doubts persisted, and I tarried*, she thought as she fumbled with the button that lay below the mushrooming collar covering her neck. *Stop fretting. Aunt Susan has always been there for me.*

Her ankle-length dress swished as she hurried while continuing to reflect. Indeed, Aunt Susan had consoled her when she needed it most. It was Aunt Susan who had heard her whimpers after her father had died and came into her room. She stroked her forehead, dried her tears, and said, *"He's in heaven now, sitting next to Jesus and saving seats for us."* Apt words for Naamah as she lay in bed, struggling to muffle her sobs. The moonlight was faint that night, and Naamah was unsure who had come. Sitting on the bed and leaning close, her aunt's face absorbed the dim light and had appeared like an angel.

Naamah crossed the street and thought of another time, ten years later, not a moonlit night, but a cold October afternoon. The cemetery's sun-soaked field, just off a main road, wasn't as warm as it had appeared on that day. She was fourteen and with her siblings, her stepfather, Eli Upton, and others. Her youngest sister Susan, barely ten, clung to her dress while Betsey, twelve, stood with arms crossed. Reverend Elliott droned on, quoting Scriptures, concerned more with ritual than offering solace. She recalled squinting that day to lessen the glare and to mask an urge to cry. She had to be strong for her baby sister, yet her soul was crumbling until rustling leaves distracted her. Aunt Susan emerged from the glare, sidled near, and grabbed her hand. She squeezed gently and mouthed, "Forgive me, I'm late."

Naamah reached Main Street and ceased reflecting. Several blocks ahead, people clustered near the tavern. She was leery as she neared until she spotted Aunt Susan. She called to her, and when Aunt Susan turned around, she waved.

Aunt Susan hurried to Naamah. "I feared you might not come."

"Forgive me, I'm late." Naamah eyes darted to the tavern's large oaken door. "There's something devilish about a preacher and a tavern."

"I waited away from the others to be easily seen." She pointed to a nearby building and said, "We're meeting there."

As they moved toward the building, Naamah asked, "Where are Uncle Washington and Cousin George?"

"Inside. The hall fills up fast. Oliver is here, too."

"And cousins Albert and Samuel?"

"No, they're home." Susanna tightened her lips and glanced away. "Perhaps someday." She forced a smile and turned to the crowd near the hall. "Oh, that's him." She rose on her tiptoes and said, "Elder Eli Maginn."

A tall, angular man with a welcoming smile approached. Several rushed toward him, and he paused to greet them. He spoke to each as he moved with a confident, comfortable stride. His following, intent on listening, took occasional stutter-steps to avoid bumping one another.

"Let's wait," said Susanna. "I'll introduce you."

"So young. Not like I imagined."

Susanna was as transfixed as those in the entourage and didn't respond. Naamah sensed the building enthusiasm, and hers built, too.

When Maginn reached them, he stopped and said, "Sister Susanna, isn't it?" His English accent added importance to a simple greeting. As he took Susanna's hand with both of his, her cheeks flushed. He released a hand to stroke her forearm. "And where are your husband and son?"

"Inside," said Susanna. "And another son has joined us."

"Splendid." Maginn turned to Naamah and asked, "And who do we have here?"

"My niece, Naamah, who I told you about."

"A remarkable name." He clasped Naamah's hand similar to the way he had held Susanna's.

Naamah arched her neck to look into his eyes that glowed as warm as his hands felt, and with his unique accent, she felt an immediate bond. "I was named for my aunt," she said.

"Two Naamahs -- even more notable."

"She died before I was born."

"And now she resides in heaven, waiting to be reunited in the flesh with her namesake. Naamah, wife of Noah, meaning pleasant, because Naamah's conduct was pleasing to God. Am I right?"

"You certainly know your Bible," said Naamah.

"God's ways are never truly known. I'm sure your aunt's death inspired your name. And quite apt, as you seem to possess an agreeable demeanor. Indeed, so pleasing it doth draw one near."

Naamah's cheeks flushed, and she and Maginn remained enrapt for what seemed like an eternity to her.

He broke his grasp and offered a gesturing hand. "Shall we go inside?"

As they moved, a voice came from the gathering tavern crowd. "Blasphemer."

Naamah turned and recognized several among the crowd; a few were her fellow churchgoers. She curled her shoulders and lowered her eyes. Maginn stood erect, projecting a dignity. *A strong, yet gentle man,* she thought. She sidled to her aunt, who by instinct put her arm around her.

"My brother, come join us," said Maginn as he gestured to the hall.

"I'm not yer brother."

"Are we not all God's children, my brother?"

"You're guided by a false prophet."

"We're guided by God as he speaks through the prophets. Come, hear for yourself."

"Never."

"Very well, perhaps later."

Maginn turned from the tavern crowd and, with arms extended, shepherded Naamah and Susanna forward. Others joined and nestled close. Naamah sensed a fellowship and felt protected until one bellowed.

"Never, Maginn. Do you hear me, you blasphemer?"

*****

The next morning, Naamah walked home from Aunt Susan's. A windstorm had blown the tree limbs bare. The magnificence of reds, yellows, and greens were gone until next autumn, replaced with soaked brown clumps littering the path to her stepfather's home.

As she entered, Betsey sat at the table with a dour expression akin to her mother's. "Where were you last night?" she asked.

"With Aunt Susan."

"And you listened to that Maginn? I know he's in town."

Naamah nodded.

"Land sakes, Amy. Reverend Elliott says, 'He's a death on a speech Englishman disguised as the devil, leading lambs down the wrong path.' "

"He's not the devil. He speaks simple truths."

"You sound as starry-eyed as Aunt Susan."

"She's inspired by what she hears, as is Cousin George."

"George," said Betsey as she shook her head. "He's always been enchanted with church. The Taggarts are like that. They're Presbyterians you know."

As Naamah passed by the table, Betsey arose and grabbed her shoulder to be face to face. She towered over Naamah and could be intimidating. "I know you're more religious than me. After Father died, those bedtime stories about heaven comforted me, too. And when Mother passed . . ." She stepped back and straightened her shoulders. "Amy, we're older now."

Naamah pursed her lips.

"It's not just Reverend Elliott. There's others. I don't want you to be hurt."

As Betsey left, Naamah sighed. Her sister could be direct, tactless, yet a caring sister still existed within. After losing their parents, Betsey adopted a gruff exterior to mask her pain. *If she would open her heart, I know Maginn could touch her soul,* thought Naamah.

She reflected on Maginn. His preaching was similar to what she had heard her entire life. But quotes from the Book of Mormon augmented her beliefs, giving her a renewal, particularly about heaven where all God's children reside with Him. Like Jesus did, they will assume a mortal life to demonstrate their obedience to God while outside His heavenly kingdom. Upon death, they will return to await God's final judgement – return to His spiritual kingdom or be condemned to outer darkness as children of perdition.

Maginn reaffirmed her core belief - to demonstrate obedience to God each day. But now believing she was like Jesus and could return to whence she had come was profound. Trying to visualize herself before God sent her to earth was exhilarating. She had discussed the concept with her aunt last night, and her ill-formed images of herself before God sent her to Earth took form. But today, those images were hard to imagine. Her thoughts of heaven drifted to the familiar. She smiled, imaging her father saving her a seat among the clouds. But Maginn had touched her, and she knew over time her view of heaven would become more robust. She wanted more.

If only I could be with Aunt Susan tonight for more discussion.

Chapter Three

Across town, Aunt Susan was preparing the evening meal for her husband Washington and five sons. Like Naamah, she continued deliberating Maginn's words. She had heard many sermons, but his always lingered and fortified her, offering more than oft-heard scripture. She knew her Bible well, but the Book of Mormon added to it, as if it was once part of the Bible and became lost for ages until Joseph Smith found it.

A dining room chair rumbled, and Susanna ceased reflecting. Washington and her sons were ravenous at supper, and she hurried with a basket of warm rolls and returned cradling the stew pot with her apron.

Twenty-one-year-old Samuel reached across and grabbed a roll. His father glared and said, "Shall we bow our heads while I offer grace?"

Samuel dropped the roll into the basket and lowered his head, but kept his eyes open.

"Heavenly Father, we are thankful for this repast," said Washington.

Samuel's eyes moved to each brother as his father continued the grace. Albert, a few years older had his eyes open, too. Samuel shook his head, and they grimaced before closing their eyes and lowering their heads further.

"We pray we have served the Lord this day and done as he would have done. If we have fallen short, draw us nearer to thee, so we may enter your great kingdom. Amen."

The heads arose, and Susanna's face glowed. "Washington dear," she said as she looked to her husband, "a-men." His appreciative smile added to Susanna's serenity. She turned to her eldest son and asked, "How was your day, George?"

"Busy. With this cold wind, folks realize they need kindling. I spent more time selling wood scraps than repairing wagon wheels."

"A cold wind, Heavenly Father's reminder to the less ambitious," said Susanna.

"It's always cold in November," said Samuel. "I doubt Heavenly Father had anything to do with it."

Washington glared at Samuel. "Honor thy mother."

"I do honor her."

"What's the matter, Samuel?" asked Susanna. "You seem out of sorts of late."

"Nothing."

"I'm your mother and know when you're not quite right. Is it your work?"

Samuel shook his head.

"Then what?"

Samuel gnawed at his lower lip. "It's Maginn. He's cast a spell on you."

"A spell?" said Susanna as Washington and George stiffened in their seats.

"Maybe not a spell, but you're different."

"Maybe I feel God's presence more than before. Is that a bad thing?'

"It's bad when it comes from a false prophet."

"Elder Maginn speaks the truth," said George.

Samuel turned to his eldest brother. "Then why is he ridiculed?"

"Those who ridicule have yet to hear him. They know not what they say."

Samuel shook his head while trying to control his temper. He hated these ever-increasing conflicts caused by this so-called prophet. What he had heard still seemed preposterous. The angel Moroni appeared unto a seventeen-year-old Joseph Smith and told him ancient writings on golden plates were buried in the Cumorah Hills near Palmyra, New York. Four years later, Maroni allowed Joseph to retrieve the plates and directed him to translate them from their reformed Egyptian into English. Using various seer stones, which he placed in a top hat, and special rose colored translating spectacles, he viewed the written words and translated them. After his translation had been published as the Book of Mormon, Joseph returned the plates to Moroni.

George's posture straightened as he scanned the table and added, "Blessed are they who are persecuted for righteousness' sake, for theirs is the kingdom of heaven."

Washington smiled at George as he said, "I'm pleased you've remembered the Beatitudes. Well said son, and quite apt."

"Must the Bible consume our entire life?" said Samuel.

"We need guidance in this worldly life," said George. "The Bible shows us the way."

"And does that foolish Maroni guide you, too?"

"That's enough, son," said Washington as he leaned off the chair.

"Reading golden tablets through rose colored spectacles is pure gum."

"Enough," said Washington as he struck the table. The squabbling ceased, resulting in an unnerving silence. Susanna, who had shut her eyes once the voices were raised, now reopened them. Albert and the youngest son, Henry, ceased cowering and resumed eating.

Samuel looked at his mother. "Promise me you will not go into the drink."

Susanna looked deadpan and didn't answer, fearing a response would provoke more conflict.

George broke the silence. "When Elder Maginn returns, I intend, as you say, Samuel, 'to go into the drink.' "

Washington beamed with pride and settled against the chair. "A big step, son. Are you sure?'

"I prayed for guidance, and God answered my call."

"Into the drink?" asked Henry.

"Baptized," said Samuel to Henry. "In the Nubanusit River."

Henry scrunched his shoulders. "Isn't it frozen?"

"There's open water," said George. "Especially where it rushes over the rocks."

Susanna still hadn't responded to Samuel's question, and he needed an answer. He said to Henry. "I remember when you were baptized." He turned to his mother. "Do you remember, Mother?"

Susanna forced a smile.

"And I remember when Reuben was baptized."

Samuel remained focused on Susanna. Her smile left as she thought about her sixth and last child, named for her father. He died after his first birthday, ten years ago. Susanna wondered, *Why is Samuel mentioning little Reubie now?*

"Remember Mother, we bundled little Reubie and trekked through snow to have Reverend Holt baptize him. When he etched a cross of water on Reubie's forehead, you cried with joy."

Samuel's commentary evoked images Susanna hoped had been erased. *Poor little Reubie,* she thought, *so sickly. Oh, how I rocked him and prayed, but nothing helped. An innocent lamb, coughing phlegm.* Her memory grew more vivid. Reubie was wrapped in woolens and peering at her, seemingly begging. *I was as powerless as Reubie.*

"You said Reubie was sealed as God's own. The devil could never claim him, and when God willed it, Reubie would be in heaven."

"Samuel, how could you?" said Susanna as a tear trickled down her cheek.

"Mother, I love you. But if Reverend Holt was good enough for Reubie, all of us," and with a head flick toward his eldest brother, "even you, George, why must you be baptized again?"

Samuel stared, hoping his mother would respond. But George spoke for her. "Faith and repentance alone is not enough. We must be baptized by immersion for salvation."

Samuel ignored his brother, remaining focused on his mother. "Will you promise?"

Susanna brushed her cheek and sniffed. "I cannot. I must do as God guides me."

Samuel's head sank. He grimaced and raised it. "Father, may I be excused?"

"Where are you going?"

"Got chores to do." He pushed his chair back to arise, scraping the floor. He ignored George, but looked at his other brothers as he spoke. "Albert? Henry?" He thought about asking Oliver, but didn't.

Albert and Henry looked toward their father.

"Go if you have chores to do."

The three grabbed their bowls and clanked them near the wash basin. The door slammed, and their raised voices decreased as they moved away from the house.

Susanna knew her answer disappointed Samuel. She prayed he would understand one day. She needed uplifting and turned to George. "I know you undertake your decision after much prayer. I support you."

"Bless you, Mother."

"I'm close, but need more time in prayer." She turned to her husband. "And you, Washington?"

"My grandfather was a Presbyterian Deacon, and we were raised with daily Bible readings. But church disagreements and now a new preacher are unsettling. There's oneness with Maginn, simple truths from God. But to reject all I heard my whole life..." Washington paused to reflect.

"I was raised on the Bible, too," said Susanna. "But the sermons left me unnourished. I've been searching for nigh on twenty years." Susanna reflected before adding, "And Joseph Smith's testaments -- well, I feel reborn again."

"I pray," said Washington, "but doubts still exist."

"Even our Lord had doubts as he dwelt in Gethsemane. But Washington," Susanna put her hand on his forearm and rubbed, "don't dwell without us."

Susanna ceased rubbing and turned to her son. "Oliver?"

"I'm with George," he said.

Susanna smiled. She wouldn't have expected any other answer from Oliver. "Now, if my other three sons would start their journeys," said Susannah. She thought further. *My three lost lambs -- no four, little Reubie.* Terror flew into Susanna's thoughts. *He must be baptized, too. I want him with me in eternity.*

Chapter Four

December 1841

Elder Maginn had returned to Peterborough. The throng waiting for the hall doors to open was larger than before as Maginn continued to expand his following. Susanna waited with Naamah beside her, hopeful of hearing more inspiration.

"Quite a chill today," said Naamah. Susanna put an arm around Naamah and drew her close. Naamah nestled, appreciating their symbiotic relationship. The snow cover tingled her near frozen toes, and she wiggled them.

The usual tavern gathering had increased, too. They milled about to keep warm while staring at the Saints. Vapor spewed from their nostrils with each breath, seemingly displaying disapproval. A few glowered their disdain. Naamah turned from the unsettling scene.

As the doors eased open, the throng shuffled back. The tavern crowd grumbled, and Naamah turned toward them. A few jeers rose above the clamor as two men lowered their heads and hurried across the snowy gulf between the two gatherings. Naamah wondered, *What can they want?*

One skidded, but regained his balance. The other one's gait seemed familiar. As they neared, they raised their heads and slowed their pace. Naamah now recognized Horace Eaton, a man for whom Betsey had a growing affection. Amused by the irony, she thought, *If Betsey would come and listen to Elder Maginn, she'd see her Horace.* She studied Horace's companion, whom she had seen before, but didn't know his name.

Inside, Naamah and Susanna moved to a bench with other sisters. They slid along it, loosened their outer garments, and inched closer. Horace Eaton stood in the rear with the other stragglers, removing his coat and stomping snow off his boots. He surveyed until he spotted Naamah. He nodded and averted his eyes elsewhere. His companion concentrated on where Maginn would soon speak.

Susanna gazed to the men where Washington, George, and Oliver sat beside one another. Years earlier, while listening to the Presbyterian clergy, her whole family was present, aligned according to age. 'Susanna and her boys' was the congregation's moniker bestowed upon her, which warmed Susanna's heart then, but now was bittersweet.

Elder Maginn approached the podium and the din subsided, along with Susanna's nostalgia. *The Holy Ghost is within me*, she thought while tingling in anticipation. Washington sat forward with an eager face. *Washington's doubts are easing*, thought Susanna. *I know he's close.*

"My return has refreshed my spirit," said Maginn in his distinctive English voice.

The crowd nodded as a few mumbled their pleasure to one another. Susanna thought of Reverend Holt's sermons, years ago.

His high-pitched, squeaky monotone was uninviting, and understandably, her boys would squirm and tease one another as Holt preached. Washington's stern eye quieted them, except for Samuel, who quieted only when Susanna slowly shook her head. *If I only could reach Samuel today, I know Albert and Henry would follow.* Susanna ceased reflecting and listened to Maginn.

"Do not allow those who howl like wolves to distress you. Your path is straight to His celestial kingdom. The wolves are lost, and only when they join us will they find salvation."

My Samuel is lost, thought Susanna. *But he's not a wolf.* As her boys matured, sibling rivalries increased, particularly between George and Samuel. George had the unique bond reserved for the eldest and the father, which George readily assumed. He had a special connection with Susanna, too, listening to the sermons, singing hymns, and discussing gospel readings with her. Samuel seemed to resent these relationships. *So much like Cain and Abel,* thought Susanna. *Lord, inspire me to see what might be.* Susanna left her worries to listen again.

"On my walk today, I prayed for guidance. God revealed Peterborough is torn asunder, as are its families. He directed me to Luke and The Prodigal Son, knowing it would comfort your soul."

Susanna's eyes widened in anticipation. Chills caused her to squirm.

"Jesus's parable of two sons, a favored elder and a prodigal younger, is so well known, I dare say I need not my Bible."

Susanna sat upright. She knew the story of the two sons who had received their inheritance, with one remaining loyal to his father and the other becoming wasteful. But she was keen-eyed, hoping for heretofore unheard guidance.

Maginn recited with eloquence, enunciating each syllable, gesturing at appropriate times, and in an accent that gave the parable a higher authority. He neared the end:

"And the elder answering, said to his father, 'Lo, these many years do I serve thee, neither transgressed I at any time thy commandment: and yet thou never gavest me a young goat that I might make merry with my friends. But as soon as this thy son was come, which hath devoured thy living with harlots, thou hast killed for him the fatted calf.' And he said unto him, 'Son, thou art ever with me, and all that I have is thine. It was meet that we should make merry, and be glad: for this thy brother was dead, and is alive again; and was lost, and is found.' "

Susanna's soul tingled with her revelation. *Samuel never devoured his birthright. He's but lost, and will be found.* Her peace of mind stayed until the rattling benches and mumbled conversations signaled the meeting's closing.

Eager, George left the congregating men and moved to Susanna. "Mother, tomorrow I plan to be baptized."

"I knew you would," said Susanna as she embraced him. She clung until her trembling eased. She stepped back and gazed before saying, "And when your father and brothers follow, I will embrace them as I have you."

"As will I."

"Even Samuel?"

George straightened his posture. "I fear our Samuel is lost. So lost, I'm unsure where to find him." He put his arm around Susanna. "As Maginn said, we're on the right path." George sensed his mother's disappointment remained, so he added, "Samuel was always slow to follow." He squeezed her closer, and Susanna cracked a smile. "And when he returns, we'll slaughter a fatten calf for him."

Susanna inched out of George's embrace and put her arms about his waist. "Bless you, my son."

Naamah looked at those in the rear. This time, when her eyes met Horace's, he did not shy from them. *Maybe Betsey will join us one day,* she thought. Still intrigued by Horace's companion, she moved to them and said, "A pleasure to see you here, Horace."

"I've been wanting to come, but with all the talk . . ." Horace gestured to his companion. "But John convinced me."

John nodded to Naamah. "Brother John Twiss, a pleasure to make your acquaintance, Sister Naamah Carter."

Naamah drew back. "Did Horace tell you my name?"

John shook his head. "I've noticed you and asked others. I didn't mean to be untoward." He glanced away and scuffed his feet. "I'm from Jaffrey and don't know many from Peterborough."

"You've journeyed far."

"To hear Elder Maginn, I would travel across lots."

"I would so opine. He's unlike other preachers."

"I've noticed as you listen to Elder Maginn. Your day of baptism is drawing nigh. I pray you join us soon."

Naamah fumbled with her bonnet bow underneath her chin. "You seem to know much about me, Brother Twiss."

"I know little. But some things are evident, especially matters of faith."

Chapter Five

Spring 1842

The hall doors opened, and the Saints swarmed out while discussing Maginn's sermon. Naamah, rapt in thought, strolled while swaying her picnic basket. When she realized she had outpaced the others, she paused.

As Betsey neared, Naamah said, "Let's wait for Aunt Susan and the others."

Betsey frowned and fidgeted.

"What did you think of Elder Maginn?"

"His accent is quaint. But he likes to hear himself talk – like an English magpie."

"Oh Betsey," said Naamah as she shook her head. "Always so negative."

"Am not. Just telling the truth."

"Were you inspired?"

"Inspired? By a preacher?" Betsey chuckled. She perused the Saints and said, "There are so many of them Mormons. I could scarcely see them all."

"You were fussing about."

"Perchance, did you see Horace Eaton?"

Naamah smiled; the pieces had come together as to why Betsey decided to come. "No. I was listening to Elder Maginn, not fussing about."

Betsey crossed her arms and resumed walking. Naamah followed until she heard from behind, "Are you not Sister Naamah Carter?" As she turned around, the man said, "I'm Brother Twiss. We met earlier."

"Ah, from Jaffrey." Naamah began swaying her picnic basket as a curious Betsey retreated back to her. As Betsey sidled near, Naamah said, "Allow me to introduce my sister, Betsey."

"Afternoon sister," said Twiss as he nodded. "Were you as inspired by Elder Maginn as I?

"I'm not that kind of Sister, just Amy's sister."

"Amy?" said Twiss as he looked at Naamah.

"Amy is what Betsey calls me."

"Well, I'm going to continue home," said Betsey.

"But I packed plenty. Won't you stay?"

"I've much to do."

As Betsey left, Naamah grimaced before turning to Twiss. "The answer to your question," she said, "is I found Elder Maginn uplifting, as always."

"Me too. His sermons are like no other."

As Twiss expounded, Naamah listened while swaying her basket. When he stopped, she asked, "Will you join us for a picnic?"

"Well, I . . ."

"There's a pleasant spot near the river."

"Where Elder Maginn baptizes?"

Naamah nodded and said, "I've given baptism much thought. I know I'm close."

"So why do you tarry?'

"I reckon I was waiting for the ice to melt."

"Which it has now. I pray you join us soon."

Naamah realized her excuse for not being baptized was lame. She hoped Brother Twiss did not think likewise. Her worrying ceased when she spotted Reverend Elliott striding toward Maginn.

As he neared, she said, "A pleasant day to you, Reverend."

He didn't break his stride, but grumbled a reply. Maginn was conversing with several gathered around him. Elliott glared as he neared and said, "I've watched your flock grow, and no longer will I stand idle."

Maginn ceased conversing and smiled. "Have you come to join us?"

"I've come to expose you and your false prophet."

Maginn's entourage grumbled until he raised his hand while keeping eye contact with Elliott. "God always reveals himself through the prophets. Did not Isaiah foretell of a Messiah born unto a virgin, and Zechariah of his return to Jerusalem on an ass, and Micah of his betrayal for 30 silver pieces?"

"Don't lecture me on the Scriptures. Those prophets foretold our Lord's coming."

"Truly. But after our Lord's ascension, did not He reveal himself unto his Apostles? And to Saul of Tarsus near Damascus?"

"Fiddlesticks, of course."

"Why would God cease revealing in this latter day? Revelations foretells a second coming."

"I'll tell you about Revelations. Revelations seventeen warns of a false religion ascending with immense influence – the great harlot of Babylon. And Matthew twenty-four warns of false Christs and prophets with wonders to deceive. Wonders that I must end."

Maginn nodded. "You know your Bible."

"And well I should. I graduated from a respected theological college." Reverend Elliot gripped his lapels and said, "And you sir?"

"I've received instruction, too. Come and join us, and we can discuss further."

"I will not lend credence to your false prophet through discussion."

The faithful grumbled, and Maginn raised his hand again to quiet them. "Verily I say, just as Thomas had doubts until he placed a finger into the Lord's wounds, you cannot believe until you open your ears and listen with a pure heart."

"You . . . you impudent, pompous fraud." Elliott released the grip on his lapels and stormed away. As he passed Naamah, she cowered and said nothing. Once he was out of earshot, she turned to Brother Twiss.

"I've never seen him so out of sorts. Once he was comforting. Now, my rock is crumbling."

"His flock diminishes, and he's fearful. It happened in Jaffrey. We're a village, unlike Peterborough, too small to avoid the wrath."

"It's growing here, too."

"We'll never find peace here. Nauvoo is the place to be."

"But it's so far."

"Still a journey we must travel."

"Nauvoo," said Naamah as she gazed west. "When I hear it, I see myself with the Prophet. Perhaps someday." Naamah ceased gazing. "For now my baby sister needs care. She's only sixteen."

"Hardly a baby."

"I reckon you're right." Naamah smiled. "We've been close, especially after Mother left us. Been more like a mother than a sister to her." Naamah took a few steps, thought further, and turned back to Brother Twiss. "Was a mother to my stepsiblings, too - Louisa, Sara, and poor little Billings."

"Billings?"

"Named to honor my father." Naamah lowered her head and took a few steps. "When Mother was lying-in . . ." Naamah paused while biting her lip. "I still hear her screams." She turned to Twiss. "Mother died a few weeks later, and then Billings left us, too. So sad for Louisa and Sara. I had to comfort them."

"Perhaps God is preparing you."

Naamah furrowed her brow.

"For when you're in a family way."

Naamah blushed and looked away.

"Forgive me: that was unfitting. You must be busy tending to your stepsisters."

"No, my stepfather remarried, and they have grown attached to their new mother." Naamah pursed her lips. "Susan may be sixteen, but she needs protection from Betsey."

"Is she cruel?"

"Not really." Naamah took a step before turning back to Twiss. "Losing parents affects us differently."

"Perhaps Susan could journey to Nauvoo with you."

"She has yet to be inspired." Naamah stared at the ground. Brother Twiss stepped closer and was about to speak before being interrupted.

"Wasn't that unpleasant," said Susanna as she neared. "Reverend Elliott was so snappish."

"Unfortunate indeed," said Naamah. "I've something more pleasant." She gestured and said, "Brother Twiss from Jaffrey will be joining us."

Susanna made an abbreviated curtsey. "Splendid as Sister Harriett Bruce is also joining us. You're fortunate as Amy is quite a cook." Susanna pointed to her husband. "Washington always rubs his belly after eating Amy's cooking and says, 'A splendid repast.' "

Washington, standing between his sons, patted his paunch and flashed a smile. Harriett stood near George, swaying her picnic basket. She shared the same birthdate as Naamah, but her girlish face belied she was twenty-one.

The group moved toward the Nubanusit and joined with others. The women, some carrying baskets, were clad in long skirts and blouses buttoned to the neck; a few wore bonnets. The men wore long pants, some with suspenders, and long-sleeved shirts; several wore vests, and a few wore tailcoats.

The Taggart group settled near a maple, close to the others. Children ran about, laughing on occasion, and lingering near the water's edge. A few removed their shoes and waded ankle deep to splash nearby friends.

Naamah had baked a mincemeat pie and cornbread. She loved maple syrup and brought a jug to trickle on them. When Twiss poured syrup on his pie, she smiled. "You seem to hanker maple syrup."

He nodded. "Hope maple trees are in Nauvoo, for I'd dearly miss syrup on my hotcakes."

While eating, Brother Twiss and George read from the Book of Mormon and led a discussion. Susanna offered occasional comments, and Naamah was content to listen, especially when Twiss spoke. Maginn moved among the groups, joining in discussion as he did.

While among Naamah's group, Maginn pointed to the river and said, "I recall when I baptized some of you. You were free of sin, as pure as the Nubanusit. To remain pure, you must refresh your baptismal covenant each day." He glanced at Naamah and said, "I hope you will join us soon."

The sun neared Mount Monadnock's peak, and the Nubanusit's roar seemed louder. "I've grown chilly," said Twiss as he arose and swept his bottom. "I must leave for Jaffrey while daylight remains. Brother Taggart, your readings have inspired me."

"As did yours, Brother Twiss."

"And Sister Carter," Twiss glanced at Washington and back to Naamah, "a splendid repast, simply splendid," he said while patting his stomach.

Naamah placed her hands against her cheeks. Washington chuckled, and Susanna cherished the affection seemingly growing between Naamah and Brother Twiss. Naamah craned her neck and watched Twiss amble up the rise and disappear.

"Such fine young man," said Susanna. "I reckon we'll see him again."

"If Amy's cooking, we'll see him," said Washington.

Sister Harriett Bruce arose. "I must leave, too. Father will be upset if I tarry too long."

George scrambled to his feet and straightened his vest. "Allow me to accompany you."

"I appreciate your offer," said Harriett. Her lips tightened as she added, "But, well… just part way. You know how Father is."

Harriett and George left, walking near one another while conversing.

"Such a sweet girl, and George seems smitten," said Susanna. "If only her family could be inspired. She endures much when she is not among us."

Nubanusit River, Peterborough, New Hampshire

Clad in a white gown, Naamah stood aside Maginn on the slope leading to the Nubanusit River. Aunt Susan stood next to Sister Amelia, who had a horse blanket draped on her forearm. Elders Gardner and Brooks held a change of clothing for Maginn. They were witnesses to attest to full immersion and that Maginn said the required words.

Naamah reflected on the events that preceded her decision to be reborn as a disciple of Jesus. As a child, Sunday sermons, saying grace, and reciting prayers with her father before climbing into bed had given her security, knowing God was always near. But after her father died, nightly prayers were said alone and from memory. But rote recitation was uninspiring, and she often avoided them and climbed into bed, wondering why she felt abandoned. And after her mother remarried, grace was seldom said. God had drifted farther from her, and weekly church attendance was insufficient to draw Him near.

But Maginn's preaching had stimulated her like when she was a child and remained to nourish her. The Book of Mormon offered fresh meaning to God and Jesus, revitalizing and augmenting her earlier Bible teaching. God had returned, and with a greater glory than when she was child. She didn't want to lose Him again, and being among a community of Saints, living the gospel daily, assured her that she would not.

"Are you ready to join us, my sister?" asked Elder Maginn.

She clasped her palms together and interlocked her opposing fingers. She lowered her head for a few moments before turning to Maginn and nodding.

Maginn splayed his arms, holding his palms opened to the heavens. "And it came to pass that the Lord spoke unto Nephi and commanded him that he should come forth." As they descended, Maginn continued. "And Nephi arose and went forth and bowed himself before the Lord and did kiss his feet."

Naamah remained rapt in the moment until Brother Twiss entered her mind. *I can't wait to tell him that I no longer tarry,* she thought. She tripped on a gnarled root and grabbed Maginn's left forearm to regain her balance as he put his right arm around her shoulder. She pursed her lips, chagrined that her clumsiness resulted from her daydreaming.

Maginn continued the descent saying, "And the Lord commanded Nephi that he should arise. And he arose and stood before the Lord." When they reached the river, Maginn faced her and raised his right hand. "And the Lord said unto Nephi: 'I give unto you power that ye shall baptize these people when I am again ascended into heaven.' "

Maginn gestured, and Naamah entered the water and sloshed farther while filled with the Holy Ghost. The spring runoff was full-fledged, and the rushing water upstream created a ubiquitous rumble. The whitecaps seemed frigid, but clad in woolen socks, Naamah didn't sense the cold. Once waist high, she turned to Maginn.

Maginn entered the river saying, "Behold, ye shall go down and stand in water, and in my name shall ye baptize them." He sloshed toward her.

As Maginn shuddered, Naamah's toes grew numb. She thought of Jesus's sufferings for her sake. His burdens were far greater than hers, and her extremities seemed to warm.

Maginn raised his right hand. "And now behold, these are the words which ye shall say, calling them by name." She gripped Maginn's left forearm with both hands, prophetically, like she had moments ago. Maginn placed his right hand on her back and eased her down. "Having been commissioned of Jesus Christ, I baptize you in the name of the Father, and of the Son, and of the Holy Ghost."

A cold shock rushed into her. She closed her eyes and felt her hair flowing about her face. Jesus was with her and experiencing what Heavenly Father commanded. Maginn's hand gathered some tresses floating on the water and submerged them; she had to be completely immersed. She sensed the devil's hellfire being extinguished, and its residue dissipating. She floated in Maginn's arms, feeling as pure as Heavenly Father had intended. She thought of Twiss. *As pure a woman as I can be.* Maginn eased her up. She exhaled and opened her eyes to his warming smile.

"Verily I say unto you the Father, and the Son, and the Holy Ghost are one."

Maginn put his arm around her and led her to the shore. They struggled until the water reached knee level, where they sloshed to the river bank. The witnesses had descended to meet them. The men moved to a stand of trees and underbrush. Gardner handed Maginn his dry clothing, and Brooks held the horse blanket to give Maginn privacy.

Aunt Susan embraced Naamah and kissed her cheek. "Welcome to His kingdom."

"It's as though I've been reborn. The air has never been so pure." She licked water droplets still about her lips. She raked her fingers through her hair and caressed her moistened cheeks until she began to shiver.

Maginn had finished changing, and Elder Brooks said, "Sister Carter have this blanket." He snapped it and threw it around her. A horsy blend of sweat, leather, and manure tainted the air.

Naamah realized she could not be forever pure. She closed her eyes and said to God, *"My soul is still cleansed, and with your guidance, will remain so forever."*

As they trudged toward Peterborough center, Naamah shivered and clutched the blanket. "'Tis odd," she said to Aunt Susan. "While being baptized I was warm, as if I was enduring much as Jesus did."

"As was I, and my baptism was in the winter," said Susanna.

Sister Amelia smiled and nodded in agreement. She turned to Maginn and asked, "Is it the same for you?"

"It's never the same, as there have been many. I rejoice knowing more will follow."

"I don't know why I tarried," said Naamah. "I can't wait to tell Brother Twiss."

"Brother Twiss?" said Maginn.

"He, like Aunt Susan, encouraged me."

"Then you must go to Nauvoo to tell him."

Naamah ceased walking, and the others stopped, too. After several moments, she gathered the blanket closer and said to her quizzical looking aunt, "I stopped because of a sudden chill."

Aunt Susan smiled, yet seemed unconvinced by Naamah's response.

"He left a few weeks past," said Maginn. "A Brother of courage who wanted to bear witness to the Prophet. Perhaps with time you'll be so moved."

She had felt Jesus with her during her baptism, which had aroused her. She sensed being near the Prophet would stimulate her similarly. *Oh, just to bear witness to him,* she thought. *God, are you calling me there to be with him?*

Chapter Six

The hope within spring's blossoms ended with autumn colors disappearing into dying leaves. Naamah's enthusiasm for Nauvoo ebbed with her growing indecision. Life in Nauvoo would be ideal, but Peterborough was familiar, bearable. She was probably inferring too much from Brother Twiss's kindness. By now, he most likely had another in his life. And besides, her baby sister needed her. She couldn't leave.

Yet within her soul, she questioned if her faith was as strong as she believed. Doubt troubled her, and as winter ensued, she suppressed it until spring returned. With the snow melting away, the Saints were re-invigorated, talking often about Nauvoo. Some would leave once the roads were passable, and when Aunt Susan left abruptly, Naamah's doubts re-surfaced. Peterborough now seemed foreign, intolerable, and Nauvoo appealing. She rued not leaving with Aunt Susan when she had a chance. *Aunt Susan is indeed fortunate to be nearing Nauvoo.*

Spring 1843

On the trail to Nauvoo

Heavenly Father, give us strength to endure, thought Susanna. She opened her eyes to wisps of dust passing by her husband and Oliver. Sitting on the wagon's edge, legs dangling, she leaned back using her arms for support and reflected on the family's life-changing decision.

She was determined not to leave for Nauvoo until the family could leave as one. She prayed for God's guidance and last autumn, near her fifty-sixth birthday, God answered her. Albert and Samuel were residing elsewhere, leaving Henry, sixteen, the sole non-believer in the house. One evening during supper, Washington grumbled about his dwindling finances and his Church tithe shortfall. Frustrated, he scolded Henry about his overdue board money. Henry arose from his chair saying, "I don't work my backside off to earn money for Old Joe. I'm leaving to live with Albert." As he stormed out of the house, Susanna realized the family rift was an irreconcilable chasm beyond repair.

Throughout the winter, as George's relationship with Harriett Bruce grew, he urged his father to leave for Nauvoo. But Washington vacillated until George announced he and Harriett intended to marry in the spring. Washington decided they would leave after the wedding, only to change his mind soon after, which surprised Susanna. He was always thoughtful, measured, and never rash, except for this momentous decision. Now, as he trudged alongside Oliver, Susanna wondered if it was God's way that she was yet to understand. She had witnessed Oliver, nineteen, maturing into a responsible adult since they left. *Maybe God knew Oliver was ready to come out from George's shadow.*

Susanna scanned the other wagons and those walking alongside. Families, some intact, each destined for Nauvoo. She dwelled on that uplifting thought until her fifty-six-year-old husband with hollowed eyes and dusty clothing distracted her. He seemed as though he was walking to his grave.

"Washington, sit for a while," said Susanna as she eased off the slow-moving wagon.

"Father, jump aboard. I'll walk with Mother." Oliver came alongside his father to quicken his pace.

When they reached the wagon, Washington shooed Oliver away while his pace slowed. He had doubts about his physical limitations, but he hastened and leapt.

"Oh dear," shrieked Susanna. Seemingly paralyzed, she placed her palms together before moving them to her lips.

The wagon halted as Oliver and others rushed to Washington. Elder Swift, who had been driving the Taggart wagon, scrambled to the rear of it.

"Brother Taggart are you hurt?" asked Swift.

Washington lay seemingly dazed. After he took several deep breaths, Oliver and Swift helped him struggle to his feet. He swatted the dust from his clothing and rubbed his hip.

"Brother Taggart, you're too old to jump into a moving wagon."

"It was hardly moving, and I'm not old."

Hunched over, Washington took several gasps before hoisting himself onto the wagon. He moved among grain sacks and crates while panting and appreciating being off his feet. The reins snapped, and the wagon jerked causing a crate's edge to jar into his ribs. Pinned in position, the edge jabbed with each wagon sway. He eventually raised his torso and adjusted his position. He rested against a grain sack and dozed.

Susanna, pleased she had insisted, hobbled with stiff muscles. When they loosened, she hurried to keep pace with Oliver. Concern etched his face as he focused on his father. Suzanna grabbed his hand and said, "I'm glad you're with us."

Oliver's vigilance remained, and Susanna began to swing their clasped hands. "God reveals himself in odd ways, doesn't he?"

Bewildered, Oliver turned to his mother.

She squeezed his hand. "I'm bearing witness to a boy growing into a man."

"I reckon." He snorted and said, "Even if I'm unready."

*****

After several days, the Taggarts neared Nauvoo. Washington's ribs had turned blue-black and ached whenever he rolled onto his side or coughed. His sleep had been fitful since the incident.

In the gray predawn light, Washington shivered and pulled his blanket closer while praying for warmth so he could nap. The cold ground had tightened his muscles and breathing was uncomfortable. But exhaustion ensued, and he nodded off until a glare woke him. The sun was not warming, just annoying, and he rolled from it as pain shot into his ribs. *God, give me strength for another day.*

He removed his blanket and lay for a minute before arising, one leg at a time. He stretched and cringed from pain. A chill came, and he shivered anew.

"Father, finish my bread. It's hard, but it will fill you."

"No porridge today?"

"A Kirkland Saint returning to Nauvoo said we're close. We need an early start to reach it in daylight."

"I'm so excited," said Susanna. "Our long journey is finally ending."

"Can't come too soon," said Washington. "Our provisions are scant."

"Elder Swift said he has plenty if we're in need."

"I may have been too frugal. Even so, all I have left is twenty-five dollars."

"Is that enough?'

Washington's eyes drooped as he shrugged.

"We'll be among the Saints soon. We'll be fine."

Washington hoped Susanna was correct. He had planned to replenish his supplies along the way and had bartered well. Yet he sensed outside Kirkland, where Joseph Smith initially led his faithful in 1831, he had been swindled. It nagged him since the cheat was a Presbyterian elder.

"Some Peterborough brethren are already in Nauvoo," said Washington.

"And more to follow," said Susanna as she smiled. "Soon, I hope."

"George and Harriett will arrive before we know it. I would have waited, but…"

"But what?"

"God said unto me, 'Do not tarry.' "

"Aha, that's why we left." As Washington massaged his ribs, Susanna asked, "Is there more?"

"Saints arrive in Nauvoo in droves. I feared the land would be all gone."

"Is that what God revealed?"

Washington shook his head and turned away. "The Saints are stirring. I daren't tarry." He looked to Oliver. "Help me gather our belongings."

Susanna's question remained unanswered, and as she helped her two men load the wagon, her concerns about Washington increased.

Chapter Seven

May 1843

Peterborough, New Hampshire

The sun shone brightly in a cloudless sky as the Saints prepared to journey west. A dozen wagons, a few covered, along with buckboards and drays queued randomly behind Elder George Bertram's Conestoga. With its four foot tailgate and white covers billowing, his wagon looked like a ship. The onlookers conversed, laughing at times, while some glared allowing their thoughts to remain within their souls.

George was loading Harriett's possessions onto a wagon. She had reasoned since George's belongings left earlier with his father, there should be enough room for hers. Now as she assisted him, she prayed everything could be stowed.

Naamah called out and waved as she approached. Harriett ceased worrying and rushed to her. "I wish you were joining us," she said.

"I can't," said Naamah as she rubbed Harriett's hand. "Others need me." She touched Harriett's cheek and added, "But I will miss you dearly."

Naamah's touch and kindness always comforted Harriett. Whenever the Saints gathered, she sat between Naamah and Susanna. Her strained family relations had worsened once she became baptized, and when she married George, no family member attended. She glanced at the Saints near their wagons. "I'll be among the Saints," she said. She stepped closer and lowered her voice. "But of all the Sisters, I feel closest to you."

Naamah beamed a brief prideful smile. "You have Cousin George now, and soon, Aunt Susan."

"My new mother. 'Tis odd."

Naamah cocked her head as her forehead furrowed.

"You're more a mother to me than my own . . . than Aunt Susan."

Harriett's remark surprised Naamah. But upon reflection, she realized the truth in it. They were the same age, yet through circumstances she became a surrogate mother early in life while Harriett had no such demands and experienced an adolescence. She was mature, whereas Harriett was still naïve.

Harriett observed the onlookers, many erstwhile friends who now gawked with seeming disappointment or loathing. She turned back to Naamah and said, "I thought Mother would come, or my sister." She lowered her head. "Father must have forbidden them."

"Someone will come."

Harriett shook her head. "Father cusses about Elder Maginn all the time."

"Betsey speaks unkindly, too." Naamah lifted Harriett's chin with her curled index finger. "Families squabble but are never torn apart."

"The Taggarts are."

"For now, but Albert is understanding. Aunt Susan prays he will bring reason." She stroked Harriett's hand. "Time heals all."

"But we're leaving today."

"We have an eternity."

Harriett embraced Naamah, seemingly not wanting to let go. She stepped back and brushed her eye. She embraced Naamah again and whispered, "I've told nary a soul, not even George." She glanced at him and turned back to Naamah. "God has blessed us. I'm in a family way." Harriett kissed Naamah's cheek and pulled back. She exhaled her relief at releasing her pent-up news.

How odd she told me first, thought Naamah. As Harriett's joy continued, Naamah felt compelled to respond. "Splendid," she said. "Aunt Susan will be thrilled."

"My monthly time still could arrive. But my heart tells me I'm blessed." Harriett blushed as she shied from Naamah. She wrung her hands and said, "Well, you know how it is."

Naamah kept her smile for Harriett's benefit, yet her mind wondered, *How would I ever know?* She wrinkled her lips as she thought further. *Never been close to a man.* Jealousy shot through her. "Well, I daren't tarry," she said. "I want to bid farewell to others."

Naamah gave Harriett an obligatory embrace and moved toward Bertram's wagon. After several steps, she turned back to a perplexed Harriett and mouthed, "You're truly blessed." As Harriett rushed her hands to her cheeks, Naamah lifted her eyes skyward. *Envy is a terrible sin. Bless you for guiding me away from it.*

Naamah's farewells were bittersweet, elated for them and saddened knowing more were leaving. She sensed she should be among them, but she dawdled. If her faith was truly strong, she would have turned her life over to God and would be leaving, too. She shook her head as if to rid her troubled mind of doubts.

Eager to leave, Elder Bertram directed the Saints to their wagons. Naamah moved out of the way, closer to the onlookers. Men climbed onto their wagons and helped the women aboard. A few were clutching infants. George, Harriett, and other walkers moved behind the wagons. Bertram moved among the Saints and raised his hands. They quieted, and he spoke.

"We journey to the City of Zion - our worldly kingdom." He scanned the Saints while removing his hat and bowing his head. George held his hat and clutched Harriett's hand. He squeezed it, and she turned to him and smiled.

Bertram continued. "God, you've enlightened us and now you call us. As ever, we're obedient to your command. We beseech you to watch over us and guide us safely home."

"Amen," said the Saints as the men donned their hats. Bertram climbed aboard and snapped the reins. His wagon moved ahead, and others followed to form a train.

"Bertram, acknowledge the corn; you journey to the Gates of Hell," someone bellowed. A few guffaws followed.

Like the Saints, the onlookers were aroused but for different reasons. They conversed and moved closer to the wagon train and Naamah. She inched away and waved to the Saints as they passed her. When George and Harriett neared, she stepped close and said, "Godspeed, and give my love to Aunt Susan."

"Good riddance – take 'em all with yah," shouted an onlooker.

The last wagon with two boys following passed by Naamah. In the distance, the sun reflected off Bertram's fluttering cover, flashing through the dust like a ship's beacon guiding pilgrims to a New World.

"Where's Maginn? He ought to pull foot with ya."

The rumble of laughter unnerved Naamah. She moved farther from the crowd. *Brother Twiss is right,* she thought. *Life would be better in Nauvoo.*

"Take that death on a speech preacher with ya."

The last wagon was distant, and Bertram's sails were inconspicuous. *Oh, I will miss them,* thought Naamah. She turned to leave for home, and a man hurried toward her. *Why that's Peter, Harriett's father.* She turned back. Harriett was too distant for him to catch her.

Peter Bruce reached the crowd and, upon seeing the distant wagons, began to sprint. He was narrowing the gap between him and the wagons until his paced slowed. He paused and hunched over. After several gasps, he took a few steps west before shaking his head and trudging back.

"Devil worshippers. Fools, following a false prophet."

"Hallelujah – they're gone."

"Gone?" said one as he took a swig from his jug. "We plumb drove them out."

As the crowd hooted, Peter glared at the last heckler. He cowered and said, "I know your daughter, newly wed and all, is among them. Sorry for your loss."

Peter lowered his head and continued retracing the route he had just hurried along. As he neared Naamah, she moved to him. "I'm Naamah, George Taggart's cousin."

"So you're the Naamah that Harriett talks about. You're one of them."

"Harriett wanted to say her farewells. She'll be grateful knowing you came."

Peter snorted. "Grateful? Why she don't even knowed it."

"Heavenly Father will let her know."

Peter waved a dismissive hand as he looked at the crowd, which had quieted to observe the conversation. He twitched his shoulder and turned to Naamah. His voiced raised as he said, "I don't believe like you and Harriett." He glanced at the crowd. Some heads were nodding.

"No matter," said Naamah. "Heavenly Father is with Harriett."

"Gum."

Naamah smiled. "A father's love never leaves."

"Never? Well, I'll never see my Harriett again."

"You have an eternity to see your Harriett."

Chapter Eight

Summer seemed to have lingered too long at spring's doorstep. But when it arrived, it came full force. The strawberry blossoms exploded with fruit, and raspberry shoots teemed with white buds, soon to redden, hopefully to a dark crimson, always sweeter and Naamah's favorite. The crude stick figure that her stepfather Eli had constructed to scare the crows was having negligible results. The strawberries were abundant, and if they were not picked quickly, the crows perched nearby would devour them. Naamah and Susan toiled as summer hissed its heat and horse flies buzzed.

As Naamah stooped, the summer sounds and a scorched back rekindled earlier years. She was alongside her mother picking berries; stooping wasn't necessary. Back then, her initial excitement gave way to irritating flies and a sweaty back that had evolved into maddening itchiness.

She pinched off a huge berry and bit into it. She wiped the oozing juice from the side of her mouth and took a last bite while watching Susan, much like her mother had once watched her. Susan paused to brush aside flies buzzing close. She bent over and arose again to flail.

"Ain't they pests," said Naamah.

"I told Eli not to sling more manure, but he did anyways. 'What's a girl know about farming?' he said."

"The flies love it. It must taste sweet to them."

"Ain't no bother to Eli, though; he don't pick them. But he sure can eat them." Susan sighed her frustration. "I wish the air would freshen. It's the buzzing that annoys me, and a breeze would drown it out." Susan raked her thumbnail near her spine. "And I'm itchy."

Naamah resumed picking while thinking of the westward bound Saints. She expected to be lonesome once her kin left, but was unprepared for its extent. With so many gone, the gatherings lacked their previous fellowship. Last week, she again questioned the strength of her faith until God enlightened her. Peterborough was different, but through faith she would endure. Close bonds would always be there, and she would be reunited, if not in this world, then in the hereafter.

She swatted at a fly on her arm, gazed at the western mountain, and stooped again. "We should near Nauvoo when the strawberries need their picking," were George's departing words. As she pushed a leaf aside to pluck, she romanticized about George seeing Nauvoo's temple as they approached. She straightened up and closed her eyes to let the vision dance in her head. *It must be truly magnificent.*

*****

The next day Naamah awoke early to begin cooking. She touched Susan's shoulder, and when her eyes fluttered, she told her to be quiet since Betsey was sleeping. They had been busy for a few hours when a door down the hall creaked.

They looked at one another, and Susan said, "About time."

Betsey shuffled into the kitchen. "Where's everyone?"

"Eli's in the field," said Susan, "and Eleanor took the girls to town."

"Is he slinging more dung?" said Betsey as she laughed. She shrugged her shoulders and grimaced. "Hate them flies. And the almighty smell. . . Don't know how you do it."

"Someone has to."

Betsey glared at Susan for her cheeky reply.

Susan's spunk surprised Naamah, too. *Good for her*, she thought.

Betsey bit into a muffin. "Still warm. I adore warm muffins." She grabbed two more and sat at the kitchen table.

"Are you going to eat them all?" asked Susan.

Betsey stopped chewing. "I've but two."

"Three."

"Already, three then. But there's plenty." Betsey took another bite. "You're a good baker, Susan."

"Thanks to Amy."

"Being a good cook will help you get a man."

Naamah looked at Betsey while stirring the batter. "That's gum. Who told you such a thing?"

"Don't know, but it can't hurt." Betsey took another bite. "Of course Eleanor got Eli, and she ain't much of a cook." She chuckled. "But old Eli had hankerings for more than just his stomach."

"Betsey," said Naamah as she shot her eyes toward Susan.

"Amy, I'm eighteen," said Susan. "I know of manly hankerings." She turned to Betsey and said, "Speaking of hankerings, how's Horace?"

Betsey straightened out of her slouch. "Fine, just fine." She settled against the chair's backrest. "Yet he still talks too much about Amy's fella, that Maginn preacher."

"I haven't seen Horace lately," said Naamah.

"I thought we'd be rid of Maginn by now. Gone with George and the rest of them."

"Heavenly Father must want him to stay to spread His good news."

"Peterborough would be a far better place if it never saw the likes of Maginn. I had to put Horace right. Told him it was either Maginn or me."

"Aha, that's why I haven't seen him."

"And you won't, if he wants to see me."

Susan was observing a familiar scene, two older sisters seeing the world differently, which had worsened once Maginn arrived. Betsey had tried to sway her against the Saints. But she had a unique attachment with Naamah and remained indifferent to Betsey's remarks. Again, she was on the sidelines wishing the squabbling would cease. But unlike previous times, she blurted out, "Stop it, both of you."

The bickering ceased. Betsey continued eating while frowning. Naamah was quiet, chagrined over being drawn into another argument. She fumbled with the button on her dress.

"Oh, the muffins. They must be done," said Naamah as she moved to the stove. With a thick padded cloth, she removed the pan and placed it on the stovetop. She dabbed the muffin tops. "Perfect. Susan, come here and press."

"Amy I know. If they bounce when you press, they're done."

Naamah smiled and nodded.

"Will you be making strawberry rhubarb pie?" asked Betsey as she arose.

Naamah pointed to the picked rhubarb near the door.

"Don't let Eli eat it all. I want a piece." Betsey fluffed a few tresses and allowed them to dangle. She adjusted her dress at the shoulders to let it drape evenly. "I'm heading to town."

"To see Horace?" asked Susan.

"None of your matter."

Betsey left, and as the door closed, Naamah sighed. "She's a whirlwind."

"And selfish, too," said Susan as she grabbed the rhubarb and began dicing.

Naamah put another batch of muffins into the oven and sat next to Susan. The two hummed as they diced until Naamah said, "Smaller pieces will taste less tart." Susan grabbed the large pieces and re-cut them. Naamah was pleased; her student still had more to learn.

Susan ceased dicing and looked at her smiling sister. "Do you think you'll ever leave?"

"Leave?"

"With the Saints." Susan arose to get more rhubarb. "Go off into the wilderness."

"I thought I'd never leave Peterborough. But of late, well, I don't know." Naamah arose to check on the muffins.

"I'd miss you."

The sincerity in Susan's voice surprised and thrilled Naamah. She wanted to hug her as she had done so often. But now Susan was taller than her, and cradling Susan's head against her chest would be awkward. So she put her arms around Susan's waist and tugged. "I'll always be here for you."

Susan broke the embrace. "Not always. Just until I can cook good enough to get a man."

Naamah's body shook as she laughed. "You sound like Betsey."

"I hope not." Susan chuckled, and then her eyes grew steely. "Amy, I can protect myself."

"I know dear, but . . ."

"Amy," and Naamah was silenced by Susan's resolve, "if your God calls you west, don't stay because of me."

Their eyes remained locked, and Naamah wondered, *Did God just untie another bond?*

Chapter Nine

June 1843

Nauvoo, Illinois

While Naamah remained in Peterborough still wondering, George, who had undergone similar deliberations, had resolved his doubts. He had just arrived in Nauvoo, and his initial impression was so overwhelming that his memory of the past several arduous weeks was already fading. He moved from the wagons to absorb more.

A massive limestone foundation lay ahead, dwarfing the workers about it. *Has to be the temple*, he thought as he visualized it complete – several stories of white stone with the angel Gabriel atop its spire, blowing his trumpet to call the faithful. He was bearing witness to the centering point for the Prophet's grand plan, an earthly Zion. He scrunched his shoulders as he thought, *If only I could see it all.*

He ambled farther away. Unlike Peterborough, the ground was flat and the streets crisscrossed one another. Hand-hewn log houses, some wooden framed ones, and even brick ones were situated on uniform lots. Each lot had ample space for a garden. *Shelter and sustenance,* he thought, a*s only a Prophet could see.* The south side, set in low lands, and the north were more heavily built upon than the east. Nauvoo teemed with commerce and optimism, unlike the desolation and resentment he had experienced east of the city. Saplings lined the streets, but he imagined when they would be as stately as Peterborough's. His previous rural community had less than a thousand residents, and amid Nauvoo's bustle he mused, *She's gotta be several times larger.*

He rose on his toes to gaze west. The Mississippi dominated the horizon, with shimmering waters drifting and occasionally swirling around shoals and flotsam. Islands and boats further defined an otherwise vast body of water. One steamed toward a wooded, uninhabited island. He squinted as he pondered. *Aha, a barge.* He turned to the uncompleted temple and nodded. *Nearby timber -- the Prophet has seen it all.*

He moved back to the wagons as sawing, banging, and men shouting instructions filled his ears, and sawdust smells and tanning odors filled his nostrils. Several blocks north, houses were under construction, and he wondered if one was his parents'. A two-story house had empty lots on either side, seemingly beckoning him to build. He gazed, savoring his thoughts, until Harriett sidled near and embraced him.

"We're finally home," she said.

George put his arm around her shoulder and pointed. "I'll build a brick house there. Two stories high for you and me." He removed his arm and glanced at her stomach. "And for George Junior."

"My lower regions have finally quieted." She sighed and looked to George with a smile. "George Junior knows he's home, too."

"Vomiting gone?"

Harriett nodded. "We endured such jostling, I feared a smart chance of losing him." She gazed at George. "I know Heavenly Father was with us as we journeyed."

The former Peterborough Saints approached the wagon train to welcome the new arrivals. As several familiar faces approached George, he saw no one from his family. He looked elsewhere, hoping to see them. Disheartened, he turned back and saw his mother among several similarly dressed women. He called to her and waved. Her smile was as warm and inviting as ever, yet in contrast to her sallow cheeks and hollow eyes.

Susanna ran to him and clung, pressing into his chest and collapsing her head on his shoulder. She said nothing, content to cling, until stepping back to kiss his bearded cheek. "More of my family has safely arrived." She wrung her hands and began quivering.

"Mother, you have the shakes."

"The excitement, I reckon." She gripped her arms and pulled them close.

George looked around. "Is Father here?"

"Still weary from a touch of ague."

George's brow creased.

"Pay it no bother. It's merely fevers and chill with occasional sweating. Everyone has a touch."

"And Oliver?"

"He's tithing, working on the temple."

George turned to the temple.

"No dear, he's cutting stone in the quarry. Only masons work on the temple."

"Perhaps with time and being attentive, Oliver could become a mason. It's a good trade."

"Perhaps, but your father needs him now."

"Where's Father's house?" George pointed to where he had promised Harriett he would build their house. "There?"

"No, they're quite dear. We're farther north. Cost Washington twenty dollars, near all we had."

Harriett had stayed back, allowing George to be alone with his mother. Susanna finally noticed her. "Goodness, my dear, come." She embraced Harriett and stepped back. "So full of life after such an almighty journey."

Harriett dwelled on Susanna's prophetic comment. She was indeed full of life and wanted to tell her, but decided to wait for a private time. She swatted at a buzzing near her head and flailed as it persisted. "Land sakes."

"The Nauvoo flies," said Susanna. "They're evil."

"More so than Peterborough's?" said George as he chuckled.

"Worse than imagined." Susanna pushed her sleeve up and extended her red blotchy forearm for George and Harriett to examine. "And at candle light, the no-see-ums and mosquitoes are fierce."

Harriett's eyes widened as she looked to George. "I've never witnessed such bites."

*****

George's initial excitement remained, growing through the week, and today, it would soar. At high noon and among a throng of perspiring Saints, he craned his neck toward billowing dust and sounds of clomping hooves and a majestic band. Two smartly dressed officers mounted on horses led The Nauvoo Militia toward him. One rose from the saddle and acknowledged the crowd while the other rode side-saddle, shying from the throng. What George had envisioned since his baptism was unfolding before his eyes. He looked to his mother.

Susanna took delight in George's twinkling eyes, just like when he was a boy. She nodded and said, "It's them."

He turned from his mother. Joseph's gold frill epaulettes swished as he bounced in the saddle. His countenance was kind, inviting, not like the old grizzled militiamen he had often witnessed - - so magnetic that George was enraptured. He turned back to his mother and said, "So young."

Susanna nodded.

He studied him and turned again. "And handsome."

Susanna blushed.

The woman riding side-saddle several paces behind Joseph was stern, seemingly tired of conflict, and older looking. She seemed saddened, aloof. George turned to his mother with a curious look.

"Emma Smith," she said

He moved farther into the crowd, nearer to the procession. Among strangers, he studied the contrasting pair until Joseph captivated him again. He couldn't take his eyes from him.

"She seems distressed," said a woman near George.

"The Partridge sisters, the Lawrence sisters, others," said another. "Too many women living in one house would distress me, too."

"Maids, nieces," the woman sneered. "I told my Ephraim, if he ever . . ."

"Sisters," said a man standing near as he turned to glare at them, "mind your blasphemous tongues."

George wondered about the conversation until blaring horns and booming drums captured his attention. He closed his eyes, allowing the rhythm to move his spirit. Basking in the sun, he inhaled and thought, *I'm truly in your kingdom.*

Once the procession had passed, the crowd headed toward a stand of trees, aptly named the Grove. George waited, savoring his experience. His mother neared with glowing cheeks unlike when he saw her a week ago.

"He's more than I imagined," said George. "And the band . . . it's still beating in my soul."

"You must join it. Don't let your God-given talents wither. Not sure where you got them. Certainly not from me or your father." Susanna turned to her husband. "Isn't that right dear?"

Washington forced a smile.

"Let's head to the Grove and you get out of this sun," she said.

The Taggarts moved with the crowd heading to hear more. George grabbed Harriett's hand and quickened his pace. Oliver locked arms with his father and took measured steps while steadying him.

Susanna paused and closed her eyes, trying to shake the image of her rapidly aging husband. She re-opened them, looked heavenward, and quickened her pace to catch up with George. Walking beside him, she sensed his enthusiasm. *If my other sons could only be so inspired,* she thought.

George thought about the earlier conversation he had overheard. What he didn't know was Emily and Eliza Partridge had lived with the family of Joseph Smith. While there, he introduced his concept of celestial marriage and asked them to enter into it with him. They had been sealed a month earlier by Heber C. Kimball. Joseph's wife Emma had initially agreed to the marriages, only to have grave doubts soon afterward.

"Mother," said George, and Susanna left her thoughts. "Who are the Partridge sisters?"

Her smile left as she turned from George. "Maids working for the Prophet."

"Why would they concern Emma? I heard two women saying . . ."

Susanna stopped, and George and Harriett stopped, too, as the crowd passed by them. "We're not always as one in Nauvoo," said Susanna. She placed her hands on her hips. "Apostates seek to undermine us with the vilest of rumors."

The edge to his mother's voice surprised George, and he instinctively cowered like when he was young and being lectured for a transgression.

"In Peterborough we knew the non-believers. Nauvoo's different, larger, so listen only to the Prophet or the Twelve, the Prophet's apostles." Susanna dropped her hands from her hips and waited for Oliver and her husband.

Feeling rebuked and wanting to hear the Prophet, George grabbed Harriett's hand and moved with the crowd. They walked among strangers, buzzing excitement from what they had witnessed and anticipating what would come at the Grove. George sensed a fellowship with the crowd.

"Quite a display by General Smith, wasn't it?" said one walking near.

"'Twas, but he'd be wise to keep his militia close. Governor Boggs won't be satisfied until he has his day. He's issued a writ or something in Missouri."

George was intrigued and veered closer.

"No matter. His legal doings are useless in Illinois."

"Should be, but I don't trust our Governor Ford neither. President Smith should stay nigh, in Nauvoo."

George grew concerned until his mother's words came into his thoughts. "*Apostates seek to undermine us with the vilest of rumors.*" He hoped he was overhearing another rumor until he heard, "Brother Snow, will our ordeals ever end?"

Chapter Ten

George remained enthralled with Nauvoo. Annoyances existed, trivial in comparison to the reward and, whenever unsettling conversations were heard, he dismissed them as rumor. But on Sunday, June 25, while at the Grove, news came he couldn't dismiss. Joseph's legal difficulties were real, and worse, Governor Ford had acted on Governor Boggs's extradition request and captured Joseph while he was away from Nauvoo. At the meeting, two from The Twelve asked for volunteers to rescue Joseph, to which many more than needed responded.

30 June 1843

George's despair from five days ago lingered with him as he headed to his parents'. He had borne witness to his Prophet once, and now he feared he wouldn't ever again. He wondered why God guided him here, only to snatch his Prophet away. Since his capture, George was hearing more about Joseph's past ordeals.

A decade earlier in Kirkland, Ohio, Joseph was dragged from his home, tarred and feathered, and left for dead. He persevered, but soon afterward his son died, which the Saints attributed to the attack on Joseph. Civility ensued, and in 1836 the Kirkland temple was completed, although at a dear cost. A church schism occurred and animosity returned. Apostates accused Joseph of promoting the failed, church-sponsored bank that financed the temple, and worse, of sexual relations with his servant girl, Fanny Alger. In January 1838, a warrant for bank fraud was issued for Joseph and, he fled to Missouri, with many faithful following later.

In Missouri, a cornerstone for another temple was laid along with renewed hope. But peace in Missouri was shorter lived than in Kirkland. In August, gentiles prevented the faithful from voting and scuffles ensued, initiating the 1838 Mormon War. Governor Boggs ordered, "Mormons to be exterminated and driven from the state." On October thirtieth, seventeen Saints were ambushed and killed, and soon after, Joseph was imprisoned. Many Saints ceased fighting and forfeited their property to flee. Leaderless, they wandered across the Mississippi to Commerce, Illinois while enduring a brutal winter.

In April 1839, after four months in jail, Joseph escaped and joined his faithful in Commerce. He renamed the city Nauvoo, Hebrew for beautiful, became a councilman, its mayor, and received a revelation to build another temple. But Missouri continued to harass him, and he was arrested in June 1841, only to be later released.

George was overwhelmed reflecting on the Saints' ordeals and paused to ponder. *Kirkland, Missouri, and now Nauvoo. Will I be like them and be driven from Nauvoo?* He had encouraged his family and Harriett to come to Nauvoo, and now he fretted about it. He glanced at the temple construction and thought of The Beatitudes his father forced him to memorize. Oddly, one came as clear as when he first recited it while his father stood over him.

"Blessed are those who are persecuted for righteousness' sake: for theirs is the kingdom of heaven."

He found new meaning in that Beatitude. He would endure life's travails, like Joseph, a speck of time before entering God's kingdom. He smiled, recalling his struggles in memorizing the Beatitudes as he walked.

He ceased reminiscing when he heard a distant band playing. He paused and cocked an ear as others paused, too. The sound grew louder as it played "Hail Columbia". Guns and cannons exploded sending shivers up George's spine. Nauvoo seemed alive again, pulsating in unison with the rhythm filling its streets. Some dashed toward the approaching sound while a few, seemingly paralyzed, wept.

"He's saved yet again."

Seemingly on cue, a breeze came to usher in the Prophet's return and to refresh George. Joseph led the celebration toward George and the growing crowd. He was bearing witness for a second time to the Prophet, and his emotions catapulted higher than before. His Prophet, seeming forever lost, was returning triumphantly yet again. His emotions had surged from utter despair to exhilaration, akin he imagined to what the early Saints had often experienced. He felt bonded with them, suffering through an ordeal, no longer a naïve, awestruck visitor, but one of Nauvoo's brethren. As Joseph passed by, he thought, *Never will I doubt. He'll always return.*

George continued to his parents' and worried anew about his father's health. As he neared his father's plot, he thought of reciting the Beatitudes in front of a youthful Father, a stark contrast to his father today.

"Blessed are those who are persecuted for righteousness' sake: for theirs is the kingdom of heaven."

Chapter Eleven

As summer wore on, more reality peppered George's initial impressions of Nauvoo. The reason he had never witnessed so many bites on his mother's forearm had become obvious. In late afternoon, the ubiquitous Nauvoo flies seemed to vanish, creating a breather until dusk when the mosquitos would swarm. His calico tent with loose netting draped on its sides was ineffective in keeping them out. One restless night as George swatted at his bothers, he concluded Nauvoo's inability to keep pace with its rapid growth and process waste suitably, coupled with the soggy marshes in the lowlands, created ideal breeding grounds for the pests.

His mother's admonition that Nauvoo isn't inhabited solely by the faithful came often into his thoughts. In Peterborough, Maginn was the common bond who inspired the Saints. Further, like the Taggarts, many in the community had kindred ties and deep roots dating back before Peterborough's founding. And while bonds fray and even break, a connection to a community still remained.

Nauvoo was different. It had a cadre of Saints who had their relationships forged from earlier tribulations at Kirkland and in Missouri. About the core of early followers were others who had arrived from various places. Thus, Nauvoo consisted of factions created from differing locales and experiences, was more diverse, and lacked of a common history.

The non-believers, some of whom lived within the city limits, grew envious as they witnessed an erstwhile undesirable marsh grow into a center of commerce. Joseph Smith instituted laws as part of the church doctrine that created a civility that was non-existent outside Nauvoo. Northwest Illinois was populated with outcasts from the eastern establishment who welcomed the freer rein the sparely settled region offered. Contempt for the law was so pervasive, at times, the region bordered on anarchy. Understandably, the Saints grew insular, preferring to trade among themselves, and when necessity required dealing with non-believers, an inherent mistrust existed.

Unlike the established eastern United States or England, Nauvoo lacked a common currency. Saints arrived with notes drawn on local banks or other script that wasn't readily accepted as legal tender, which caused Joseph Smith to declare, 'paper currency an evil, a canker that saps out our life'. He decreed gold and silver the only legal tender within Nauvoo, making script virtually worthless. Since many had arrived with little, if any, specie, self-sustaining and bartering became their means for existence.

Just prior to arriving in Nauvoo, George had passed a cemetery on the city's eastern edge with numerous grave markers. He thought it odd at the time that a city less than a few years old would have so many graves. Later, when he learned of two more cemeteries, he wasn't surprised as he sensed Nauvoo's death rate far exceeded Peterborough's. What caused him special concern was the many children listed in the obituaries of the *Wasp*, Nauvoo's newspaper. He worried for George junior and the world into which he would soon come. But his mother eased his worry saying that it's just the sickly season, and this will pass with the autumn frost.

George had an understanding why August was known as the sickly season. He had endured hot August days in Peterborough all his life, which were often cooled with nightfall or with northwest breezes. But Nauvoo's heat and humidity were incessant, smothering him like a scratchy, foul-smelling blanket. He perspired often, and his clothing reeked, a constant reminder of this hell hole. He hoped September would bring a respite.

*****

George stared at holes evenly spaced apart that outlined the foundation for his father's home. Some holes were only partially dug. The stone pile laying near should have been depleted by now. He shuffled to the tent and paused to wipe his sleeve across his forehead. The construction nearby had progressed since his last visit. He wondered if his father lacked money or if his ague had sapped his energy.

He lifted the tent netting and peered in. His father lay, eyes sunken and gazing, seemingly unaware of George's presence. His pillow's sweat stain appeared like a black halo. A hand stroked down George's back, and he wheeled around.

"Let your father rest," whispered Susanna.

He let the netting drift from his hand and followed his mother. She sat on the crude bench near her garden and patted a spot next to her. She extended her legs and fluffed her dress as George joined her.

"So humid," she said.

"We need an almighty dose of Peterborough air right now."

"I miss Peterborough. Didn't fancy I'd have the courage to leave," said Susanna as she swatted to shoo away a fly. "I reckon my courage comes from Father. He'd say, 'Susanna, you've got Scotch courage. You get it from great-grand pappy John Law.' "

"Great-grand pappy John Law?"

"Our kin. He came here as Cromwell's prisoner years ago. Scotch courage," Susanna laughed. "We're more English than Scotch. But Father always hated the English, the war and all, felt more akin to the Scots. After the war, he packed his sled and trudged to Peterborough Slip to build a new home."

"Grandfather never feared a thing. I reckon he got his courage from this John Law."

"How he endured I'll never know, suffering through the first winter, toiling the days, sleeping on his favorite rock at night."

"He was a pioneer -- like you Mother."

"Oh pshaw," she said as she turned from George. She pondered and turned back. "Never thought of myself as a pioneer. But if I am, so are you."

George bowed his head. "Grandfather's favorite rock is where we listened to your sermons when we were young."

She waved a dismissive hand. "They weren't sermons, George. Just words the Lord inspired me with."

"Not according to Grandfather. He'd always say, 'If my Susanna was a man, she'd be a damn good preacher.' "

"I miss him. Been two years since he left us." Susanna glanced toward the temple and back to George. "Once the temple's complete, we must have Father baptized. I want him with us in His heavenly kingdom.'

George nodded.

"And his namesake, little Reubie." Susanna grew sad thinking of her infant son's suffering.

"He's at peace now."

"True, but he's not in His heavenly kingdom."

"There's time to redeem them both," said George as he sat more erect. Sensing his mother's sadness remained, he added, "I promise."

Susanna didn't respond, seemingly preoccupied and drifting deeper into sadness.

"Is Father getting better?"

She shook her head. "His lower regions ailed before we arrived. I fear his fever now resides in them, too."

"What did the physician say?"

"Said quinine would ease the fever. But the druggist's walls are empty. A shipment is due within a fortnight." Susanna sighed. "But the cost will be too dear."

"Should we bleed him?"

"Physician Tate says it's too primitive."

"Then what should we do?"

"Pray to God for certainty on the matter."

George bowed his head as he thought, *Grandfather was right. She would be a damn good preacher.*

They remained deep in thoughts, barely moving in the oppressive air, until George shifted on the bench while frowning and staring at the rock pile.

"Oliver must be better," he said. "Even though he hasn't worked a lick."

"He still ails, but is tithing today."

George arose. "I've seen Father's building sketches. I could come on and help. Completing the holes and stoning should take a few days, and if Father has ordered the timber, I could . . ."

"George, we've not enough money for timber. And with Washington and Oliver ailing, we have little to barter." She pointed to her garden. "Only a few crops."

George pursed his lips and took a few steps. He turned to his mother. "I still have a double eagle, half eagle, and a few shillings."

Susanna arose. "Keep your coins. But if you could help . . ."

"I will," said George. "Besides, my thoughts of a brick house were but fancy."

"You could live here."

George wrinkled his brow. "Too crowded, and George junior will be born soon."

"And soon," said Susanna as she closed her eyes, "I dread my tent will be uncrowded."

George came to her, and as she reopened her eyes he saw her anguish.

She gulped and said, "While in Peterborough, Heavenly Father told Washington not to tarry, and we left in haste. Last night while wiping his brow, he bore his testimony. 'I led us to Nauvoo. My work is done. My time draws nigh for me to return to the Lord.' "

Susanna spoke without passion, resigned to the inevitable. George covered his mouth, and his hand drifted through his beard to grip his neck. He clenched his other hand, unable to speak and reassure his mother until her stoic presence gave him strength.

"Then so be it. Father has fulfilled the Lord's purpose."

"Bless you my son."

They embraced as they often had through the years. But George sensed desperation to his mother's cling, as if she was trying to unite her tired soul with his for strength. After a few moments, she broke their embrace.

"Mother, I'll finish the house, and if Oliver could . . ."

"Oliver? I know not Heavenly Father's plan for him." Susanna looked to the ground while rubbing a hand. "I know not his plan for me." She looked at George. "Life is uncertain, is it not?"

George said nothing, sensing his mother had more.

Susanna pondered while taking deliberate steps. She sighed.

"Death is the only certainty we have."

Chapter Twelve

27 August 1843

Susanna's stoic presence while stating the inevitable demonstrated a concept George heard often – accept God's will with a strength to endure. A father will die and his eldest son will assume his role is innate. Fathers dying occurred often in Nauvoo, reminding George his rite of passage would occur. Unlike other rites, like marrying Harriett and having children, he had no control over this one. He prayed for guidance and the strength whenever it came to pass.

*****

On an unexpectedly cool Sabbath, George walked with Harriett to the Grove. He arose early, committed to arrive ahead of the throng to be close to the podium. Today, he needed inspiration, wanting to hear all that would be said.

Seeing no signs of activity as they neared his father's tent, he paused and called out. As others passed them, Oliver emerged from underneath the tent flap, buttoning his shirt and pulling a suspender over his shoulder. Sensing George's displeasure, Oliver hustled.

"Is Father coming?"

"Too ill, and Mother won't leave him."

George was not surprised -- another reminder of what his soul knew was imminent. "You have added strength this Sabbath," said George.

"Mother opened the tent last night, and my fever's gone."

George glanced at the stone pile. "So by tomorrow the stones will be in place."

"I reckon, but my head's a swirl."

"The stones," said George as his eyes narrowed. "By tomorrow?"

Oliver cowered and nodded.

George and Oliver walked with other men while Harriett drifted to some nearby women. The buzz of anticipation was pervasive, buoying George. "Today, I'm reminded of Peterborough," he said. "And gathering at the Nubanusit."

Oliver scanned the crowd and turned to George. "But this an almighty gathering." After several steps, he pointed to the Mississippi. "And that ain't the Nubanusit."

"Just Peterborough on a mighty scale."

They chatted more and eventually were among some English men.

"Odd, isn't it?" said Oliver.

Confused, George looked at his brother.

"Just like Peterborough, and we're walking with Maginn." Oliver chuckled. "Lots of Maginns."

"There's only one Elder Maginn."

"I still fancy their accents. It's why I was baptized."

"Because of Maginn's accent?"

"I reckon."

"What about his preaching?"

"Never really listened to his words, just his accent."

Oliver's words troubled George, and he considered rebuking him. But he let it pass and pondered. Oliver always admired him and followed him as he became a Saint. He wondered if Oliver was truly inspired or only parroting him. Soon he would assume his father's role, and Oliver would need to assume more responsibility, too. He glanced at a grinning Oliver, still amused by the English accents, and wondered, *Will he be strong enough to endure?*

At the Grove, the early arrivers had gathered by gender near the podium, where a few from the Twelve were talking among themselves.

"We must sit close," said George as he hustled to an open spot near the front.

Oliver followed at a relaxed pace, and Harriett moved with some women to a bench far from the podium.

George eased to the ground and pulled his knees toward him, enjoying the solitude until the ever-swelling crowd disturbed him. When Joseph stepped onto the low-rise podium, the crowd quieted. One from the Twelve arose and spoke, and George listened, hoping for inspiration. Other speakers followed, but George was drawn to Joseph too often and was inattentive to them.

As Joseph arose, George's heart pounded. He made a few inaudible remarks to the last speaker before strolling to be front and center. He welcomed the assembly and commented on the temple's progress. He was of average height and spoke in ordinary tones, unlike Maginn's towering presence and commanding voice. But his face was smooth with rounded features, more attractive than Maginn's rawboned one with its prominent nose. He opened his arms to the heavens, drawing George seemingly face to face to bear witness. Joseph's eyes seemed oblivious to the crowd, focused elsewhere as he related what he saw.

"We're all sons of God the Father sent here like Jesus to endure as he endured. And when we're called to leave, we will return to God the Father, leaving our sons to be fathers. And like unto them, they will reunite with God the Father. Your earthly burdens are brief, and your salvation will be to reside again from whence you came, in eternal paradise."

George squeezed his eyes, trying to envision eternal paradise. His grandfather Reuben and infant brother Reubie floated against a softened mix of shadowy, reflective clouds. His father appeared suddenly, yet George was unafraid. He seemed as welcoming as Joseph when he said, *"My blessed son, of you I'm well pleased"*.

George grew lightheaded and his eyes reopened. Joseph's eyes were no longer elsewhere, but riveted upon him. He nodded an approval, and George nodded back.

Joseph lowered his eyelids and turned from George. "And for the son who cannot endure yet follows in faith, you will see paradise, too. For God only gives unto a son what he can endure."

Joseph ambled to those seated behind him. As they arose and offered praise to Joseph, "Amen" came from the congregation. George pondered what he had just witnessed before arising and dusting his bottom.

Oliver followed George's lead. "Must have been several hours," he said. "I still fancy Maginn."

George ceased brushing his pants, unconvinced that Oliver was prepared for what would come.

Chapter Thirteen

5 September 1843

Like walking to the gates of hell, George trudged with Harriett and his mother beside two recently-crafted pine boxes upon a wagon while pondering. He had left the Grove ten days earlier, reconciled to a logically sequenced rite of passage and prepared to endure. But Oliver's death a day before his father's was unexpected and illogically sequenced in the world order. His ague had passed, only to return with a vengeance. He had accused Oliver of malingering and bullied him to complete the foundation. *Was I too hard on the boy?* Oliver's dying words were his regret for disappointing George. *Was God's vengeance meant for me and not Oliver?* His earlier proselytizing was like his recent badgering, utter intimidation. If he had not evangelized, Oliver would still be in Peterborough. *Did I, like Cain, slay my brother?* He had replayed that question often. Now the answer would come when he was reunited with Oliver in eternity.

His hand pushed down his thigh and across several coins in his pocket. The gold double eagle, which was to be used for his house, was gone, replaced with a half eagle and several silver shillings. The unadorned pine coffins lacked black lining and were

unstained, yet were still expensive. To save more, George dressed
the bodies for viewing by those coming to offer condolences. His
guilt weighed heavily while dressing Oliver, and Harriett needed to
finish for him. Elder Gardner donated his wagon, and George
believed he had no other expense until Susanna insisted she must
write to her sons. George pulled from his pocket the half eagle
needed to pay the seventy-five cents for paper and postage. He
pondered it before sliding it back into his pocket.

The wagon veered to allow room for a returning wagon. Two
women clad in black and a man with a snowy beard sat upon it; a
few others walked behind. One woman sobbed, and the others
seemed deep in thought or simply dumbstruck. As the wagons
passed one another, the old man removed his hat and placed it across
his heart. George nodded his appreciation.

The wagon reached the gravesite, and Elder Gardner and
George removed the coffins. Susanna stood between Harriett and
Gardner's wife, looking as dumbstruck as those whom they had just
passed. Elder Wright, another Peterborough Saint, had helped
George dig the two graves earlier. His wife had typhus pleurisy, and
George planned to return the favor when Elder Wright's wife died.

A last shovelful of dirt was thrown on the two coffins.
Gardner moved to the women at the foot of the graves. George
assumed his new role at the head, alone, and facing the others.

"Heavenly Father," he said as Gardner removed his hat.
George paused as the lump in his throat persisted. He shifted his
eyes to the blinding sunlight and became lost within it.

"Heavenly Father, we return them unto thee. They came to live among us according to your will. We pray you are well pleased with them. We will endure here until you call us to return."

George lowered his head and flashed his eyes. His temporary blindness left. His mother's face still reflected the burdens she would endure, emotionless, as if his words had no meaning. He worried. *Have I failed in her time of need?* He wrung his hands as his eyes welled. He shifted them to the sun and saw his father and Oliver. *"Of you, my blessed son, I'm well pleased"*.

His worry left until Oliver's image drifted from his father. While staring at Oliver, George thought, *I was too hard on you, and I beg forgiveness*. Oliver morphed into the clouds, and George heard nothing.

Chapter Fourteen

October 1843

Peterborough, New Hampshire

The rising sun melted the garden rime, and dew glistened while vapors rose from the pumpkins. Albert Taggart scrunched his shoulders and blew on his hands. *Going to be an almighty cold winter.*

As he entered the house, an ashen Samuel was holding a letter. "So what did Mother pen us?" asked Albert.

Samuel tossed two sheets of paper onto the table. "Look for yourself."

Albert grabbed and flipped through them searching for the beginning.

"Mother wrote first, then George." Samuel snorted and said, "They're so poor they can barely afford paper."

Albert glared at his brother before returning to the letter. His hand trembled upon seeing his mother's handwriting. His eyes moved across the letter to see:

"*Nauvoo September 6th 1843. Dear Children, I now take my pen in hand to write you a line to inform you of my health, which is pretty good. But the subject upon which I must write makes the task a painful one for I must tell you, my children, you are fatherless.*"

Albert's hand trembled so much he couldn't read further. He dropped it and stared.

"Yup, Father's dead. Read on, it's worse."

Albert gripped with both hands, and through teary eyes only salient words were seen. "*Father ... bowel complaint . . . never was well of it while he lived . . . Oliver . . . fever . . . ague.*" He dropped his hand to his side. "Good God, not Oliver."

Samuel nodded.

"And Mother?"

"She and George still live. Mother wrote she prays that we will be saved." Samuel shook his head. "Prayed to her false God to save us. How loony is that?"

"She's always prayed for us. Stop being harsh."

Samuel frowned and turned from his brother.

"What did George write?"

"Said what Mother said -- they're poor as church mice and praised Old Joe." Samuel slammed the table. "Damn him, it's all his fault."

"Old Joe's?"

"Old Joe, Maginn, George -- all of them. It was George who turned them."

"You can't blame George. Mother and Father always had deep faith."

"Didn't George go into the drink first?"

Albert shrugged and nodded.

"Mother, Father, Oliver, even Cousin Amy followed him."

Albert cowered from his brother's continuing tirade.

"Albert, you're the eldest with any sense left at all. Go to that hell on earth and fetch Mother back."

"I doubt she'd return. She believes in Old Joe. What did George say about him?"

"Ah, I forget. Give me the letter."

Samuel grabbed the letter and fumbled through it. "Listen to this gum. 'Now something concerning Old Joe, so called. He is a young-looking man for his age, which is near thirty-eight years, and one of the finest looking men in the country. And he does not pretend to be a man without failings and follies.' "

Samuel snapped the letter down. "Without failings? I hear tell he chases every woman who crosses his path."

"Who told you that?"

"I forget, maybe Old Sym."

"Before he entered the tavern or after?"

"No matter. It's an orgy out there, like Sodom and Gomorrah."

"Mother would never go to such a place."

"You don't understand. Old Joe is like Maginn, a fancy talker, thinking he's the second coming. Listen to this."

Samuel scanned the letter for a few moments. "Ah, listen. 'He is a man that you could not help liking as a man, setting aside the religious prejudice that the world has raised against him.' " Samuel mumbled before speaking more clearly. " 'And I assure you it would make you wonder to hear him talk and see the information which comes out of his mouth, and it is not in big words either, but those which any one can understand.' "

"George hasn't mentioned orgies yet."

Samuel glared at his brother. "Not directly, but there's more." Samuel returned to the letter. "Now concerning public reports and stories concerning Joseph Smith and the Mormons, so called, they are false as the Devil or those that may make such stories. I say this as a fact knowing it to be so. Therefore if you ever believed me to be one of truth, I am still the same."

"Still no orgies."

"Not exactly, but," and Samuel crumpled the letter and tossed it on the table, "George is hiding it. He's different than us."

"He's always been closer to God. And Samuel," Albert paused to gather his brother's attention, "he's always been far more truthful than either of us."

"Ah, c'mon Albert, you've heard the stories about Old Joe."

"I have. But people always talk, especially after you depart. Even early Christians were misunderstood. People called them cannibals."

"Huh?"

"Yup cannibals, because they ate Jesus's flesh and drank his blood."

"That's communion."

"'Tis, but the pagans misunderstood. Maybe people misunderstand Old Joe."

"You sound as loony as George. I know the truth. We'd be better off without Old Joe and without Maginn, too." Samuel threw on his coat. "I've got chores." The door slammed, and amid the sound of crunching leaves, Albert heard, "Damn them all." The ranting continued.

Albert smoothed the creases on the crumpled letter. He read until his eyes blurred. He bowed his head and prayed until the crunching leaves grew louder. He looked to the door.

Samuel opened it and stuck his head inside. "Mother's going to pray for us, is she? Well, here's my prayer." Samuel looked heavenward. "God, strike down that evil Old Joe, and while you're at it, Maginn, too."

The door slammed, and Albert closed his eyes. He thought of earlier times with his father and Oliver. A gust roared and swirled the leaves to drown out Samuel's anger. The fury grew, seemingly vengeful. Albert opened his eyes and held his breath, waiting for a calm that did not come, and he grew fearful.

Chapter Fifteen

Spring 1844

Peterborough, New Hampshire

The snow that had clung stubbornly in the shadows finally melted. Spring had arrived, and "the worst winter ever remembered" had ended. The air warmed, and when tree buds exploded with leaves, Peterborough came alive.

Near the tavern, Henry Thornton picked his teeth with a straw reed while studying a gathering crowd. John Mackenzie approached and asked, "Whatcha looking at?"

He pointed. "Them Saints."

"Maginn must be back."

"There's the mystery. Old Sym said Maginn met his maker, down in Massachusetts. Lowell, I think."

"You're joshing. He's too young. You sure Sym's right?"

"I ain't seen Maginn."

"Can't miss him: tall, quoting scriptures." John chuckled. "He told our Reverend a thing or two about the scriptures."

Henry ceased picking his teeth and stared at John.

"It weren't a fair fight. Maginn gave our pompous Reverend his comeuppance."

Henry shifted his eyes to the crowd. "I figure with Maginn dead, them Saints would die off too."

John observed the crowd while pondering. "Maybe they're having some kind of funeral for him."

"Ah, that's probably it." Henry ceased watching. "Maybe by and by, they'll become Christians again." Henry spat on the ground. "If we'll have 'em back."

"Doubt they'll do that. They got a meeting brewing for this summer."

"But Maginn's dead."

"It's bigger than Maginn. Big as all creation."

"You saying Joe Smith is coming?"

"Maybe."

"Why would he come here? Hell, a boodle of them Saints have traipsed out to see him."

"Don't know. But Old Sym said it's going to be almighty big,"

"Ah, sweet Jesus."

John stared at the crowd filing into the hall. "Shame about Maginn. I kind of fancied him."

"Well, head across the street, go into the drink, and you'll see him in paradise."

Henry laughed as John shook his head and continued along. Henry continued to chuckle, amused by his last retort. He tossed the straw reed aside and sucked through the newly-cleaned gap between his teeth. He put his hands in his pockets and spat while watching the Saints. Once they had filed into the hall, he thought of his friend. *John's got to acknowledge the corn. With Maginn gone, them Saints will be gone, too.* He spat again and lowered his head to shuffle home.

*****

Inside the meeting hall, Naamah sat amid unoccupied spots on either side of her, delineating each clique. Last year, every seat was occupied, and others stood around the perimeter or listened from outside the eight foot open windows. She didn't sense the fellowship of earlier times, even though the faces were familiar.

She glanced to her left where her aunt had sat and thought, *Grant her peace. Let her find joy again.* She glanced where Harriett had sat and smiled. *Grandchildren always bring joy.* A warm breeze drifted in and sunbeams illuminated dust particles, creating an enchanting light. *Springtime, a renewal from the dead of winter.*

She ceased daydreaming to listen to Elder Glenn. The podium was nearly as tall as him, and he could barely be seen. After a few minutes of his tinny monotone, her mind drifted, as it often did lately, and she wondered, *Is my faith fading?* When Maginn spoke, she was mesmerized, sensing his words came from the Prophet. She glanced about the hall and realized tinny rhetoric wasn't the sole reason for her ennui. She missed the camaraderie.

Her reasoning for remaining in Peterborough had grown lame. Her younger sister Susan could fend for herself. She now realized the irony - she needed Susan more than Susan needed her. She could have left with the Taggarts, but didn't. Her grandfather, Reuben Law, would say, 'We have Scotch courage. We fear nothing.' *I reckon Aunt Susan and Cousin George got all of my Scotch courage.* To leave now she would have to go alone, requiring more Scotch courage.

Elder Glenn completed his sermon, and the meeting disbanded. She said a few perfunctory goodbyes to Sister Amelia and others as she left. A year earlier, she would have lingered to discuss Maginn's preaching with Aunt Susan. But today as she walked home, she was captive to an iterating loop. *Is my faith fading? Will Nauvoo strengthen it? Will I muster Scotch courage to journey alone? My faith was once my strength. Now it's my distress.* She paused to sit on a nearby bench and arched her neck to bask as springtime scents perfumed her thoughts. With each inhale her racing mind throttled back.

Two women she had known since childhood approached while conversing with one another. When one noticed Naamah, she halted. Her befuddled companion stopped and saw Naamah, too. They exchanged a few words and crossed the street, avoiding eye contact. Naamah grimaced and arose, absent her earlier inner peace.

She entered the house and hung her shawl on a peg.

Betsey entered the room. "Back so soon? Was your meeting cancelled?"

Naamah shook her head.

"I reckon with Maginn dead, it ain't the same. I don't want to speak ill of the dead, but Horace doubts he'll ever return."

"I haven't seen him."

"He's working in Lowell. But upon his return . . ." Betsey began to blush. "I think he has designs on my heart."

Betsey seldom blushed, and Naamah was caught off guard. "Marriage?" she asked.

Betsey gave a hesitant nod.

"And what will your answer be?"

"Yes, of course." Her coyness disappeared as quickly as it had come. "Every woman needs a man. Goodness, remain a spinster?"

Naamah ceased listening as Betsey continued lecturing on the importance of having a man. Naamah's companions were mostly women. She was comfortable being around them while men were still strange, perhaps because she knew few of them. They could be comforting, but too often, she found them intimidating. She smiled as she thought of Brother Twiss, the exception -- comforting, strong, but not intimidating.

"With Maginn gone," said Betsey, "one problem is solved."

Betsey's remark broke into Naamah's thoughts.

"Horace wanted Maginn to do our wedding vows. Dash it all, I want a Christian wedding."

Naamah thought about correcting Betsey's misconception, but didn't. *Oh, to be away from this commotion and in Nauvoo would be heavenly.*

Chapter Sixteen

Nauvoo, Illinois

26 May 1844

As George waited to hear from Joseph Smith, he reflected. Several weeks earlier, he had attended a general conference, which occurred shortly after the death of Elder King Follett. Joseph took the occasion to speak about death in general rather than eulogize his friend's tragic demise. George had hoped for inspiration since at the time he was still grieving his father's and Oliver's deaths. He received more, which now replayed as he waited.

On that day, Joseph approached the podium as dark clouds loomed and trees swayed. He gripped his lapels and said. *"May the Lord strengthen my lungs and stay the winds."* The leaves continued to flap, yet George heard every word Joseph had said.

"God himself was once as we are now, an exalted man, who sits enthroned in yonder heavens. If the veil were rent today, and God was made visible, you would see him like a man — like yourselves."

When George first heard those words, he was confused. "How can I or any man become a God?" But as quickly as he had questioned, the Prophet answered.

"When you climb a ladder, you must begin at the bottom and ascend step by step until you arrive at the top; and so it is with the principles of the gospel—you must begin with the first, and go on until you learn all the principles of exaltation."

As the Prophet continued to expound, George reflected on his life. He had taken his first step toward exaltation when he was baptized, and his father's and brother's deaths had brought him higher up the ladder, closer to God. "Am I becoming more Godlike?" He had pondered, still unconvinced and hoping for answers.

"The mortal body has a beginning and an end. Thus, here is your eternal life -- to know the only wise and true God. Learn to be Gods yourselves by going from a small degree to another, from grace to grace, from exaltation to exaltation, until you sit in glory with those who sit enthroned in everlasting power."

As Joseph continued, George had realized mortal existence is brief and the spirit is eternity, a spirit the same as God. As the sermon ended, the clouds had parted, creating darkness on either side of the blue skies above Nauvoo; and the winds had been stayed. As George left, he had an enriched view on living his life - as he was now, God once was; and as God is now, he could be.

Soon after Joseph's King Follett sermon, the apostates had proclaimed Joseph a fraud saying, "Mortal men becoming Gods is utter blasphemy." The apostates' rhetoric continued, and William Law, the most outspoken, accused Joseph of adultery, creating deeper church schisms and fanning anti-Mormon flames. The hullabaloo that followed continued to trouble George.

Now as Joseph arose to speak, George prayed he would respond and vanquish the apostates' mistruths. Joseph's stride lacked its usual vigor. His smile seemed contrived. He appeared as beset upon as George was feeling. He didn't grip the podium with authority, but slouched, using it as a crutch. His opening remarks were barely audible. George feared his Prophet's recent tribulations had taken their toll. But Joseph cleared his throat, and a vigor came into his voice.

"I, like Paul, have been in perils, and oftener than anyone in this generation. I have suffered more than Paul did, and as Paul boasted, 'I should be like a fish out of water, if I were out of persecutions.' "

Joseph's last word, 'persecutions', was a trigger for George. *Blessed are those who are persecuted for righteousness' sake: for theirs is the kingdom of heaven,* he thought. *My Prophet has been as persecuted as much as Jesus.*

Joseph let go of the podium and puffed his chest. His words flowed and came with zest. He commanded the stage and was determined to extend his reach. His voice resounded in defiance.

"Ye persecutors, ye false swearers, all hell boil over. Ye boiling mountains roll down your burning lava," Joseph threw his arms heavenward. "For I will come out on the top at last." He gripped the podium and roared, "I have more to boast of than ever any man had. I am the only man that has ever been able to keep a whole church together since the days of Adam."

Those around George were as electrified as him. He feasted on the excitement while shivers in his nape caused his shoulders to scrunch. He craved more, and His Prophet delivered.

"I am in the bosom of a virtuous and good people. How I do love to hear the wolves howl. When they can get rid of me, the devil will go also."

His Prophet turned from boasting to a sober discussion of the forty-three warrants for his arrest. George grew somber, too. *The persecution my Prophet suffers,* he thought. After a few minutes, Joseph broached another topic.

"I had not been married scarcely five minutes," said Joseph, "and had but made one proclamation of the Gospel, before it was reported that I had seven wives."

George squirmed in his seat. He had heeded his mother's early advice when he asked about the Partridge sisters. But rumors persisted about adultery and polygamy, cloaked as "spiritual wives" or "celestial wives". The crowd grew uneasy. Some sat erect, and a few inched forward, wondering what the Prophet's next words would be.

"This new holy prophet, William Law, has gone to Carthage and swore that I told him that I was guilty of adultery."

George squeezed his hands together as Joseph's voice grew louder.

"This spiritual wife-ism, why a man dares not speak, or wink, for fear of being accused of this." Joseph continued to refute various claims of his adultery before saying, "A man asked me whether the commandment was given that a man may have seven wives, and now the new prophet, William Law, has charged me with adultery."

Seven wives? Such almighty gum, thought George. He waited for Joseph's vehement denial. But Joseph digressed again, and

George rubbed his hands while he waited, hoping. And when he feared a denial would never come, it did.

"What a thing it is for a man to be accused of committing adultery," said Joseph as he gazed lovingly at his wife Emma. "And having seven wives?" Joseph paused as an anticipatory silence came over the crowd. He eyeballed women clustered together in front of him and returned to Emma to answer the seven wives question he posed. "When I can only find one." Joseph smiled and bowed his head in obedience to Emma.

George exhaled and eased back as Joseph finished. George had doubts about polygamy, and with Joseph's public denial, his doubts had been vanquished. He prayed the apostates' false accusations would cease.

George looked toward the women. Harriett was untying five-month-old Eliza Ann's bonnet ribbons to calm her fussing. Susanna flicked her index finger on Eliza Ann's lips until she began to suck them. She took her granddaughter from Harriett and swayed her as Harriett looked over her shoulder. The tingles George had felt when Joseph spoke returned. He looked heavenward and thought, *I, too, can find but one wife, and am blessed to live each day in your earthly kingdom.*

*****

The following morning, Joseph continued his fight. He rode to Carthage, accompanied by several brethren and his brother Hyrum, to address the charges against him. By nightfall, he returned, freed yet again of the spurious charges, reassuring George that his Prophet was infallible. George prayed for normalcy to replace the strain of repeated persecution. But as he thought more, he wondered if each persecution was another rung toward his ultimate exaltation.

Chapter Seventeen

7 June 1844

Susanna sat and gazed, occasionally blinking, while Harriett sat near and rocked Eliza Ann. George had abandoned his dream of a brick house after his father's death. His father had believed George's idea was frivolous given the family's meager resources. He had expressed his concerns to Susanna, and she agreed and prayed someday George would agree, too. She squirmed as she wondered, *Was Washington's death God's answer to my prayers? Could God be so cruel?*

Eliza Ann squalled, and Susanna left her gloomy thoughts. "Let me hold my little cherub," she said. "You seem weary."

Rocking Eliza Ann wasn't tiring, but soothing, a blessing Harriett savored. But she sensed Susanna needed comforting so she handed Eliza Ann to her grandmother.

Susanna held her granddaughter at eye level, gazing until her arms tired. She cradled and swayed her while cooing. "Oh, such delight." She wiggled Eliza Ann's chin, evoking more smiles. "Oh how I prayed for a daughter." Susanna ceased wiggling, and her eyes lost their sparkle.

After a few silent minutes, Harriett asked, "Why so doleful?"

Susanna broke her stare and turned to Harriett. "When last in a family way, and having only sons, I prayed for a daughter. And God blessed me with little Reubie." She stared at the floor. "I should have prayed for a healthy baby. God must have found my prayers too bold and therefore . . ."

"God would never be so cruel."

"I reckon," said Suzanna as she shook her head. "I've been out of sorts lately, so almighty melancholy." Eliza Ann cooed, and Susanna smiled "After Washington and Oliver died, I died too. But then . . ." Susanna wiggled Eliza Ann's chin.

"Eliza Ann, a gift from a loving God." said Harriett. "Not a cruel one."

Susanna nodded and returned her attention to Eliza Ann.

A peaceful solitude ensued until George stormed in, waving a crumpled newspaper. "Blasphemy to rile the gentiles." As Susanna swayed Eliza Ann to calm her, George read the paper's masthead aloud.

NAUVOO EXPOSITOR.

-- THE TRUTH, THE WHOLE TRUTH, AND NOTHING BUT
THE TRUTH. --

He snapped the paper to his side and glared at his mother. "Gum, almighty gum."

Eliza Ann squalled, and Susanna began to rock. "I've never heard of this *Expositor*," she said.

"It's William Law and other apostates." He raised the paper. "Listen to this." George scanned for a few moments. "Ah, from their preamble; 'If that God who gave bounds to the mighty deed and bade the ocean cease, if that God who organized the physical world and gave infinity to space be our front guard and our rear ward, it is futile and vain for man to raise his puny arm against us.' "

He snapped the paper and said, "Puny arms? Why Old Joe will raise his puny arms and fix their flint."

Eliza Ann's squalling grew louder. "Such talk of violence is unnerving," said Susanna as she pressed Eliza Ann to her bosom. Eliza Ann quieted.

Harriett's eyes had widened. "Sounds like a war is brewing."

"Could be," said George. "These apostates attack like all creation. Accuse the Prophet and the Twelve of whoredom."

"Whoredom?" asked Susanna.

"Law's vulgarity for the principle of spiritual wives." George turned the paper over and scanned it. After a few moments, he read, "Wicked and corrupt men are seeking our destruction by a perversion of sacred things, for all is not well while whoredoms and all manner of abominations are practiced under the cloak of religion."

Harriet gasped, and Susanna caressed Eliza Ann's head, seemingly oblivious to George's last words.

George ceased reading aloud and offered occasional grimaces. After a prolonged silence, he shook his head and lowered the paper. "Too vulgar for your ears."

His response didn't satisfy the women's curiosity.

He bit his lip. "They say the Prophet lures females to Nauvoo solely for him to . . ." George grimaced.

Harriett's darted her eyes to Susanna, who was still preoccupied with Eliza Ann. "Nauvoo's a beautiful place. Not a place for . . . for whoredoms." Harriett avoided looking at George.

"Not according to the *Expositor*," said George. "Law likens Nauvoo to Rome, the Popery with Joseph as Pope."

Susanna left her enchantment with Eliza Ann and said, "Us? Catholic? I'm grateful Washington has been spared such slander."

"Our Legion should march over there and destroy Law's vulgar press," said George.

"George, we come from a land of steady habits and must respect the freedom of the press," said Susanna.

George's ire cooled. "Law was once with us, and now he turns on us."

Susanna eased back in her chair and stared at the wall, oblivious to Eliza Ann's stirrings. She spoke without emotion. "Apostates always bring ruination. Jesus was a Jew. The Pharisees, the Sanhedrin, even Judas turned on him. Peter denied him thrice before the cock crowed. Jews against a Jew, and now Joseph has his Apostates."

"You know your Bible well, Mother."

"Too well, I dread." Susanna turned to George and said, "The moneychangers . . . Gethsemane . . . Pontius Pilate . . . Crucifixion . .

. violence, then doubts, then death . . . and resurrection." Susanna paused for several moments. "Are we to bear witness again?"

George placed the newspaper on the table. "Mother, your melancholy has returned." He took Eliza Ann from Susanna and gave her to Harriett. "Come, rest will freshen your thoughts."

*****

The following day with a rage akin to Jesus's when he overturned the moneychanger's table, Joseph ordered the *Expositor*'s press destroyed. Upon hearing the news, George was elated that his Prophet had stood tall, striking down falsehoods and vulgarity. He believed justice had been served until he remembered his mother's caution about respecting freedom of the press. He grew uneasy when he recalled her last words before retiring.

"Are we to bear witness again?"

Chapter Eighteen

11 June 1844

Governor's Mansion, Springfield, Illinois

While Illinois Governor Thomas Ford and an aide were conversing, a rap on the Mansion's dark, oaken door interrupted them. The door creaked as John Jenker peered in. "Pardon, but there's something burning."

"Dash it all, what's so almighty pressing, JJ?"

"Joe Smith destroyed the *Expositor* last night."

"The *Expositor*?"

"Another Nauvoo newspaper. It published one issue, and that was enough for Smith. He torched it."

"Under whose authority?"

"He's Nauvoo's Mayor."

"I know."

"His City Council found the paper guilty of libel and slander."

"Libel and slander? Do you know how many presses I could destroy for that? Doesn't Smith understand?" Governor Ford turned to his aide. "Hancock County is a powder keg. Everyone wants a piece of Joe Smith. Now he goes and makes it easy for them."

"I know," said the aide. "Higbee said Joe's house would be burned asunder. Wouldn't be a Mormon left in Nauvoo in ten days."

"Higbee?"

"Another apostate who was once one of them."

"Don't it just beat the devil - Mormon against Mormon?"

"Perchance, there's your answer," said the aide as he smirked. "Let one of his own kill him, and your problem goes away."

"Wouldn't end there. Smith's militia would seek revenge, and I'd have a bloodbath. I don't need any of their blood splattered on me."

"True. Best to stay clear."

"I intend to. But it could reach all the way to Springfield."

"Higbee is heading to Carthage to file his complaint," said JJ. "So Smith will be locked up for a while."

"For destroying a press? Damn, he'll pay a fine and be loose in a day."

"Charge him with other crimes. Can't be hard."

The Governor stroked his chin and took a few steps as he thought. "Who's my Justice in Carthage?"

"Robert Smith, and he don't fancy them Mormons, neither."

The Governor's worried face eased. He paced for a few moments before turning to JJ. "How far between Nauvoo and Carthage?"

"Twenty or so miles."

"Damn it all," said the Governor as he grimaced. "Smith won't come alone. He'd bring his militia and stir up all creation."

"Insist he come alone."

"He'd never do that. What did Tom Sharp just say in his paper, the *Warsaw Signal*?"

JJ grimaced and avoided eye contact. "Said Joe Smith ain't safe outside Nauvoo. He'd be dead if he ever left."

The room quieted, except for the Governor's boots squeaking as he paced, until his aide said, "Maybe a lone assassin could get Joe."

"And make him a martyr."

"Um, well, not a martyr, but . . ."

"Damn it all. There's ten thousand of them Mormons, and plenty of them sympathizing Jack-Mormons, too. They believe Smith is their Prophet – a second coming. His militia would cross lots for revenge. And Nauvoo is larger than Carthage and Warsaw combined." He slammed the table. "We'd have a damn civil war."

The Governor ran his stubby fingers through his hair. He moved to the large window and pushed the curtain aside. Sun streamed in as he pondered a while. "Never wanted this

Governorship to begin with," he muttered. "And I sure as tarnation don't want Joe Smith's blood on my hands." The curtain drifted from his hand, and he turned from sunlight.

18 June 1844

Nauvoo, Illinois

Joseph Smith, atop a building under construction, rose above The Nauvoo Legion assembled between him and The Mansion House. George, a Legion member, held his fife and admired his Prophet dressed in his General's uniform -- a midnight blue, cutaway waist coat with gold epaulets, beige breeches, and knee high black boots, with a sheathed cavalry saber dangling from his belt. His usual entourage from The Twelve were on mission, some campaigning for his Presidential candidacy. Joseph stood alone, like Jesus without his disciples; unusual, troubling, and indicative of George's past week, which he now pondered.

His immediate gratification with the *Expositor*'s destruction faded once his Prophet was charged with crimes. The summonses energized the apostates who were unyielding in their constant attacks. As talk of violence escalated, George's emotions surged and ebbed. He was unnerved when Joseph declared martial law a week earlier, which eased once he realized interrogating strangers disembarking at river docks or traveling roads into Nauvoo would ensure tighter security.

Harriett's worry never ebbed and fed upon the growing hysteria, particularly among her quilting bee sisters. After last night's bee, he had tried calming her fears as they lay with Eliza Ann between them. Harriett caressed her daughter's head, seemingly oblivious. After several minutes, she ceased and glared at him. Anger seethed when she said, "I never should have left Peterborough. Never should have left my family." She resumed stroking Eliza Ann's hair, saying nothing. But her outburst had triggered a guilt within George that still lingered.

Now he pondered returning to Peterborough, which triggered other guilt. If he hadn't proselytized and bullied Oliver, he would still be alive. He shook his head and thoughts about Oliver were replaced with Harriett clinging to Eliza Ann. A lifeless mother with a vapid stare came to haunt him until his aged father enduring a death march appeared. Each image he envisioned was of those he had urged to Nauvoo. His gloom was teetering toward despondency, so he returned to the moment.

Joseph strode on the roof top while speaking, towering like a man atop a mountain. George heard only bits of his rhetoric, but being in his presence was heartening. Joseph had ceased pacing and become animated as he roared, "Will you stand by me?"

The deafening response created an electricity, vaporizing George's worries.

Joseph unsheathed his sword and said, "If you had not stood by me, I would have gone there." He flung his arm and pointed his sword to the Mississippi. "I would have gone west and raised up a mightier people."

The crowd grumbled. "Never leave us," one near George bellowed. "With you for eternity," another offered. George couldn't imagine life without Joseph and joined his Legionnaires to offer several huzzahs.

Joseph lowered his sword, and with it hanging at his side, absorbed the adulation until the crowd quieted. He waited, readying to offer more while surveying his multitude.

"I do not regard my own life. I am ready to be offered a sacrifice for this people. What can our enemies do?" Joseph paused, allowing the faithful to ponder before answering his question. "Only kill the body, and their power is then at an end."

Sacrifice? Wondered George. *Did He just prophesy His death?* He lacked an answer, and he fretted until Joseph nodded to the band. George raised his fife and blew while twittering his fingers. As he stepped in place, the sound pulsated through him. With sword raised, Joseph led his Legion along the crowd-lined street with faces admiring their unvanquished leader.

George's tweeting fife rekindled a childhood remembrance. His grandfather, Reuben Law, was asking him to play "The White Cockade", a tune Reuben fifed as he marched to the Concord Bridge during the War for Independence. Now, George sensed he was marching for Nauvoo's independence. He glanced heavenward and thought, *You weren't fearful then grandfather, and I'm not now.*

George relished being a band member as it evoked another memory of his grandfather. *"My great grandfather was a bagpiper who led us Scots to victory over Cromwell. You have his talent, laddie."* Later his mother told him Grandfather was mistaken. Old age had settled into his mind. Yet George never lost the image of a kilt-cladded warrior piping triumphantly. *Aye, my Scotch blood,* he thought. His grandfather's words encouraged him to develop his passion for music. He lifted his eyes. *Talents from God through my kin.*

The Legion halted, and the band ceased playing. Still exhilarated, George reflected on his earlier gloom and realized it was caused by doubts.

Just like Jesus, we all have doubts.

Chapter Nineteen

23 June 1844

Bedlam had replaced the customary Sabbath tranquility, forcing George to arise in an eerie pre-dawn light. He dressed and went into the other room as Harriett stirred in their bed. Susanna had arisen and was sitting, gazing at the wall.

"What in creation? Did the noise awaken you, too?" asked George.

Susanna shook her head. "I had been awake before it started."

George finished tying his boot laces and opened the door. "There's an almighty light down by the Mansion House." He turned to his mother. "I'll be back."

As the door shut, Harriett came into the room, still in sleepwear. She brushed a sleep seed from her eye. "What's the clamor?"

"More of the Prophet's plan, I reckon." Susanna shifted in her seat. "Or Heavenly Father's."

"Plan?" Harriett's eyes widened as she waited for Susanna to respond. But Eliza Ann's intermittent fussing had grown into squalling. "I know that sound. She's hungry." Harriett returned to the back room. "Don't worry, Mother would never leave you."

Saints milled about Nauvoo's streets conversing with one another; a few sobbed. Concern was etched into every face. Joseph Smith had left Nauvoo. George prayed it was just another rumor, but questions lingered in his mind. Had he been captured? Was he in peril? Had he left to raise an army? Would he return victorious? Had he gone to find a new Zion? Each lacked an answer, creating doubts. He tried to avoid one question, but couldn't -- had his Prophet forsaken him?

George was not alone with his doubts, and with the Twelve away and the Prophet gone, Nauvoo lacked leadership. Chaos prevailed.

Montrose, Iowa

Joseph Smith had gone with his brother Hyrum across the Mississippi for solitude and to reflect. Should he head to the Rockies and begin Zion anew, or to Washington for a fair hearing, or to Carthage for whatever might come? Many options offered hope, except the last one, which seemed a death wish. *Is this thy command?*

On the Mississippi's west bank, Joseph's eyes drifted across to the lowlands and up to the promontory. He thought of the desolate land that within a wisp had become a burgeoning metropolis. The sun had yet to arise, and Nauvoo's silhouette was as he had imagined earlier. The majestic temple, a beacon gathering his flock, was

nearing completion and would be his signature achievement. The
Legionnaires' torches glowed as they patrolled Nauvoo, accentuating
his city. He was mesmerized, buoyed by knowing his faithful were
living according to his preaching in his city.

He turned west and inhaled the cool prairie air. He moved
from the river and, upon cresting the rise, gazed heavenward.
Western stars dotted the darkness, and without them, he would have
been looking into an abyss. He glanced from star to star without
purpose before focusing on a tight cluster. After several moments,
the cluster appeared as a mushrooming light, signaling a city below.
He pivoted to Nauvoo's light and wondered, *Kirkland, Missouri,
Nauvoo – is there more left undone?*

When he had left several hours earlier, he believed fleeing
was the answer, but doubts arose. A mushrooming light now seemed
to be beckoning, *"Go west and build a new Zion."* He raked his
hands through his thick hair, hoping to ease his swirling mind. He
paced and pulled his hair with both hands, tangling his well-coifed
locks into a thicket similar to his torn, addled thoughts.

He sat propped up by a boulder to gaze at Nauvoo. Its earlier
mesmerizing light had muted to a dreary grey, seemingly a
discolored wasteland. The sun inched up the horizon, creating a
blaze except in Nauvoo. He grew uneasy, fearing the blaze came
from apostates' torches. He feared for his pregnant wife Emma and
for his flock searching for their shepherd. He closed his eyes, and
when they reopened, his magnificent temple appeared dilapidated
and soon to be rubble.

He turned from the horror, west to the serenity of a new Zion.
He stretched his arms atop the boulder and rested his head upon
them. The western light cluster still beckoned. He ignored it and

searched, hoping Heavenly Father would reveal more. He ceased searching and collapsed his head on his arms. He rolled it on his forearms for several moments.

"Why hast thou forsaken me?"

He remained face down. His breathing accelerated and filled his nostrils as he envisioned a new Zion in the Rocky Mountain basin. He struggled to resist the image's magnetic pull and the sweet intoxicating prairie air. He lifted his head heavenward.

"Are you calling me west, or is it my fears that drive me thither?"

Heavenly Father did not answer. Joseph lowered his head and was alone with his dilemma. A sudden warmth descended his head into his nape and spine. A distant cock crowed, and he turned east. The sun blinded him. He shielded his eyes, and Nauvoo came into focus.

"Art thou revealing thyself, Heavenly Father?" He arose, still focused on Nauvoo. "Is this thy plan?"

He was unsure if he had received a Divine answer, but headed, nonetheless, up the rise to his brother Hyrum.

*****

Throughout the day, Joseph's dilemma remained. But at two o'clock on Sunday, June 23, he sent a letter to "His Excellency Governor Ford". He would leave the Iowa shore and proceed to

Carthage on the morrow. He asked for a safe escort with a posse and a fair trial. Soon after he sent the letter, doubts returned.

A safe escort or am I merely Daniel heading to a lions' den?

Heavenly Father didn't answer.

Chapter Twenty

As promised, Joseph rode with seventeen co-defendants to Carthage on June 24. When he passed a wooded area, he thought of earlier preaching at the Grove. He remained upbeat until a hullabaloo disturbed him. The Carthage Greys, a ragtag militia, cordoned either side of the road, and as he neared, insults were distinct among the cacophony. A wild-eyed, stubble-bearded militiaman strode toward him, long rifle swaying with each step. Joseph squirmed in his saddle and girded for a possible attack. But the militiaman slowed his pace to be eye to eye with him.

"Prophet, are ya," he said as they moved together. He spat some chew toward Joseph. "Well Prophet, we're going to string yer up, and then we're going to shoot yer." His eyes grew fiendish; his laugh was devilish. He stopped walking and pumped his long rifle skyward. "Death to the Prophet." Cheers ensued, along with hoots and jeers.

The following day, Joseph was in court, and the proceedings went worse than he imagined. Governor Ford's "man in Carthage" did his job. Justice Robert Smith established an outrageous bail that Joseph could not meet. Further, two apostates filed added charges accusing him and his brother Hyrum of treason for placing the Legion under martial law. His lawyers disputed these charges, but Justice Smith, also the Captain of the Carthage Greys, ruled them meritorious. Joseph and Hyrum were taken to the recently built, two-story brick jail. While incarcerated, Joseph's legal woes continued as rumors now circulated that Nauvoo was running a counterfeiting operation.

Joseph had assumed a fine and restitution to the *Expositor's* plaintiffs would resolve his legal issues. He should have been back in Nauvoo by now, not imprisoned and surrounded by hostility. If found guilty of treason, he could be hung. The grizzled militiaman saying, "We're going to string yer up." preyed upon his mind. *Was he the devil incarnate uttering foolishness, or the angel Moroni heralding Heavenly Father's plan?*

His mind drifted to his last reunion with Emma. He sensed the sweet aroma about her, her warm embrace, and a squirm from within her midsection as she clung to him. His thoughts grew sweet, wondering if his unborn would be a son, before they turned bitter, wondering if he would ever see him.

Am I Daniel in the lions' den?

He raised his eyes, hoping for an answer. There wasn't one.

27 June 1844 8:00 AM

Like Joseph, Governor Ford's worries haunted him, too. The early morning rain had dampened the rabble-rousers' enthusiasm, but once it stopped, the day grew hot and humid -- ugly enough to blow Hancock County's powder keg. As Ford stared from The Hamilton Hotel's second story window, several men guarded the

Carthage jail. The Greys were a few blocks from the jail, re-enforcements if needed. Their soaked tents were pitched helter-skelter among liquor bottles and other debris. They appeared as motley as the citizens who milled among them, bored, itching to finish whatever, so they could return home.

He turned from the window and reflected. Parading the Smiths through Carthage was a stroke of genius. The rabble seemed satisfied until the treason charge increased their appetite; and now counterfeiting rumors made them ravenous. Going to Nauvoo to substantiate the counterfeiting could sate their appetite, and being far from Carthage was appealing.

Within an hour, the Governor led a small contingent for Nauvoo. As he rode out of town, the curious citizens on the common moved toward the Governor's procession. Some grumbled, a few jeered, and many simply stared. Militiamen smiled and nodded as the Governor passed them.

"It's growing hotter. Best you leave Carthage today," said one among the Greys. As the Governor pondered, he heard, "We'll do the job for ya."

He turned toward the voice. Several militiamen had sappy smiles. He moved in his saddle to eyeball them before spurring his horse and riding west.

Carthage Jail

Midday

As Ford rode toward Nauvoo, Joseph enjoyed fellowship with John Taylor, Willard Richards, and Hyrum. The sympathetic jailer had moved his family elsewhere and allowed Joseph and Hyrum to use his living quarters. Upstairs and freed from the ground floor cell, Joseph ate while discussing plans for his trial.

After lunch, Hyrum read from Josephus, one of Joseph's favorite historians, choosing a passage dealing with James, Jesus's brother. James was brought before the Sanhedrin to face charges and ordered to be stoned. Joseph wondered while listening to Hyrum, *Is my brother to be stoned because of me?*

When Hyrum finished, Joseph said, "The passage you chose this day gives much to ponder."

Hyrum grabbed his brother's arm and drew him near. "If God so wills it, then so be it."

The day wore on and, encased in a two-foot thick brick building, the room seemed like an oven. Joseph removed his shirt and breeches, and the other three followed his lead. Sensing despair, Brother Taylor began to sing Joseph's favorite hymn, which Taylor had learned while on mission in England.

He sang in his usual melodious voice, "A poor wayfaring man of grief hath often crossed me on my way."

Hyrum joined in, and Joseph hummed while imagining. The poor wayfaring man of grief endured life's hardships – want of bread, thirst, beaten near death, imprisoned, and condemned to meet a traitor's doom by morning. Joseph's image grew more vivid as the swarm outside jeered throughout the singing. He continued to hum as his three disciples sang the final stanza loudly to rise above the outside commotion. The poor wayfaring man was none other than

The Savior, Jesus Christ. Joseph ceased humming and sang as if he was Jesus.

"Of me thou hast not been ashamed. These deeds shall thy memorial be; fear not, thou didst them unto me."

The outside uproar ebbed once the singing stopped. Joseph knew in death he would be not be shamed, but immortalized, but he worried for his disciples. *Will they die for their good deeds they didst unto me?*

Wooded lands along the Warsaw/Carthage Road

4:30 PM

The Warsaw Militia was a mile from Carthage, no doubt spurred by Thomas Sharp's constant rhetoric in the *Warsaw Signal*. Sensing their time had arrived, over a hundred trickled out of the woodlands. They were en route to reinforce the Carthage Greys. But with mud smeared on their faces, they appeared more undisciplined than the Greys. Many wore their uniforms inside out. A few towed whiskey kegs behind them. They were dead-set on meeting their destiny.

Nauvoo, Illinois

As armed men moved toward Carthage, George waited with anxious Saints near the Mansion House where nine days earlier, his

Prophet had inspired him. Since then, only confusion had ensued, and he hoped for clarity. What was the status of Joseph's charges? When would he return? Was he safe from harm?

As Ford stood atop the same rooftop where Joseph had stood, George was struck by the contrast. Ford was short, pale, and furtive as he surveyed the crowd - an uninspiring presence oozing distrust. George feared his concerns wouldn't be addressed. But when Ford extended his arms much as a father welcomes his children, George had a hopeful moment.

"Citizens of Nauvoo, had you rendered Joseph Smith unto me when I so commanded, you'd be safe today. My hands are washed clean of this turmoil. Yours, I dare say are not."

George's shoulders slumped as one from the crowd yelled, "Where's our Prophet?"

Ford pointed to the questioner and said, "You caused the turmoil, and you must remedy it." He swept his arm across his body. "Nauvoo, surrender your arms and your tumult will be swept away."

George creased his brow and thought. *Arms? He took our arms a few days earlier.*

"Your religion is for the peculiar. But you are not militiamen." Ford pointed to the temple. "Go, pray, and ask for forgiveness. For if you do not, your temple will be reduced to rubble."

Ford paused and reached for his pocket watch. He snapped it open. It read five o'clock. The crowd grumbled as Ford turned east. He checked the time again and thought about returning to Carthage. But the eastern horizon was a sun-soaked glare, appearing like a road to perdition. He snapped his watch cover shut and turned to the Saints to pontificate further.

Carthage Jail

5:00 PM

As Ford remained twenty miles away, Warsaw men arrived in Carthage. Inside the jail, a sweltering Joseph moved to the open window and looked out. The sun was lowering, and hopefully the heat would dissipate. The Greys were still ensconced on the common; some played cards and all appeared ill-prepared to protect him.

He followed the Carthage/Nauvoo road west until it disappeared. As he gazed farther, he didn't visualize Nauvoo, or the Iowa shore, or Far West, Missouri, but a new Zion in a Rocky Mountain basin. He wondered anew about his decision to return and come to Carthage for trial. He gazed heavenward, but as he suspected, heard nothing.

As he lowered his eyes from the heavens, men with mud-smeared faces moved toward the jail. A shot rang out, and he dropped to the floor and crawled to the pistol that had been smuggled into the jail earlier. The roar increased as the mob neared the jail's ground floor. Hyrum and Willard Richards shut the door and pressed against it. Boots clomped the stairs leading to the second floor. Shots were fired, and splinters flew from the door. Hyrum screamed, fell backward, and crashed onto the floor. Blood spurted from his disfigured face.

Joseph rushed to the door, ripped it open, and fired his revolver. But his firepower was meager in comparison, and his attackers continued their ascent. John Taylor was hit in the side and crashed against the windowsill before rolling under the bed. Joseph scurried to the window as Hyrum lay near, oozing blood. He stuck a leg out of the window and gazed west, longing for his previous serenity to replace the pandemonium. A shot struck his hip, causing him to tilt farther out of the window. A deafening volley came from below. One shot tore through his heart and another struck his collarbone.

He teetered between the faithful with him and the mob below. He struggled to resist gravity's inexorable pull before resigning his fate to a celestial force, to Heavenly Father. He toppled out and crashed near the mob.

"The Mormons are coming," said one in the group that had ascended the stairs. They retreated and dispersed into the crowd. Willard Richards was too shell-shocked and John Taylor too wounded to move. From outside and distinct amid the clamor, they heard, "Go to hell, Prophet, and see your spiritual wives."

As the shooting continued, John Taylor slumped, knowing each was ripping into his Prophet and eviscerating his body. He pressed his side to stanch the blood flow and felt his pocket watch. A bullet intended for him had struck it. As he removed his watch, he wondered why Heavenly Father had so blessed him.

His watch hands had stopped for eternity at sixteen past five.

Boston, Massachusetts

As the Carthage rabble spurned a fallen Joseph, Brigham Young waited in a Boston train depot with his travelling companion, Elder Wilford Woodruff. He flipped open his watch cover and read the time. The watch was ticking, yet its hands appeared to resist movement. He jiggled it and looked at the hands again before closing the cover. He turned to Wilford sitting next him and said, "Be awhile before we depart."

"So be it," said Wilford. "Been a glorious summer day as we prepared to preach the next few days. Hopefully, those suffragettes will not interrupt us this week."

Brigham grunted.

"A day inspired by the Prophet. Did you sense his presence?" Wilford paused but didn't receive a response, not even a grunt. "Well, I did." He thought further and nodded. "Verily I say, the Prophet was among us."

Brigham arose and took several hurried steps toward the train tracks. He stopped and scanned the station's massive vault. After a few minutes, he furrowed his brow and returned to his seat.

"Off to Salem again," said Wilford. "Will you see your daughter Vilate?"

Brigham didn't respond. Passengers bustled near, but Brigham didn't notice them. His brow remained furrowed.

"Salem with those witches," said Wilford. "Those Puritans were good at condemning, truly not our Prophet's way." A commotion near a train platform distracted Wilford, and he ceased chatting.

After a few minutes, Wilford's curiosity was satisfied. "We'll be in Peterborough soon. Elder Maginn had such success there." He turned to Brigham and asked, "When you were in Lowell, did you receive particulars on his death?"

Brigham continued to be distant, and Wilford grabbed his forearm. Startled, Brigham turned toward him. "What ails you so?" asked Wilford.

"A heavy depression of spirit suddenly came upon me. A melancholy that rendered me speechless."

"That's odd. This week in Boston will be joyful – preaching the gospel and fireworks on the fourth. If not Boston, perhaps Peterborough will cure your ails."

Brigham grunted, hoping his melancholy would leave long before reaching Peterborough.

Peterborough, New Hampshire

As the Greys reached the jail too late to reverse destiny, as assassins dispersed into the countryside, as Wilford relived his joyous day while Brigham, for unknown reasons, had great melancholy, Naamah sat at the kitchen table fanning herself. It was hot and humid, unmerciful weather for Peterborough, but not as sizzling as Hancock County. She ceased fanning and grabbed a damp cloth. She wiped her face before sighing and grabbing her makeshift fan.

The fan had been crafted from a circular Sister Amelia had given her. She ceased fanning and unfolded it to read again. In less than a fortnight, some from the Twelve would be in Peterborough. Joseph Smith was rumored to be coming, which she believed was false until she heard Joseph longed to return to his New England roots.

The kitchen felt like an oven, and fanning was futile. She went outside where the sun was lowering while a breeze stirred. She meandered, listening to her full length dress swooshing against knee-high grass while pondering the conference. She paused and gazed at Mount Monadnock while envisioning Peterborough Saints listening to Joseph by the cooling Mississippi. *How fortunate they are to be in Nauvoo this day,* she mused.

An easterly breeze freshened, and she turned to face it, allowing perspiration to be whisked from her face. The winds stiffened, seemingly pushing her west. She turned and allowed the breeze to cool her clinging, sweat-soaked dress. Her spine tingled, and while staring at an impassive mountain asked, *Nauvoo, you call again, and I will tarry no longer. I'll leave with Sister Amelia.*

Chapter Twenty-one

28 June 1844

Hancock County

As Naamah waited, determined to leave Peterborough, George and fellow Legionnaires escorted two creaking wagons back to Nauvoo. An open box lay on each wagon, one with a blanket and another with prairie brush to shade the corpses from the sun's decaying effect. The wheels lifted a lifeless dust that drifted past him toward Carthage. The pungent odor above each wagon drifted east, too.

George cleared his nostrils and turned to Carthage to lessen the unpleasant smell. Several hours earlier, he had been there to retrieve the bodies. The Greys weren't on the common as he had expected. They had dispersed into Hancock County, leaving Carthage an eerie, nearly abandoned town rife with animosity. He turned back to Nauvoo. The stench of death was less unpleasant than the acrimony he felt in Carthage.

As the cortege neared the city limit, the Saints joined the procession. Ten days earlier, George had marched and fifed amid a multitude. He imagined Joseph now with sword drawn vowing to defend his city, which aroused George from his defeat. *With my almighty strength, I'll defend Nauvoo.* That thought came like a

battle cry and stimulated him more. *I'll slay every last assassin.*
Revenge, a sweet elixir to invigorate the soul, isn't a cure, and soon
his gloominess returned.

As he entered Nauvoo, the band blared a funeral dirge,
bringing the weight of sadness. His initial shock upon hearing of the
assassination returned. The crowd swelled around the Legionnaires,
some frantic for a closer view, perhaps hoping the coffins were bare.
The procession wended through the crowd to the Mansion House.

There, the Saints jammed close together. Some climbed upon
the roof where Joseph had stood ten days earlier. The crowd's
countenance varied. Some wailed, or sobbed, or wrung their hands.
A few covered their mouths in disbelief, more folded their hands to
pray, and many seemed paralyzed into silence. The scene
overpowered George. Shock, denial, sadness, anger, and revenge
were no longer distinct. He was as beset upon as each Saint he
witnessed, and unable to endure their pain, he grew numb, feeling
abandoned and alone among thousands,

29 June 1844

Nauvoo

With his arm around his mother, George stood in the
mourners' line that snaked from the Mansion House. Close to him,
Harriett bounced Eliza Ann since waiting under an afternoon sun
was tiresome for an infant. The queue inched forward, sporadically
at times, but eventually turned the corner next to the Mansion House.
A sobbing drone, sprinkled with occasional shrieks and moans, was

omnipresent, triggering George's emotional whirlwind. Perspiring, he wrung his hands while wondering what the sight of his Prophet would do to his fragile psyche. He squeezed through the Mansion House entrance into the hall. The stairway to the second floor lay ahead. Joseph's and Emma's portraits hung above the fireplace in the women's sitting room to his left. The gentlemen's parlor where Joseph had recently entertained politicians for his Presidential bid was to his right. His portrait in his military garb hung on the wall.

The house was packed with mourners, and the air was oppressive and malodorous from the thousands that had preceded George. Eliza Ann squirmed, and Harriett loosened her clothing and fanned her. George wiped his brow with his sleeve. The bodies lay close to the windows further magnifying the sun's effect. They were more odoriferous than when George had returned with them from Carthage.

The stench of death triggered the hostility that George had sensed when in Carthage. Would the Greys attack, and if they did, would he be called to defend? He worried until he visualized himself thrusting a sword into an attacker to avenge his fallen Prophet. He relished the image until a breeze from Harriett's fanning brought back reality. The women in his life needed him, and if he died, they would be left to flounder. He fretted, and when Eliza Ann squalled, his eyes welled.

Harriett rocked Eliza Ann until her squalling ceased. The Prophet's wife Emma winced and massaged her side. Harriett thought of her joy whenever Eliza Ann had stirred within her womb. She couldn't comprehend the anguish Emma must be feeling. And when Emma winced again, Harriett realized Emma's unborn child would torment her with every squirm. *She'll never have the joy of being in a family way. And once her child is born?* She couldn't ponder further and clutched her sweltering daughter close. "How fortunate are we?" she whispered.

Harriett feared mob retaliation, too, although she never expressed her worries. Those fears returned, and her enchantment with her daughter left. *When will an attack arrive?* She glanced at her husband. *Will George be needed? Will he survive?* She fretted and drew Eliza Ann close for comfort. *Will I survive?* And with that horrendous thought, she clutched her daughter so tight she squirmed.

Eliza Ann grew heavy and cramped Harriett's bicep. She handed her to George to flex her arm. But loneliness came quickly, and she grabbed her back from George and clung.

The Prophet's mother, Lucy Mack Smith, captivated Susanna, and she reflected on her sorrow after Oliver's death. Her thoughts were broken when Mother Smith cried out.

"How could they kill my boys? Oh, how could they kill them when they were so precious? I am sure they would not harm anybody in the world."

Her wailing tore through Susanna's soul. She lacked answers for Mother Smith and felt helpless. In her quiet sorrow Susanna thought, *The almighty grief that has been visited upon that poor aged woman -- upon us all.*

*****

Later that evening, Susanna sat in her usual chair listening to the increasing winds sweeping through Nauvoo to freshen the muggy air. She thought of Emma Smith, now a widow like her. *I remember my first night without Washington. God eased me into it, but poor Emma hath been hurled into hers.*

Other widows, even those widowed while their husbands carried on the Church's mission, came to her thoughts. Sisters always comforted one another, particularly the widows. *"There but for the grace of God go I."* That expression before Washington's death had entered Susanna's mind whenever she comforted a recent widow. At times, she uttered it glibly. But after Washington died, a widow expressed a more apt sentiment to console her. *"There with God's grace now go I."*

Images of church leaders on mission filtered in and out of George's thoughts. Who would fill the void left by the Prophet, if indeed, anyone could? His thoughts swirled to worrying anew about an attack. But as he gazed at Eliza Ann asleep in Harriett's arms, he ceased fretting to enjoy the blessing of a loving wife and child.

Harriett sensed her daughter was asleep and considered putting her to bed. But clutching her baby gave her a sense of worth and contentment. After a few minutes, she kissed Eliza Ann's head and arose. *My night will be restless, but yours need not be.* Harriett left the room.

Upon her return, she reflected on the day's events. The house was quiet until the winds increased. George arose to open the door and air the house. Harriett and Susanna smiled to acknowledge his thoughtfulness. The room freshened as did the moods until the winds roared. Lightning crackled and lit up the sky. A furious storm ensued, and George rose to close the door.

The crying from the other room could now be heard. Harriett sprang from her chair. "And she was sleeping so peacefully," she said as she left for her daughter. A thunder clap rattled the house, and Susanna said with deliberate pauses, "It . . . is . . . finished."

She remained catatonic as the thunder and lightning continued. The storm drifted farther from Nauvoo, and a downpour ensued, stirring Susanna. She turned to George and said, "Heavenly Father's way of protecting us this night."

George left his thoughts and gazed at his mother. His brow wrinkled.

"The storm gives us peace this night," she said. "The mobs will seek shelter and not attack."

"And tomorrow?" asked George.

Susanna shrugged. "I know not about tomorrow."

Chapter Twenty-two

Peterborough, New Hampshire

Peterborough was poles apart from Nauvoo's shroud of despair. The sun's brilliance shimmered on the Nubanusit as Naamah listened to Elder Glenn. The recent oppressive heat had its moisture squeezed out with last night's rain, and now a Quebec breeze brought invigorating air. She basked, enjoying wildflower scents while observing white clouds contrasted against a sapphire sky, adding an exclamation point to an ideal July day.

Glenn moved among the gathering, more attentive to his scribbled notes than his audience. His voice was still bothersome, and even standing, he was chest high with the heads of those sitting. He would never command like Maginn, yet today Naamah had renewed inspiration, a feeling she feared had been lost.

She wondered if she had finally stopped trying to hear Maginn and simply listened to Glenn. She inhaled and thought, *Or is it this joyous day that inspires?* A foolish thought. She had enjoyed many summer days, and besides, her belief wasn't so shallow that weather affected it. Glenn's remarks moved to the impending conference, and she listened more intently than ever. When she realized why, she squirmed from the shivers in her nape. *God is teaching me to listen, so I'm prepared for what will be revealed at the conference.*

Glenn's discourse concluded. But Naamah continued pondering until Brother Otis Clark spoke to her.

"And what delights have you brought?" he asked.

"Well, let's see," she said as she opened her lunch basket. She removed a folded cloth and spread it on the ground. "Chicken, cooked last night, and fresh baked bread." Naamah placed each item on the cloth as Otis's eyes filled with anticipation. "Peas still in their pods and strawberry pie."

Otis rubbed his palms together. "Sister Carter's strawberry pie, and it's all for me."

Sister Eleanor gave Otis a playful nudge.

"Of course," said Naamah as the men groaned. "But I know Brother Clark will share."

He made an animated frown, and the group chuckled.

Naamah had been attracted to Brother Clark and tried getting closer to him. But her contrived attempts had seemed bungling, lowering her self-confidence. And when he gravitated to Sister Eleanor, she had ceased her efforts and remained friends with both. Yet doubts about her ineptness lingered.

The group enjoyed their meal while discussing the coming conference. Naamah fed off the enthusiasm and allowed the rumors of Joseph Smith's appearance to be a momentary fact. As usual, what she had brought was entirely consumed, and she enjoyed the compliments. Eleanor's food basket was nearly full, which delighted Naamah until she realized she was being petty.

Otis wiped the strawberry smudge from his mouth and tossed the cloth aside. "Sister Carter, by far your best pie ever."

"I should say so," said Eleanor. "You had three servings." As Otis patted his stomach and leaned back onto an arm, Eleanor turned to Naamah and said, "You're blessed. Men so appreciate a good meal."

Otis arose off his arm. "Sister Carter, is the rumor true?"

"About the Prophet coming? I pray, but I fear it is not."

"No, about Brother Eaton and your sister. Marriage?" Otis surveyed the area. "Although I haven't seen him for a while."

"He's in Lowell, working," said Naamah.

"And will he return for Betsey?"

Naamah shrugged.

"If Betsey cooks like you, Brother Eaton shouldn't tarry a moment."

Eleanor nudged Otis and said, "Stop with your prattling."

Naamah had heard at times that men always appreciated a woman who could cook. She had accepted it as true, only to realize it offered a false hope. Betsey seldom cooked, and, though younger, would soon marry, while Naamah had no marriage prospects. She wondered if she was destined to be a spinster.

13 July 1844

A weary Naamah lay on her bed, urging herself to arise and make breakfast. But she nodded off until the aroma of baking buns stirred her anew. She dressed hurriedly and scurried to the kitchen, where Susan was cooking and Betsey sat frowning, waiting impatiently.

"My, aren't you a fright today," said Betsey.

Susan placed the muffin pan down and turned to Naamah. "Didn't sleep well?"

Naamah shook her head as Betsey said, "Isn't today your big day?"

Continuing to ignore Betsey, Naamah pressed on the muffin tops and said to Susan, "Perfect, dear, they're done."

"Well, you need to do something," said Betsey. "You look plumb tuckered out."

It was indeed Naamah's big day, and the reason for her fatigue. Brigham Young had arrived yesterday and met with some Brethren. Joseph Smith had not come, much as she had expected. Brigham would speak today, and she had been restless, wondering what one so close to the Prophet might say.

On her way to the conference, she thought of her breakfast with Susan: fresh strawberries with cream, muffins, and eggs prepared to perfection. Her student had graduated. As they ate, Susan had talked about a young man who had caught her fancy. Once she sensed Susan was searching for advice, Naamah had grown uneasy, as both Susan and Betsey knew more about men than her.

"Land sakes, your eyes are so fleshy." Betsey's parting remarks to her returned, and Naamah pressed on her baggy eyes. She smoothed the rice powder on her cheeks, fluffed her hanging tresses, and pressed her eyes again. As she neared the gathering, she sidled up to Sisters Eleanor and Amelia.

"I'm so excited I could burst," she said.

Sister Eleanor turned around with a gleam in her eyes.

Naamah brushed her cheeks and dabbed beneath her eyes. "I scarcely slept. Do I look a fright?"

"Fright?" said Amelia. "Why, you look like a porcelain angel, as you always do."

Naamah ceased primping and touched Amelia's forearm. "Bless you for such kind words." She pursed her lips and thought, *That Betsey, why do I listen?*

The Sisters moved toward the hall. Inside, Naamah hurried to some open seats, as the room was filling fast. She fluffed her dress while surveying and nodding to the familiar faces. They appeared as pent-up as she felt. She noticed some less familiar faces. *Ah, the saints from Jaffrey,* which provoked another thought. *I wonder how Brother Twiss is faring.* She lingered over thoughts of him, wondering why he suddenly came to mind.

The din subsided as Elder Glenn approached the podium. He was barely noticeable behind the stand, and Naamah thought, *Such a little man.* When he said, "Today's preacher is Elder Brigham

Young," Naamah looked to him. She knew of him, but had never seen him. Even seated, he seemed formidable. She glanced at Glenn and was drawn back to Brigham. She studied him, not hearing Glenn at all.

Brigham gripped the chair's sides to arise and marched to the podium as Glenn moved away. With each step, Naamah's anticipation grew. He was neither tall nor angular like Maginn, but compact, a dominating presence. His broad forehead and thin, tightly drawn lips projected authority. He gripped the podium sides with the same resolve he had gripped his chair, a powerful man able to crush it at will, if he so desired. He didn't speak, just scanned, and when his eyes approached Naamah's, he paused. The resolve in his eyes frightened her until they eased to become a window into his soul. She was awe-filled, feeling as though through Brigham, she was a step from the Prophet, closer than she had ever been.

He ceased surveying and spoke. He lacked prepared notes, unlike Glenn, and didn't quote scriptures like Maginn. He spoke from his soul, to which Naamah had just borne witness. Erect, gripping the podium, his voice thundered as he slowly scanned to ensure his audience remained captivated. He paused to focus on Naamah again and said, "The death of one, or of the Twelve, will not destroy the priesthood, nor hinder the Lord's work."

His eyes shifted away, and Naamah believed those words were meant for her. Perhaps she had been too critical of Elder Glenn, always comparing him to Maginn. The truth came from the Prophet through the elders, regardless of one's speaking ability.

Brigham concluded and strode back to his chair. Others followed, but Naamah's thoughts drifted often to Brigham's words. She tried to concentrate on the other speakers but couldn't keep her eyes from Brigham. He sat, legs crossed and listening, still commanding the stage. *If he hath filled my soul*, Naamah wondered, *what would the Prophet do to me?*

The final speaker concluded, and Naamah remained seated, reflecting, until the stirring broke her interlude. She turned to Sister Amelia. "I'm exhausted. I've never been so aroused in my life. Oh, and Elder Young was . . ." Naamah paused to reflect more.

"I reckon," said Amelia. "But each touched my soul."

Naamah gathered with some sisters for further discussion. Amelia talked again about going to Nauvoo, and Naamah was determined to leave with her. On her walk home, she was buoyant, filled with the Holy Ghost. She thought of Betsey's remark: *"Isn't today your big day?"* She smiled as Brigham returned to her mind. *More than I could imagine.*

When she opened the door, she heard its distinctive squeak. "Susan," she said as she stood in the doorjamb. She moved to the kitchen. "Betsey?"

She looked around and noticed paper folded twice to form an envelope propped against a tin with wildflowers in it. She grabbed it and saw *Sister Naamah Carter Peterborough, New Hampshire.*

Her heart raced as she turned it over and broke the red wax seal. She unfolded it and saw.

8 April 1844, Nauvoo

Dear Sister Naamah Carter,

I have taken my quill in hand often to write to you, only to put it down for fear of being too bold. Today, while listening to our Prophet discuss the passing of Elder Follett, by chance I happened upon Brother George Taggart. He said writing you would indeed be fitting and proper since we had been earlier acquainted.

Naamah's heart fluttered, and she moved to a chair. She inhaled and continued reading:

I have not been blest with words to describe the peace I receive whenever the Prophet speaks. His simple truths are straight from God. I know in my heart the truths Elder Maginn spoke came from God through the Prophet. Nauvoo is truly His heavenly kingdom on earth.

Naamah squinted as she tried to decipher the scrawl among the smudges. Her heart fluttered anew once she realized what was written:

My prayer is for you to come and experience the Prophet's words. With God's help, I trust your baby sister's needs no longer require your tending. My heart would be almighty filled to see you again.

Brother John Twiss.

Naamah eased against the chair rest and placed the letter to her bosom. After a few minutes, she eased forward and re-read it, noticing the April date. *Hmm, three months past, I wonder . . .* She recalled others lamenting delays in receiving letters from Nauvoo.

The door squeaked, and Betsey stormed in. "Aha, you found your letter. Was it from your fella?"

"Fella?"

"The postmaster said it was from Nauvoo. And I reckoned it . . ."

"When did you get this letter?"

"A while ago."

"A while ago, when?"

"My mind's been elsewhere. I'm getting married you know." Betsey stepped away before turning to face Naamah again. "I don't rightly recall."

Naamah settled back against the chair.

"So," said Betsey as she inched closer, "was it from your fella?"

"It was from a dear, dear friend," said Naamah. She arose and left.

She re-read the letter, and while clutching it to her bosom, reflected on her day. *First Elder Young, and now Brother Twiss.* She looked heavenward. *Both signs are from you, this I know is true.* Her blissful thoughts were interrupted by Betsey muttering about something that displeased her. Naamah shook her head. *I shant tarry further. Everything I desire is in Nauvoo.*

16 July 1844

Like Naamah, Brigham had heard Joseph Smith rumors, too -- not of his coming to Peterborough, but of his death. His first inkling came while enjoying fireworks on Boston Common. In the morning while at Brother Bement's house, a letter arrived confirming Joseph's death. Later that day, Elder Woodruff received another letter with the same news.

Brigham experienced emotions similar to George's and Nauvoo's faithful – shock, anger, fear, and panic. He was stoic, keeping them in check until the cycle of grief continued and amassed. His thoughts turned from self-pity to worry about Nauvoo. Who would lead them? Had the church's authority died, too? Had the Prophet taken the Keys to the Kingdom with him?

His questions lacked answers, which frustrated him further. His headache intensified, preventing him from rational thought until a revelation came. He slapped his knee with conviction as he arose to aver, "The Keys to the Kingdom are here with me."

He saw a clear path forward: return to Nauvoo, console the distraught, and lead them forward. He left for Boston and spent the night there with Elder Woodruff. He lay in bed planning with doggedness while Woodruff slouched in a chair and wept.

*****

The news of Joseph's death spread immediately around Peterborough. The Saints were as thunderstruck as their Nauvoo Brethren had been. Having Elder Young in Peterborough was comforting. But when he left suddenly, loneliness and abandonment were added to the Saints' despair. The nonbelievers, Peterborough's majority, feigned sorrow before becoming self-righteous. Many believed "the Mormon cult" would fade away.

Naamah's emotional drop had been most dramatic. She had inferred much from Brother Twiss's letter -- courtship, marriage, a family -- and at night, alone in bed, her inferences were reality. But now, she wept and spent hours alone, mired in a bleak future. She suffered for Brother Twiss, Aunt Susan, and the Peterborough Saints whenever she thought of Nauvoo.

On Friday the nineteenth, the Saints held an impromptu gathering. As Naamah walked to it, she pondered the shattered pieces of her dream. She accepted that the closest she would ever come to the Prophet had been when she bore witness to him through Brigham's eyes. She thought more about Brigham until one thought tingled her. *"The death of one, or the Twelve, will not destroy the priesthood, nor hinder the Lord's work."*

She scrunched her neck. *He wasn't referring to Maginn at all. He was preparing us for what he knew was to come.* The significance of his words began to dawn, something that had eluded her in her despair. *The Prophet does live for an eternity.*

She strode with newfound energy until she spotted a crowd of non-believers in her path.

"The devil got his comeuppance," said one.

"With Old Joe dead, you Mormons will die, too," said another.

She scurried past them to the Saints. They were gathered as they had a few days earlier. But today their mood was somber and their numbers sparser. She moved to a group with Eleanor and Amelia. She listened to the lamenting until it became too much.

"The Prophet is still among us," she said, "and will be for eternity."

"Sister Naamah speaks the truth" said Amelia. "We must endure." She rubbed Naamah's arm. After a few moments, she stopped. "I know we've talked about Nauvoo. But not now, there's much uncertainty there."

Naamah looked at her and nodded.

"Sorry for your loss," came in a smarmy tone. Guffaws followed.

Amelia glared toward the crowd before turning back to Naamah. "Besides, if we leave, they'll believe they hastened us."

On Naamah's walk home, Brother Twiss's letter came to mind. She knew it by heart. He never mentioned courtship, marriage, or a family. And the April date was before Joseph's death. *If he wrote today, would he still encourage me to go to Nauvoo?*

Chapter Twenty-three

Nauvoo, Illinois

August 1844

While Naamah mourned far from Nauvoo, the Taggarts grieved, mired in a chaotic city and in constant fear of attacks. The bustling city that once enthralled George had ground to a halt. The Saints were lost sheep, needing a determined shepherd.

Initially, rumors swirled about Joseph's kin succeeding him. But Hyrum died along with Joseph, and another brother, Samuel, died suddenly in late July. The lone surviving brother, William, was claiming to be the rightful Presiding Patriarch. Among Joseph's children, Joseph III, the eldest, was eleven and an unlikely choice. Joseph had revealed earlier that his unborn son would become President and King of Israel one day. But the faithful needed immediate leadership.

With none of Joseph's kin likely candidates, the buzz centered on his confidantes, particularly from the Twelve -- but who? Four were in Carthage. Joseph and Hyrum were dead, Elder Taylor was severely wounded, and Elder Richard was still recovering. Others were on mission. Elder Page and Sidney Rigdon, who was Joseph's First Counselor in the First Presidency, were in

Pittsburgh, and others, including Elders Woodruff, Young, and Kimball were in the East.

On August 7, the inner circle met, Rigdon articulated his Church involvement and insisted that as Joseph's First Counselor he was the rightful Guardian. Brigham Young was blunt and brief. He didn't care who led, but he should manage the Church succession. As revealed unto him in Peterborough, he held the Keys to the Kingdom, and thus, the means of knowing God's mind. The August 7 meeting concluded without a decision, opting for a formal vote at a general assembly on the thirteenth.

8 August 1844

George, like most Saints, had not been privy to the inner politics regarding succession. As the Twelve returned, his sense of abandonment left, creating hope to counter his despair. Rumors about Rigdon spread upon his return, and George thought about him and others among the Twelve. Knowing Brigham Young was a New Englander, George felt a closeness to him. He prayed Brigham would take a greater role in the Church leadership.

On the morning of August 8, word spread of a general meeting. The faithful, eager to hear more, streamed into the Grove. George was among them when Sidney Rigdon stepped onto the raised platform.

"I stand above you where our blessed Prophet so often stood." Rigdon raised his arms. "Brethren, open your hearts today as I open a meeting of prayer. Let us . . ."

Rigdon's words were lost in the blowing wind as he turned. The animated Rigdon moved about the stage and onto a nearby wagon bed. And with the winds, his preaching moved among phrases, muffled words, and roaring gusts. His speech seemed as disjointed as his movements.

Unable to hear Rigdon's every word, George reflected on his opening remarks. Unlike when Joseph had said at King Follett's funeral, "May the Lord strengthen my lungs and stay the winds," the Lord chose not to stay the winds for Rigdon. As George scanned the gathering, he sensed its initial optimism was waning. He noticed the sun's height and concluded Rigdon had preached for nearly two hours. *If not for this breeze, the sun would be insufferable,* thought George.

Rigdon moved off the platform to mingle with the congregation. As he neared George, he heard, "Brethren, I humbly have put before you my credentials. Dwell on them in prayer as you consider the Church's guardian. The Prophet is among us, and . . ."

Rigdon turned and whatever he said was lost for eternity. But George understood the gist of Rigdon's remarks. He was usurping the Church leadership. George sensed his disillusionment was shared among many gathered with him. He closed his eyes and shook his head until gasps rose from the crowd followed by a unified murmur.

Brigham Young stepped onto the platform and glared at Rigdon who was still among the congregation. His voice boomed through the buffeting winds.

"I will manage this voting for Elder Rigdon." He pointed to Rigdon as he scurried to regain the platform. "He does not preside here. This child," Brigham thumped his chest thrice, "this child of

God, Brigham Young, will manage this flock for a season. We need not possess a hurrying spirit. The Council of Elders has returned and will decide the leadership in due course."

George was as awestruck as the crowd while Brigham continued. He commanded center stage, unmoved by blustery air. Rigdon was obscure, dwarfed as he shifted from side to side, seemingly eager to interrupt Brigham but lacking conviction to do it. Brigham had risen for the battle and became a barrier between a confused faithful and a usurping Sidney Rigdon, who in Brigham's mind was an erstwhile apostate whose eloquent preaching had led some faithful to the gates of hell. Brigham concluded, stating the assembly would reconvene in the afternoon.

George moved to his mother and Harriett. "I didn't know Elder Young had arrived," he said to his mother. "I reckoned him still traveling from Peterborough."

"His Peterborough journey hath transformed him," said Susanna. "A journey much like Saul of Tarsus's journey from Damascus. Brigham will carry us forward."

"Saul of Tarsus?" George said as he looked to Harriett, who seemed as perplexed as he. "You mean St. Paul."

"Without St. Paul carrying Jesus's teaching to the multitudes, Christianity would have withered away."

George looked to Harriett again, who tilted her head and raised an eyebrow.

"As Elder Young spoke, I heard his words," Susanna said. "But they came unto me in Joseph's voice. And as I cast my eyes upon him, he stood taller than ever before, like Joseph, and not square-set like the Elder Young I once knew."

In the late afternoon, Rigdon, Young, and several of the Twelve took the stand. High priests gathered and sat nearby to the right, the Seventy sat in the front seats, and the Aaronic priesthood sat behind them. As Brigham spoke, George tried to hear Joseph's voice. Unlike his mother, he heard Brigham, speaking in short, and at times disjointed sentences, sprinkling in anecdotes, humor, and an occasional barb, but most importantly, his words came from his soul.

His style was a sharp contrast to Rigdon's, but effective, and his unexpected mid-morning arrival, which awoke the crowd from Rigdon's pontificating tedium, was fortuitous timing. As the day drew to a close, George prayed for Elder Young to lead the Church. He wasn't alone in his prayer. The succession crisis ended with Brigham chosen to lead the faithful.

Chapter Twenty-four

Brigham Young took immediate charge, and the Saints arose
from ashes of despair. He re-organized the leadership, made
appointments, and dispatched high priests into the world – Wilford
Woodruff to England, Parley Pratt to New York, and Lyman Wight
to Texas. They were tasked with building their ranks to the size of
Nauvoo.

Enthusiasm returned. Nauvoo grew and prospered again to
the gentiles' dismay as they had anticipated Mormonism dying along
with Joseph. And when it didn't, they created obstacles. In January
1845, Nauvoo's Charter was revoked ending local rule and stripping
militia protection from the citizens.

In Peterborough, the Saints recovered from their initial
shock, too. The local gentiles' compassion for the Saints' loss was
brief, and they awaited with smugness for 'those erstwhile Christians
to return to the fold.' But instead, the Saints became more devout,
and as they did, the gentiles' smugness grew unfriendly and openly
hostile. The Saints avoided the ill-will and insulated themselves
further from the community.

*****

Naamah answered Brother Twiss's letter soon after learning of Joseph's death, saying she appreciated hearing from him, lamenting the Prophet's death, and concluding with a vague reference to other matters needing her attention. By the time she received another letter, her mood about Nauvoo had brightened. Brother Twiss was still vague about his intentions, yet Naamah inferred more than was written. She responded in December, which went unanswered. She wondered if he had received it, or if his response was lost or never sent. Regardless, Sister Amelia and a small group were leaving in the spring, and Naamah was determined to go with them.

Peterborough, New Hampshire

March 1845

A blast of cold air accompanied Susan Carter as she entered the house. Naamah scrunched her shoulders and turned from the oven as snowflakes drifted in.

"Land sakes, will winter never end?"

Susan slammed the door. "Not for a while." She removed her coat and put it on the hook. Still shivering, she moved to the oven and rubbed her hands. Sensing her sister's disappointment, she said, "But spring's coming. The snow will melt."

"You always bring cheer."

"I know you're eager to leave, but you'll have to wait a tad longer."

"Sister Eleanor said the same thing to me."

"Eleanor - the one recently married?"

Naamah nodded. "They desire to have their marriage sealed for eternity once they reach Nauvoo."

"Sealed for eternity – what a pleasing way to say it." Susan mused for a few moments. "I don't understand your Prophet, yet some things seem better than what I've always been told."

"You could add 'sealed for eternity' to your wedding vows."

"If I ever get married."

"You seemed close to Thomas."

"I thought so, but you know men."

"I doubt I do," said Naamah as she sat down at the table.

Susan moved to sit across from her. "Any news from Brother Twiss?"

"I sense I expect more than he can give."

"Men are that way."

They both chuckled, and Naamah smoothed her apron across her lap. "Brother Twiss and I believe in the Prophet," she said. "It's our strength and our bond."

"Betsey says you follow your Prophet because of Aunt Susan."

"Betsey has always been all-fired certain, even when wrong." Naamah fiddled with the cloth napkin before saying, "Except for Brother Twiss, my closest Saints are women."

"Is that unusual in your religion?"

"I reckon not." Naamah fiddled for several moments before saying, "We're an odd family, aren't we Susan? Many sisters, and but a brother we never see."

"He's married and has his own life in Reading."

Naamah folded the napkin and then unfolded it. "Father died so young, and then our stepfather."

"You always feared Eli."

"He's gruff, not a gentle man like Father. If not for Aunt Susan, I don't know what I would have done."

"What are you trying to say?"

Naamah pushed the napkin aside and folded her hands. "I've never known a man and am unable to judge Brother Twiss's affection for me, if indeed, there's any."

"Perhaps the answer will come from your Prophet in due time."

"Oh Susan," said Naamah as she reached across the table and rubbed her sister's forearm. "Except for you, there's nothing in Peterborough for me."

"I understand. But soon you'll be with Aunt Susan and others who left."

"And little Eliza Ann." Naamah rushed her hands to her face. She leaned from her chair and shielded her mouth. "Sister Harriett confided in me first when she was in a family way." She settled back. "Oh, we have much to discuss. She's probably in a family way again. Maybe soon, huh?"

Susan was enjoying her sister's changed demeanor and let her ramble. Naamah jumped among thoughts with infectious enthusiasm and animated gestures. Susan's cheeks still stung from the cold, but inside she glowed while listening to Naamah and enjoying the pleasing aromas -- a familiar milieu soon to be gone for eternity once Naamah left.

"I pray one day I'm in a family way, too -- blessed with many," said Naamah.

"Many boys? To help with the chores?"

"Oh, I don't know; it's up to Heavenly Father." Naamah settled back. "But I doubt he would bless me with boys."

Susan cocked her head while trying to follow Naamah's logic.

"I know not a hooter about men. I couldn't possibly rear boys."

They both laughed, and Susan treasured what soon would be another remembrance.

*****

As Susan predicted, spring arrived. As the days grew longer and warmer, Naamah's enthusiasm magnified. Sister Amelia stopped by to discuss their final plans for their life-changing journey.

"I'm almighty obliged to Mr. Upton for use of his shed to store my belongings," said Amelia. "Right neighborly of him."

Naamah smiled at Amelia's naïve remark as she recalled Eli's exact words. *"My shed? Well, I reckon so, and if it's going to help you Mormons to move on, all the better."* Naamah placed cups and a teapot on the table and gestured to Amelia to sit.

"As you know, I've been fearful about having enough money," said Amelia.

"My savings are meager, but we'll persevere," said Naamah as she poured the tea. She blew on the cup and took a sip.

"You remember Sister Caroline?" said Amelia.

"Surely."

"Well, her husband died a month ago."

"Oh dear," said Naamah as she lowered her cup.

"And she's in need of boarders. I wrote her to tell her of our interest."

"Brother Herbert was so young and such a devoted husband," said Naamah. "I grieve for Sister Caroline."

"She's among our Peterborough sisters. They'll tend to her."

Naamah nodded and smiled as she thought, *The sisterhood is always there.*

A rap on the door was followed by, "Cousin Amy, are you home?"

Naamah turned to Amelia and shrugged. The door opened, and Albert Taggart walked in carrying a letter.

"Oh my, Cousin Albert." Naamah gestured toward Amelia. "Sister Amelia and I were just discussing our plans to journey to Nauvoo."

"Sister Amelia," said Albert as he removed his hat and nodded slightly. "My visit is indeed fortunate."

Naamah arose and pulled out a chair for him. "Would you like a spot of tea?"

"Please, not to bother," said Albert as he sat and placed his hat on the table. "I must go to Nauvoo and hoped for a smart chance to catch on with your group."

"Nauvoo?" Naamah said as she looked at Amelia with surprise. Amelia seemed equally as surprised. Naamah thought further and smiled. "Aunt Susan will be delighted. And should Samuel and Henry join us, she'd be..."

Albert sneered, cutting off Naamah. "It's their badgering that drives me to Nauvoo. I'm to fetch Mother and bring her home."

Naamah grimaced. "She'll never leave."

"It beats the devil what you see in this Nauvoo. Listen to what George writes." Albert unfolded the letter he was carrying and read:

"My health now is pretty good, Mother also, and my little daughter Eliza Ann are in comfortable health, although they have both been sick the past three months each, this past winter."

He lowered the letter and frowned as Amelia cowered. "Your Nauvoo is unhealthy. I fear Mother will not live another winter." He shook his head. "George knows it, too. Listen," and he raised the letter.

"I think my life has been one of sorrow and tribulation since I came to Nauvoo, but I do not feel like complaining, for sorrow and perplexity is the common lot of mankind here in this life."

"Cousin George is right," said Naamah. "We have a common lot to endure, and faith eases our burdens. Where better than in Nauvoo among the Saints? I pray you understand."

Amelia nodded an approval and straightened off her chair.

Albert grimaced and continued. "George says there's some almighty conference on the sixth." His eyes flashed over the letter. "Ah, listen. George says, 'It's going to be the greatest you ever had.' " He lowered the letter.

Naamah touched Albert's forearm. "You'll bring joy to Aunt Susan. George and Harriett will be happy, too."

"Harriett?" said Albert. "Harriett's dead."

Naamah's mouth dropped as she looked aimlessly around. Amelia arose and came beside Naamah to rub her back. Naamah collapsed her head in her hands and rested her elbow on the table. Amelia kept caressing.

"I thought you knew," said Albert. He raised the letter and read:

"My wife has ceased to live. She now lies in the grave by the sides of Father and Oliver. She died on Feb 19th after a lingering illness of six months."

Naamah raised her head to brush a tear. "Poor Aunt Susan." She remembered her last image of Harriett beaming about being in a family way. It was too much, and Naamah whimpered. "Poor Eliza Ann."

Amelia ceased caressing and hugged Naamah. "Remember what George wrote, 'Sorrow is a common lot for us to endure.' " She lifted Naamah's head with her palm. "Harriett's with the eternal, awaiting George and Eliza Ann."

Naamah smiled. "And with Uncle Washington and Oliver - an eternal family awaiting all of us."

Albert felt dreadful being the bearer of distressing news and helpless to offer comfort. He was relieved Amelia was there for his cousin. He thought of his sorrowful times and his longing for a comfort that never arrived. He was envious of what he was witnessing between two believers in 'this so-called Prophet'. But soon his skepticism returned.

Nah, he thought as he shook his head. *Perhaps this Joe Smith works for them two, but not for me.*

Chapter Twenty-five

Nauvoo, Illinois

Spring 1845

Naamah, Sister Amelia, Albert, and several others from Peterborough arrived in Nauvoo shortly after the general conference George had mentioned in his letter. News of their arrival spread among the erstwhile Peterborough Saints. George, the recently widowed Sister Caroline, and others came to greet the arriving contingent. Naamah hoped her aunt would be there, and possibly Brother Twiss, but as she perused the crowd, she saw neither of them.

George stepped out from the welcoming group and moved to his brother. Naamah stood aside to give them time to reunite, hoping for a peaceful meeting. George put both his arms around Albert and squeezed him near. Albert was deadpan, girding against displaying affection, in contrast to his brother's enthusiasm. George released his arms and stepped back.

"Welcome to Nauvoo, my brother."

"And where is Mother?"

"Home, with Eliza Ann," said George. "She has slept but a tad since hearing of your coming. I insisted she rest and promised to fetch you as soon as you arrived."

Hearing 'fetch' triggered Albert's reason for coming. He thought of telling George, but the Saints' joy was apparent and far greater than his. He was the lone outsider. *Later would be better,* he thought. He smiled and said, "Well George, you've fetched me. Let's go to Mother." He stooped and grabbed his two carpet bags.

"Let me ease your load," said George as he took a bulging, barely shut bag.

"Give my love to Aunt Susan," said Naamah.

"Cousin Amy," said George. "How thoughtless of me." He lowered the bag and went to hug her.

"Your mother needs time with her sons," said Naamah. "Tell her I'll visit soon."

George nodded and returned to Albert. They walked beside one another, carrying a bag each to their outside. After several strides, George said, "Remember the story of the Prodigal Son?"

"Can't say I do." Albert scratched behind his head. "From The Bible?"

"A parable our Lord Jesus told to his disciples. It's about two sons who…"

The brothers had moved out of earshot, but Naamah heard enough. She was leery about the reunion, knowing her aunt's expectations differed from Albert's.

Naamah ambled toward Sisters Amelia and Caroline. Caroline's watery eyes glistened with joy that barely masked her sadness. Naamah clutched her hand with both of hers. "I'm sorry. Brother Herbert was a saint, and . . ."

"Sister Naamah, so pleased you're finally among us. I was telling Sister Amelia, 'Heavenly Father tends to us all.' " She looked to the ground. "And He does work in ways we can't fathom."

Amelia nodded as Caroline raised her eyes. "Now, my bed has room for another, and there's straw gathered nearby on the floor. Sister Amelia is in need of a room, and says you are, too."

"I wouldn't want to be a bother," said Naamah.

Caroline gripped Naamah's hand like she had done to her earlier. "A woman's loneliness is dreadful, and most dreadful at night. Having you near will ease my burden." She glanced heavenward. "My soul tells me it's His plan."

"Then so be it," said Naamah.

Caroline brushed under her eyes and smiled. It seemed genuine this time. She gestured to a man sitting on a small cart, observing them. "You remember Brother Wexford."

As Naamah faced him, he slowly lifted his hat and lowered it, the only acknowledgement he seemed able to muster.

"He's been a widower for a time," said Caroline, "and an almighty help to me. Helps other Sisters, too. It gives him purpose." Caroline smiled for a moment. "God's way, I reckon."

Brother Wexford loaded the luggage onto his cart. He spoke not a word, seemingly captured in distant thoughts. Once the cart

was loaded, he climbed aboard and flicked the reins to bring the
luggage to Sister Caroline's.

As the cart creaked away, Naamah gazed at the temple until
she heard Caroline say, "Shall we go?"

"If I may, I'd like to tarry a while."

"My house is at Warsaw and Cutler, several blocks away. It's
easy to find." She glanced at the temple. "Tarry as long as you
fancy."

Deep in thought, Naamah ambled randomly within the
confines of Mulholland Street similar to the Mississippi flowing
between its banks, lacking urgency and content to absorb all the city
offered. Nauvoo was unlike Peterborough -- tenfold larger, set on a
treeless, never-ending plain, and this April day was more humid than
Peterborough in August. The river was a constant reminder of
Nauvoo's western limit. She felt like she was at the edge of
civilization, isolated and protected by a great river from whatever
might lay beyond. She had been in Nauvoo for a wisp of time, yet
sensed a cocoon forming. She passed strangers and heard from one,
"Morning, Sister," and "Welcome to Nauvoo," from another.

So unlike Peterborough, she thought, *where I shied from
those who once were friends.* The ambiance gave the sprawling city
a togetherness that once existed in Peterborough. She left her
thoughts and moved toward the temple until its dominance
overwhelmed. She paused to gaze. *Brother Twiss was right, I tarried
too long.*

She grimaced while thinking of her lame excuses for
delaying. *Odd,* she thought as she studied a man hurrying toward
her. Her heart raced, and she turned to the temple. *Could it be?*

"Sister Carter?"

Naamah turned back. *Indeed, it is.* She hurried toward Brother Twiss before pausing to wait.

"I heard the news and prayed you'd be here." He reached her and caught his breath. "I feared you tarried, and had …" Twiss inhaled and scuffed the ground, ". . . had lost your desire."

Naamah's eyes widened.

"I meant your desire for Nauvoo." Brother Twiss's eyes darted from Naamah's.

"Nauvoo left neither my heart nor my soul. Did you receive my letters?"

"Letters? I received one, months ago. And when you didn't respond to my others, I thought you …"

"Others?"

"I wrote several." Twiss pondered before dropping his head. "The gentiles." He shook his head. "Once letters leave Nauvoo and travel through Hancock County, we just never know."

"What did you write?"

"My fervent desire was for you to come and be among us." He scuffed the ground and added, "And to see you again."

Naamah moved a hand to her mouth and shied from Twiss. She sensed her cheeks reddening.

"May I accompany you on your walk?" he asked.

Naamah nodded, and they moved along Mulholland back to the temple.

"Magnificent, is it not?" said Twiss as he gestured to the workmen about the grounds. "Elder Young wills it to be completed this year. I spend one day in ten working on it."

As Twiss expounded on his temple work, his enthusiasm was charming, spurred in part by nervous energy. Naamah had been anxious, too, but now, oddly, his unease was calming her. She remained comfortable until they paused a few blocks from the temple. His commentary ended, and Naamah's eyes darted about, apprehensive with the conversation's lull.

Twiss gestured to the house in front of them. "My home, and as I said in my letter, three blocks from the temple." He grimaced. "The letter you never received."

"Do you board?"

"I've had boarders in the past. But not now."

"Oh, you own it."

"Ain't much, but she's mine."

"Well, I think she's lovely."

"And with houses so dear, I know it will fetch more than I paid." As Twiss smiled, Naamah sensed his pride in his business skills. "And will you be boarding?" he asked.

"With Sister Caroline on Warsaw and Cutler."

"I know the house." He wrung his hands. "If you fancy, I'll show you the way."

"Then I shall follow after you, Brother Twiss."

They took several steps east along Mullholland toward Warsaw before Twiss said, "And if you fancy, you may say Brother John."

"And please, Sister Naamah has always been pleasing to my ear."

While escorting Naamah, John offered to guide her around Nauvoo so she could witness more. She didn't hesitate to accept his offer. He had to tithe the following day, convenient for Naamah as she needed time to get settled, but was available thereafter.

*****

As promised, John arrived and the guided tour began. They paused often at the temple, which helped each to overcome their initial anxieties. He pointed out specifics and discussed various tasks he had performed as part of his tithe. His initial enthusiasm hadn't waned; he was genuinely upbeat.

They moved past the temple to the hillcrest. For Naamah, the Mississippi hadn't lost its initial appeal, and as she gazed west she felt on top of the world. She inhaled and took in the panorama until she heard, "Sister, turn around."

John pointed above the temple's scaffolding. "When complete, its spire will be the highest in Nauvoo. So high," and he slung his arm west, "even the gentiles will see Joseph's Zion." He stepped closer and with reduced volume said, "And with an angel atop blowing a trumpet, they'll hear His calling."

Naamah glanced west and back to the temple and closed her eyes to enhance the image John had just described.

He waited, listening to twittering birds and gazing at Naamah until her eyes reopened. He wrung his hands and said, "Come, we've more to witness."

They turned south onto Durphy and proceeded down the hill toward flat land. Along the way, he pointed to Elder Woodruff's recently completed two-story brick home with four chimneys and white curtains in each of the nine windows. They turned west onto Munson and paused at Elder Heber Kimball's house, brick, two stories, and with several chimneys. Naamah sensed the houses on the flat lands were stately and affluent, unlike those on the bluff and farther north where Aunt Susan and many from Peterborough resided.

As John discussed the Kimball house, Naamah sighed and placed her hand above her bosom.

"Yes, it's magnificent," said John. "And worth its weight in gold." As Naamah breathed deeply, John said, "Feeling faint? Nauvoo's heat, I reckon."

"No," said Naamah as she lowered her hand. "Elder Woodruff and Elder Kimball were but names to me. Now, being drawn nigh and among them . . ." Naamah stared at Kimball's house and back to John. "Truly, I sense the Prophet among us."

"As I told you," John beamed his self-satisfaction, "Nauvoo is heaven on earth."

After moving two blocks, they turned south onto Main, strolling by Stoddard's Tin Shop. Main Street had a unique bustle. Naamah knew nary a soul, but the smiles and occasional welcoming comments she had experienced earlier were still as sincere. Her protective cocoon was nestling closer and growing warmer. Across the street were brick buildings appended to one another, one with a sign above its entrance: "J.M. Browning GUNSMITH".

John gestured. "The Lord's work indeed. We're fortunate to have Browning among us, making his harmonica guns for our protection."

"Guns frighten me."

"As they do me." John rubbed his hands on his pant legs while observing Naamah's distress. "Let's take leave. I've more to draw you nearer to the Prophet."

Naamah's anticipation increased as she passed a print shop and turned west onto Kimball. In the middle of the block, Twiss paused in front of another two-story brick building.

"Elder Young's," he said.

Naamah gasped and rushed both hands to her face. "I've seen him but once, and if I could see him again . . ."

"You will see him many fold, I'm sure."

Turning south onto Granger for a block and west onto Parley, John stopped in front of the Seventy's Hall. "In there, our leaders make important decisions." He extended his arm northeast. "And when the temple is complete, their decisions will be made while being closer to God."

They meandered east from the Hall until its door rumbled. Naamah turned, and several well-dressed men stepped out and dispersed. One strode toward them before turning north onto Granger.

"That's Elder Young," said Naamah as she looked with disbelief at John. She turned back and studied Brigham until he disappeared among the houses.

"You've witnessed much," said John. "Let's refresh."

He strode, and Naamah followed, occasionally raising her full-length dress to keep pace. They stopped at the water's edge and sat on a pile of hides. In front of them, boys with yokes on their necks and water buckets in hand queued to fill them.

"Many ferries arrive here, bringing Saints from afar," said John.

"And these boys?"

John flicked his hand toward the bluff. "They carry water to the temple workers."

John beckoned to one, who came with filled pails. He took a ladle off its hook and dipped it. He offered it to Naamah, which she took and drank. When she had finished, he re-ladled and gulped. He dipped again and offered it to Naamah, who flashed her hands to signal 'no'.

He replaced the ladle and thanked the boy. As the boy doffed his straw hat, John said, "I've seen thee at the temple."

"Yes sir. My pa says carrying water learns me to tithe."

The boy returned to his yoke, and John knelt to dip his handkerchief into the river. He offered it Naamah.

"Bless you, Brother John." Naamah untied her bonnet and wiped her face. She returned the handkerchief to Twiss, who dipped it again and gave it back. She wiped again before clutching it on her lap.

A young boy with determination in his flushed face moved up the ramp. His pant legs were soaked, and his shirt damp with sweat.

"He's too young," said Naamah. She glanced at the temple. "So far and steep -- will he make it?"

"With God's help, he will."

Along the river the air was cooler, and Naamah was content to rest. Boys trudged shouldering their yokes with buckets hanging from either side. When one with unevenly filled buckets veered toward them, John sprang from pile of hides. He took the buckets from the boy's yoke, evenly refilled each, and re-hung them. He patted the boy's head and watched until he crested the rise.

"So thoughtful," said Naamah.

"Someday I'll have boys, and a Brother can repay me."

John sat next to Naamah, and bounced his fingers on his thigh. Without looking at her, he said, "Maybe you'll have boys someday, too."

Naamah thought of her conversation with Susan when she confessed to "not knowing a hooter about boys." She smiled until she wondered if John was implying more in his statement. She squirmed and fumbled with his handkerchief before stuffing it into her pocket.

They left the landing and moved north across Water Street. A few sisters and several girls had gathered under a tree, singing a hymn while they stitched. Naamah looked to John and back.

"The Women's Relief Society offering instruction and encouragement," said John. "Its founder was a seamstress."

Naamah recognized the hymn they were singing and hummed along. What Naamah didn't know was Sarah Granger Kimball and her seamstress, Margaret A. Cook, began The Society to sew clothing for Temple workers. With support from Joseph Smith and other elders, the Society's mission was broadened, and by March 1844, its membership grew to thirteen hundred. But Emma Smith, its President, used the Society to preach opposition to plural marriage, and Joseph, shortly before his death, suspended their meetings.

When the hymn was over, Naamah asked, "Can any sister join?"

"It was disbanded, yet sisters continue to gather." John eased his arm around Naamah's shoulder and turned her to face a two-story building.

Surprised by John's touch, Naamah twitched. But his arm lay gentle and was comforting.

"The Mansion House, where I last saw the Prophet."

Naamah's mouth dropped.

"Never before had I been succumbed by such almighty grief." He released his arm from Naamah's shoulder. "And with the Twelve not among us . . ." John stepped away as his eyes welled. He sniffed. "But Heavenly Father had a greater mission for him. More will see Joseph as a true Prophet." John brushed his tears with both hands.

Naamah rubbed his back. She felt his quivering ease and back muscles relax with each caress.

"You're God's angel," said John.

Their eyes met, and Naamah wasn't intimidated or uneasy. The conversation lulled, but she was content, allowing Nauvoo's ubiquitous sounds to fill the void.

Once John had gathered his composure, they strolled toward the Temple. As they walked, John talked about Nauvoo before Joseph's death and his adoration for the Prophet. As he elaborated, his mood brightened. Naamah offered little, allowing his monologue to flow, sensing it was therapeutic for him.

They arrived at the corner of Warsaw and Cutler and paused at Sister Caroline's house. Each thanked the other for "their day". Awkward lulls occurred, but they continued to chit-chat with neither wanting the day to end.

With one prolonged silence, John said, "I must return home, but I promise to call again."

As he left, Naamah remained on the corner, watching John heading to his home. When he was distant, she headed to the house. A bulge in her side surprised her, and she removed John's crumpled

handkerchief. She smiled as she thought, *I know thou shall return.*
She clutched the handkerchief close to her heart and went inside.

Over dinner, she gushed about John as her roommates smiled
and offered brief comments. When she paused and inhaled deeply,
Amelia said, "You seem smitten by Brother Twiss."

"Smitten? Mercy no," said Naamah.

"He's respected among the Brethren and dedicated to the
gospel," said Caroline. "And land sakes, always at the temple." She
chuckled. "Better to be smitten by him than some others around
here."

Naamah yawned and said, "I'm more fatigued than I thought.
Time to retire."

In the twilight, Naamah lay on her straw bedding next to the
bed that Caroline and Amelia shared. Reinvigorated, she talked
about her day again until the room darkened. She lay quiet, listening
to Amelia's sleeping wheeze while thinking of John.

She hadn't been forthright when she said she wasn't smitten.
Was it Brother John, or what I bore witness to? She parsed the
day's events and concluded John wasn't just a piece of it, but the
keystone. She smiled as she thought, *Hmmm, I reckon I am smitten.*
She grew woozy. *I sense he's smitten, too.* With that thought, she
drifted into a peaceful sleep.

*****

On the Sabbath, John and Naamah were at the Grove for prayer. The speakers lacked Maginn's charisma and elocution, but being in the Grove and among a throng created an ambiance that more than compensated. Her faith had been refreshed, and on the walk home, John words nourished her more. Nauvoo was enwrapping her, and John was its centering point.

They were together often and frequently discussed a future together. His marriage hints increased and were more pointed. Naamah sensed he was building toward asking her. Amelia and Caroline told her to accept whenever it came, and others offered positive encouragement. She was sure of her answer but needed the advice of the person she trusted most, Aunt Susan.

*****

When Naamah arrived at George's home, Aunt Susan hugged and clung while trembling before stepping back and saying, "Mercy, far too long." She eyed Naamah and embraced her again. "Come, let's sit."

I'm truly home at last, thought Naamah as she sat.

Eager for Peterborough news, Susanna asked about former friends. She was methodical with her questions, moving from house to house and street to street to assure no one was overlooked.

As Naamah listened, her aunt's voice was as ever, evoking memories of previous chats. Yet her passion was more muted, and her ever-twinkling eyes were weighed with sorrow. *She's aged so,* thought Naamah.

"Look at me," said Susanna. "I've not seen you in nigh on two years, and I ask about Peterborough."

"Do you miss it?"

"I reckon I do." Susanna looked away and thought. "I miss the people dearly. Even those who never understood."

"Would you go back?"

She shook her head and snorted. "Albert asked the same question. Said I must return and leave this God-forsaken hell hole."

Aunt Susan's sadness confirmed Naamah's concerns. Albert could not comprehend the depth of his mother's faith.

"When George said Albert was coming, I believed my prayers had been heard. Even believed Samuel and Henry would be with him. How foolish." Susanna sighed. "Reckon it's not to be."

Naamah reached across and rubbed Susanna's arthritic hand.

She smiled to acknowledge the gesture. "Families shouldn't be torn asunder," she said. "I wanted . . ." Susanna bit her lip. "And I have little time."

Naamah continued rubbing. "You have an eternity."

Eliza Ann toddled into the room and became the center of attention. Eighteen months old and clad in a coarsely woven, full-length gown, she stood rubbing her eyes. She stared at Naamah, and when her curiosity became threatening, she looked to her grandmother.

Susanna held out her hands. "Come meet your Cousin Amy."

Eliza Ann looked back and forth before taking halting steps to Susanna. Susanna lifted her onto her lap, and Eliza Ann sucked her thumb. She stroked Eliza Ann's fine, curly locks as she lay against Susanna's bosom and grew sleepy.

"Have you seen Brother Twiss?" asked Susanna. "Land sakes, he questions George about you often."

Naamah beamed and said, "Yes, and often."

Susanna smiled.

"If not for him, I'd be in Peterborough," said Naamah. "We were apart for quite a spell, yet now, it's as if we never parted."

"I remember. We picnicked along the Nubanusit. I sensed an early fancy."

Naamah blushed and shied away. "Was it obvious?"

Susanna grinned. "Washington noticed, too."

Susanna listened to Naamah talk about Brother Twiss. Naamah was in love, much as Washington and she had been thirty years earlier. Back then, they planned to have children and instill them with Christian principles to leave the world a better place. Their belief was their bedrock, formed from Washington's Presbyterian upbringing. And when they found a better way, they followed the Prophet. Susanna had some misgivings as she reflected on her idealism then and reality today. She ceased reflecting to enjoy the moment.

Eliza Ann was asleep, but Susanna continued caressing while listening to an enthusiastic niece. Naamah paused to inhale and added, "Forgive me, I'm chattering like a jay bird."

"Understandable, you're in love."

"Am I?"

Susanna smiled as she nodded. "And Brother Twiss is considerable of character, respected by Nauvoo's Brethren."

"But is it too soon?" Naamah fumbled with her dress. "He's hinting at marriage."

"You've known him since the picnic, and he waited while you tarried."

"I tarried for Susan, and then . . ."

"He'll ask soon."

"I reckon, but . . ."

"Amy," and Susanna eased off her chair, "it's meant to be. He's waiting for you to be certain, and then he'll ask."

Naamah had what she needed, Aunt Susan's assurances. She exhaled her relief, and her face glowed.

"Nauvoo does bring sorrow, though," said Susanna. "But when two are sealed, it's easier. You and Brother Twiss will need one another." Susanna eased back, and her sadness crept back.

"You've endured much."

Susanna nodded. "Losing Washington and Oliver, I died, too." She stroked Eliza Ann's hair. "But this angel, truly God's blessing." Her smile was brief. "Poor Harriett, so sickly before she finally left us. And George . . ." Susanna kissed the top of Eliza Ann's head. "His faith is unshakeable, like his father."

"You and Uncle Washington were close. Not like Mother and Eli."

"Your mother and Billings were close. But after he died . . ." Susanna paused and kissed Eliza Ann's head again.

"After he died -- what?"

"Your mother was frightened, six children and all. And lonely."

"But to marry Eli?" said Naamah as she frowned.

"Don't be harsh, dear. Loneliness is a terrible way to live." Susanna exhaled and pursed her lips. "I was committed not to tell you." She sighed before saying, "But I must."

Naamah edged forward as concern came to her face.

"Albert didn't understand when I told him, and I doubt George does either, although he would never say such. The widower Brother Jolley asked me to marry him, and I'm going to accept."

"I'm . . ." said Naamah as she fumbled with her dress button. "I'm happy for you. But why didn't you want to tell me?"

"Our wedding shouldn't distract from yours. You and Brother Twiss are young with a life ahead of you. Brother Jolley and I are surviving as best we can until the end."

"And thereafter?"

"We live according to the Prophet and will be in God's eternal kingdom, I with Washington, and Brother Jolley with his Frances."

Naamah wrinkled her brow. "Sealed to Washington, and now to Brother Jolley."

"You can't understand, and may you never endure my quandary." Eliza Ann squirmed, and Susanna repositioned her. "I pray you and Brother Twiss live long together."

"I pray you're right."

Susanna kissed her granddaughter's cheek. "My blessing is for you to bring many precious angels like this into the world."

Naamah blushed. "My John speaks often of children."

"I'm so pleased to hear you call him John."

Chapter Twenty-six

Naamah had her aunt's blessing and was eager for John to ask, so she could say yes. The next day as they walked to Sister Caroline's, the conversation drifted toward marriage. Naamah hoped John's hints would evolve into a direct question, but they didn't. A similar experience occurred a few days later. Now Naamah was anxious, fearing he would never ask.

After Sabbath services, they attended a community supper with many from Peterborough. She reminisced with others about earlier times. Oddly, Peterborough seemed foreign, another place in time, even though she had been in Nauvoo for just a short while.

After supper, they strolled while reliving their inspirational day. The day cooled as twilight drifted toward nightfall. Sporadic cricket chirps had grown to a constant clatter. Their conversation shifted when John remarked about Sister Madeline's good fortune of being in a family way, which led him to remark on the joy of children.

Naamah listened, hoping his rambling would come to a point. When he said, "Someday, I pray Heavenly Father so blesses me," she stopped walking.

"Fatigued?" asked John as he retraced his steps back to her.

She sighed as she brooded over a response. "John, if you desire Heavenly Father's blessing, you first must be sealed in marriage." She focused on John with a resolve akin to her aunt's when she said, "It's meant to be."

"This I know," said John as he shifted his eyes away from Naamah.

Naamah stepped back and stood with arms akimbo. "And?"

"And," said John as he removed his hat, "will you marry me, Sister Carter?"

"Of course I will." Naamah dropped her arms and stepped closer. "Why didst thou tarry?"

"You tarried in Peterborough. I sensed you still needed time."

"Time?"

"Guess I needed time." John fumbled with his hat brim. "To be sure you'd say yes." He put his hat on his head and looked directly at Naamah. "If I'd been spurned . . ."

"Spurned?" Naamah stepped closer. "Dear, dear John, never."

He put his arms around Naamah's shoulders and squeezed her close. "My prayers have been answered." He squeezed again as a few on Mullholland stared at them. Self-conscious, John broke his embrace and kissed the top of Naamah's head

She wanted more, but John ended their embrace much like her father did whenever he wanted to reinforce, "Everything will be all right," which gave her some comfort. Once she realized they had caused an inappropriate scene, she glanced at John with admiration. *The Brethren know what they say. He is a man of considerable measure.*

That night when Naamah told her roommates, they uttered, "Finally, at last." They were as excited as her and talked about the wedding plans. John insisted the wedding's time and place were his responsibilities, yet he seemed to be dawdling. Naamah became concerned, wondering in a gloomy moment if he had second thoughts. But he remained true; they would marry this Friday at Elder Ormus Bates's home. Naamah now regretted having doubts.

30 May 1845

Naamah's wedding date arrived, and with stomach fluttering, she walked with Amelia and Caroline. Her long-sleeved white dress swished about her ankles, an ordinary dress, except for three clamshell buttons centered from the neckline to her bosom. She toyed with one, wishing her aunt could attend. But she was recently married, and Naamah understood. She thought of Aunt Susan's words as she stitched on the third button. *"There, my special gift to you."*

They moved past the temple and down the rise to the flat land. Amelia sighed and said, "Such an almighty journey. Why?" She hastened to Naamah's aside. "And who is Elder Bates?"

"It's a surprise is all I know," said Naamah.

At the intersection of Main and Kimball, John, a half block away, waved. Another man stood beside him, studying his watch. When he spotted Naamah, he closed the watch cover and slid it into his vest pocket. Naamah raised her dress and hastened.

John's companion doffed his hat and said, "I'm Elder Bates. Welcome to my home." Naamah gave a nod and abbreviated curtsey as Bates turned to John. "Escort the Sisters inside, and I'll wait. Should be but a moment."

John ushered Naamah up three steps and into a well-furnished parlor. Several familiar men were near the fireplace, except one with an arm on the mantle and away from the others. The women clustered near the six-foot high window.

Naamah gasped and placed a hand on her chest. "Mercy, such a wonder."

Aunt Susan stepped out from the group. "You look lovely, dear." She sniffed. "Your mother would be so happy."

"I thought you couldn't . . ." said Naamah. She turned to John. "Is this your surprise?"

John shrugged as Naamah turned back to Susan.

"I've been of ill health, but Brother Jolley helped me gather my strength." Susanna pointed to the man leaning on the mantle. As Naamah dropped her hand from her chest, Susanna said, "The buttons are lovely. The clamshells' purple add a touch of color. Purple, the color of advent." Susanna shielded her mouth and whispered, "Advent proclaims good news. Perhaps some good news will soon come."

Bates opened the door and allowed the man behind him to enter first. As he did, Naamah thought she would swoon. She spun to John and mouthed, "Elder Young."

John nodded while trying to contain his smile.

A Sister entered after Brigham, carrying a basket. Brigham gestured to a table and said, "Place it there, Sister Partridge."

Sister Partridge complied and moved to Naamah. She grasped her hand and pecked the side of her cheek. "A special day, isn't it?" She gestured to the basket. "Teacakes from Mother Young. If you would be so kind, return the basket later."

"I will, Sister Partridge."

"You may call me Sister Emily." Her smile was warm, genuine, and soothing to Naamah's nerves.

As Emily moved near the door, Brigham took charge, moving John to Naamah's right before opening his book. Naamah was fascinated at being so near Brigham. Whenever he looked at her to ask a question, she responded as best she could with a dry mouth and racing heart.

The questions ended, and Naamah and John were pronounced husband and wife. She turned to a chorus of amen and exhaled her relief while gazing at a teary-eyed Susanna. Naamah sensed she might cry, too, and turned back to Brigham. He stared, and Naamah moved her tongue to moisten her mouth. When he said, "Sister Twiss," it seemed foreign at first. He placed his right hand on her head, and she grew faint at the touch

"Sister Twiss, my blessing for you," he said. "May you live long and bring many into His kingdom."

He released his hand to clutch her shoulders and pull her near. He kissed the top of her head and patted it before releasing his grip. He smiled, and Naamah's knees grew weak.

Brigham nodded to Elder Bates and left with Sister Partridge following him. Aunt Susan and the sisters gathered around Naamah, gushing their congratulations. The Brethren clustered near John. While the two groups continued chatting, John and Naamah looked often to one another. The irony struck Naamah: she just had been married, yet she was with the sisterhood. John eventually drifted near. Naamah, anxious to leave, gave her aunt a prolonged hug and left with John. When he shut the door behind them, the parlor din ebbed.

Naamah sighed and said, "At last."

The newlyweds walked hand in hand up Main toward Mulholland. Along the way, many congratulated them, and at one point Naamah, with cheeks aglow, said to John, "Are we so obvious?"

John squeezed her hand, still captivated and seemingly oblivious to the pedestrians.

As they started their ascent toward the temple, he released Naamah's hand. She reflected on her whirlwind day, trying to slow the events to savor each. "I'm still amazed Elder Young was present."

"Elder Bates has known him for some time," said John. "We worked together on the temple, and I told him if Elder Young could marry us, I'd double my tithe."

"Ah, and that's why he came."

"Don't know. But I will honor my promise, nonetheless."

They paused on the hillcrest in front of the temple. John looked down the rise. "That's an almighty climb." He took Naamah's hand and stood aside her. She continued to reflect until John released her hand.

"Isn't that Cousin George with the wheelbarrow?" he said.

Naamah looked to where John was pointing. "Yes, and Eliza Ann bouncing in the bucket." She called out and waved, and George veered his wheelbarrow toward them.

As he neared, he said, "I'd hoped to attend, but today is tithing day." He lowered his wheelbarrow.

Eliza Ann was curled against a dirt mound among some stones. Her hair had been gathered and looked like a rat's nest. Several tresses curled near her mud-streaked cheek. "Nama, Nama," she said as Naamah removed her from the wheelbarrow.

"George, she's soiled," said Naamah as she brushed dirt from Eliza Ann's dress.

"I had no choice. Mother is at your wedding. Others were busy."

Naamah cuddled Eliza Ann and reflected on her wedding blessing. *I pray I'll bring many like Eliza Ann into His Kingdom.* Her contentment lasted until Eliza Ann squirmed. She lowered her and brushed her soiled dress. Eliza Ann ran helter-skelter, enjoying her freedom.

"My tithing is not complete," said George as he raised his wheelbarrow. He called out to his roaming daughter.

The soiled cherub stopped and stood knee-high among bustling workmen, out of place and confused, and Naamah wanted to cuddle her again. George called again while beckoning, and Eliza Ann's forlorn expression disappeared into twinkling eyes. She bounded to George, who lifted her into his wheelbarrow and moved away.

"I pray Elder Young's blessing will come true," said Naamah.

"To live long?" said John as he furrowed his brow.

"No, to bring many into the world."

John took Naamah's hand. "May you be so blessed, and may we grow old together to enjoy our blessings."

Naamah tossed her head toward the temple and said, "And be sealed for eternity."

John released Naamah's hand. "Perhaps."

Naamah stared and moved to be in front of him. "What?" she said.

"I didn't want to alarm you," said John. "But Elder Bates confirmed what I've only heard."

Naamah grabbed John's hands. Worry creased through her brow.

"Elder Young will complete the temple to fulfill the Prophet's vision, and then we'll leave."

"Leave Nauvoo?" Naamah released John's hands and stepped back. "I've just arrived. It's my home, our home." She wrung her hands while looking forlorn.

John put his arm around her shoulder. "You've not traveled outside Nauvoo. Hancock County is dangerous. The Brethren are in peril. Mobbers are at the Kingdom's gates."

Naamah wrung her hands. "But if they drive us away, what will become of the temple? Of the Prophet's vision?"

John shrugged. "Only He knows."

*****

Later, they sat on the steps to John's house looking toward the Mississippi. The sun was a fiery semicircle nearing the water, and Naamah wondered what lay beyond. Nauvoo was once 'west', and now where the sun still shone was 'west'. She came to Nauvoo believing she would never leave. Now doubts had been thrust upon her. She had many questions that for now would remain unanswered. Her immediate concern was questions surrounding their wedding night.

John kissed Naamah's cheek, and they went inside. As they lay side by side, Naamah, like John, was an anxious virgin. Even though awkward, they made love that night. Naamah's night was enhanced as she cherished her wedding blessing while making love, believing an 'Eliza Ann' would soon come.

Their intimacy continued for a fortnight until Naamah's monthly time arrived. She would have to wait for her 'Eliza Ann'. Several days ensued, and the couple resumed their closeness. But John's ardor seemed muted, lacking energy, which Naamah attributed to his fatigue from double tithing.

Chapter Twenty-seven

July 1845

Driven by guilt, Naamah bustled along a rutted street while carrying Mother Young's basket. Being newly married, John had occupied her time and thoughts, and she forgot her promise to Sister Emily Partridge. Winded, she paused while looking at the temple. Her thoughts were now bittersweet. If John was correct, as soon as it was completed, they would leave. It seemed nonsensical, and she hoped he was mistaken. The basket weighed on her arm, reminding her of her purpose. *I daren't dawdle.*

She reached the Youngs' home and paused. It seemed as daunting as Brigham, and having not met his wife, she worried about her reaction to her forgetfulness. She girded her resolve and moved to the door. A woman in the side garden dropped her hoe and waddled to intercept her. Her brim shielded her face, and Naamah was anxious about the approaching woman until she raised her head.

"Sister Emily, I didn't recognize you at first," said Naamah.

"Ah, Mother Young's basket. She was wondering."

"My mind has been elsewhere, and …"

Emily patted Naamah's hand. "I know, my dear." She gestured. "She's inside if you'd like to return it. Sister Lucy Decker paid her a visit this morning." Sister Lucy Decker was Brigham Young's first plural wife, who he married 14 June 1842. Their first child was born on 19 June 1845.

"I daren't bother them."

"No bother, and you can meet Sister Lucy's newborn."

Naamah's eyes widened, and Emily led her to the door and entered.

Mother Young and Lucy sat beside one another at a table with chairs around it. Behind them was a brick fireplace with a Dutch oven beside it. A bedroom was on the right, and a closed door to the left. Lucy was cradling her newborn as Mother Young looked on.

As Emily introduced Naamah, Mother Young arose. She was similar in age to her husband, Brigham, and nearly twice the age of the other women in the room. She had a round face with a prominent nose separating her eyes. Her forehead was high, and a small bonnet covered the crown of her head. Her countenance was imposing, like her husband's.

"I've come to return your basket," said Naamah.

"Basket?" she said.

Naamah gulped and said, "Elder Young brought it to my wedding,"

"Ah, now I remember. Please sister, come join us."

Her hospitality was sincere, dispelling Naamah's initial impression and easing her worry. Naamah placed the basket on the table and sat across from Emily facing the bedroom with Mother Young and Lucy between them. As Emily leaned to look over Lucy's shoulder, Naamah wondered when she might be as blessed as Lucy. Mother Young unfolded the cloth on the basket.

"Oh my," she said as she looked at Naamah. "And what are these?"

"My gratitude," said Naamah. She eased against the chair's backrest. "And an apology for my tardiness."

Mother Young flashed a dismissive hand and took a bite of a muffin. "So moist." She offered the basket to the others. The preoccupied Lucy declined, and Emily took one and bit into it. She brushed crumbs from her mouth and confirmed Mother's Young's assessment.

The four chit-chatted while looking often at the sleeping child. Lucy was quiet, being weary from lying in, yet had a new mother's radiance. Naamah bit into a muffin and surveyed the room, as comfy as the conversation. She felt nested and not a stranger to sisters she had just met.

After a while the door behind Naamah rattled, and the conversation paused. Naamah turned as Brigham and two other men came from the adjoining room. Her heartbeat quickened.

"And was your meeting successful?" asked Mother Young.

Naamah remained transfixed on Brigham as he grimaced and went to Lucy to ask, "And who do we have here?"

Lucy smiled as she said, "Brigham Heber, born a few week ago."

"Why, Heber is a better sounding name than Brigham," said one of the men. "Perhaps it should be the child's first name."

They all laughed, and a confused Naamah offered a chuckle, not knowing Elder Heber Kimball had just spoken.

Brigham peeled back the baby's covering, and with his index finger and thumb, shook the infant's hand. "Welcome to His kingdom, Brigham Heber." He looked at Lucy and said, "Bless you for allowing me to bear witness to him." The affection in their eyes seemed mutual and persisted. Mother Young's eyes darted about the room until Brigham and Lucy broke their eye contact.

The scene enthralled Naamah, and her admiration for Brigham soared. He was the Church leader, by necessity busy, yet took time to marry her and John and now to welcome a baby and bless his mother. She wondered if he would do likewise when she and John had a child. *Perhaps Elder Bates could speak on John's behalf again,* she thought.

Brigham turned to Emily. "And how have you been faring?"

"Better. My morning travails this past fortnight have finally left."

Brigham held Emily's hand and said, "May your remaining months be free of travails."

Brigham continued to hold Emily's hand until Mother Young said, "This is Sister Twiss, whose wedding you presided over."

"Truly, I remember." He turned to Naamah and nodded. "Welcome to our home."

The men exited, and the chit-chat resumed until Brigham Heber squalled. "I'd hoped little Brigham would have slept until I returned home," said Lucy. The noise grew louder and constant. Lucy sighed and arose. "Might I have privacy?"

Mother Young nodded and watched Lucy move into her bedroom to nurse. As the door shut, the squalling became muted and eventually ceased, replaced by Lucy's cooing and the babe's sucking. Mother Young continued staring with saddened eyes.

Emily squirmed, seemingly unnerved by the scene, and arose. "Well, I mustn't tarry. Got my garden chores before returning home."

Mother Young broke her stare. "I'm appreciative of your help. With this heat . . ." Mother Young glanced at the door. "Well, I'm not as young as I once was."

Emily pressed her hands against her dress and ran them down her thigh while looking at Mother Young, seemingly wanting to respond.

"Oh Brigham, you bring such joy," said Lucy from behind the bedroom door.

Mother Young fumbled with the basket's cloth as Emily departed. The room was quiet, except for occasional pleasure from the bedroom. Naamah arose. "I've tarried, too."

Mother Young ceased toying with the cloth. "Such ado in our lives. Some days I wonder." She gestured for Naamah to sit.

"Brother Brigham has many worries, and these mobber attacks . . . Last night three Brethren homes were put to the torch."

"In Nauvoo?" said Naamah.

"No dear." Mother Young pointed. "East, toward that dreadful Carthage." She sighed while reflecting. "At night, in my doleful moments, I see them gathering, becoming almighty powerful and driving us into the Mississippi." As Naamah's eyes widened, Mother Young added, "Brother Brigham says my nightmares are the devil's work. Heavenly Father will watch over us. I pray he's right."

A muffled delight came from the bedroom, and Mother Young glanced toward it.

"Elder Young is truly a Saint," said Naamah as Mother Young turned to her. "Leading us -- powerful, yet gentle with the youngest among us. To have him as your husband to comfort you must be a blessing."

"Yes, yes, truly." Mother Young turned to the bedroom. She moved her thumb and index finger around her chin and down to her neck. She tugged her sagging skin, dropped her hand, and turned to Naamah. "Brigham follows the Prophet in every way." She closed her eyes and when they reopened, she seemed rejuvenated. "And you dear, a new wife and all, tell me about it."

"As Heavenly Father intended, we're united as one, and if we can be as blessed as Sister Lucy . . . We pray we have many." Naamah straightened in her chair. "Elder Young's blessing for me was to bring forth many."

Mother Young nodded. "Then it shall come to pass."

Naamah beamed for a moment before growing somber. "Of late, Brother Twiss has been weary, feverish at times."

"A touch of ague. It's common."

"He's doubled his tithe and wants to complete the temple for Elder Young."

"A noble effort. Your Brother Twiss is truly a Saint, too."

Naamah looked around the room and bit her lip. "He said when the temple's built, we will leave. I doubt it's true, though."

Mother Young sighed. "I fear Brother Twiss is right."

"But he labors hard, and if we leave . . ." Naamah shook her head. "I don't understand. What will become of the temple?"

"It's Brother Joseph's vision. Only he knows, and he has yet to reveal it unto us."

The door opened, and Sister Lucy entered carrying Brigham Heber on her shoulder while rubbing his back. Mother Young arose and embraced them both. She stepped back and gazed.

"I've tarried too long," said Naamah as she arose. "A pleasure to meet you."

"The pleasure was mine," said Mother Young. She caressed Brigham Heber's head and looked at Naamah. "You've been an added comfort to me this day. More than you know, Sister Naamah."

Those words tingled Naamah's spine. She had been anxious, and it ended with Mother Young appreciating her coming. *My worries were for naught,* she thought as she left.

Outside, Sister Emily had ceased cultivating to cup her forearm underneath her stomach. She rubbed her stomach bulge with her other hand. When she spotted Naamah, she ceased caressing to wave. Her smile appeared more blissful than before, and a tinge of envy came to Naamah. *I pray Elder Young's blessing for me comes to pass*, she thought as she waved back.

The ambiance at Brigham's house remained with Naamah until she neared the temple. She had hoped John was mistaken, but Mother Young's confirmation squashed her hope. *No one's closer to Elder Young than her,* she thought. She shook her head. It still seemed absurd to build something magnificent and then depart.

As she entered her home, John had arisen and was at the table, still pale and sweating. Naamah's worries about him returned until he smiled and asked, "How was your day?"

She thought of Mother Young, Brigham, a pregnant Emily, Lucy, Brigham Heber, and two distinguished elders, like a family, and she was a small part of it.

"My day was better than I could have possibly imagined."

Chapter Twenty-eight

12 July 1845

Naamah held Eliza Ann while George and Sister Fannie Park recited their wedding vows. She reminisced on her words uttered six weeks earlier while swaying Eliza Ann. The house grew stuffy, and Eliza Ann weighed on her arms, becoming more of a burden than a joy. When her stomach constricted, she winced and handed the child to Aunt Susan.

"Can you hold her?" she whispered. "I'm feeling faint."

Aunt Susan took her granddaughter, and Naamah tiptoed to a chair away from the gathering. Using her hand, she fanned while tugging her sweat-dampened dress to free it from her body. Her monthly time had come, the second occurrence since her marriage. She was disappointed yet not surprised, as intimacy this past month had decreased. She winced as her cramps seemed more severe than ever before. *Could be this ungodly weather,* she thought. Her eyes drifted to Eliza Ann. *Or maybe just my dismay?* She squirmed. *Maybe cramps just worsen once one's virginity is lost?*

The ceremony concluded, and several offered their congratulations. Naamah struggled from the chair to mingle.

"Cousin Amy," said Fannie, "delighted you came." She rushed her hands to her mouth. "May I call you Cousin Amy? I know George does."

"Pay it no bother, Sister Fannie Taggart."

"Oh," said Fannie as she gushed, "you're the first to say it."

Naamah smiled as she thought, *Elder Young was my first.*

"And is Brother Twiss working at the temple?"

"Brother Twiss is home, resting for tomorrow's temple work."

"Such dedication. There'll be a better place for him among the angels one day." She turned to Susanna and wiggled Eliza Ann's chin. "Speaking of angels." She looked to Susanna and asked, "May I?"

Unsettled by the exchange, Eliza Ann squalled. Fannie caressed her face, which quieted her. Fannie moved to George and the men. He stepped from the group and placed his arm around Fannie while gazing at his daughter.

"I'm delighted for George," said Susanna to Naamah. "Sister Fannie is what he needed."

"And what Eliza Ann needs," said Naamah. The two were silent, content to watch the new family, until Naamah said, "You'll see less of her now. Will you miss her?"

"I reckon," said Susanna. "But a young child is tiring. Being a grandmother will be fine." Susanna stayed with that thought before shielding her face and lowering her voice, "Will I be a great-aunt, soon?"

Naamah grew somber as she tugged at her clinging dress. She turned toward the newlyweds as she shook her head. "No."

"Forgive me. My question was indecent. It's, well. . ." Naamah turned back to Susanna. "Sometimes I feel more like your mother than your aunt." Susanna looked forlorn when she said, "You're the only girl I ever had."

Naamah embraced her aunt. As she stepped back, Susanna asked, "Still feeling faint?" Naamah shook her head as Susanna asked, "Is everything well?"

Naamah's worries flashed through her mind – cramps, John's ague, not being with child, and fear of mobber attacks. This day, she was more distressed than usual and could use some motherly comfort. But Aunt Susan seemed exhausted, too weary for added burdens. Naamah had been in Nauvoo for a few months but had learned its ways. Shoulder your burdens and sustain yourself in faith, knowing a better world will come.

Naamah reached into her being and forced a smile. "Everything is well, as the Lord is my shepherd."

*****

Summer wore on, and Naamah's worries morphed into habitual fears. John worked at the temple every fifth day but needed to rest in between his tithes. He was unable to maintain their garden properly, their source of sustenance with the meager remains used for barter. By late August, Naamah did all the gardening.

When not doing household chores and gardening, she was at the temple, baking and washing the hired workers' clothing. She wanted to contribute more, but John was her primary responsibility. And when his health further declined, her temple work lessened, adding more guilt. Her only valuables were a locket and child's ring that her mother gave her just before she died. One day, Naamah had planned to pass that legacy to her daughter. But now the Church's need was immediate, and prospects of a child seemed distant.

A wistful Naamah looked at the jewels before placing them on the table with other contributions. "Bless you, dear," said a sister while offering a smile. Sister Amelia rubbed her back as others nodded their pleasure. *Mother, our meager treasures have found God's purpose.*

Naamah felt closer to the sisterhood, making sacrifices for a common purpose while working near a magnificent edifice. They discussed their faith while they worked, more so than in Peterborough, perhaps since Nauvoo's daily burdens were more trying. Her contributed jewelry sparkled in the sunlight, seemingly as bright as the sisters' smiles. Naamah nodded as she thought, *I'm living the gospel each day, no longer a Mormon, but a latter-day saint.*

9 September 1845

As evening crept into Nauvoo, the crickets' chirps, usually a harbinger of cooling air, were mistaken this night. Humidity lingered in the house like an odorous blanket, suffocating John and Naamah. With his eyes closed, John lay upon the straw-stuffed matting drenched in sweat and shivering. Naamah knelt beside him, and by routine, removed the cloth from his forehead and dipped it into the bowl beside her. She wiped his head and face, folded the cloth, and replaced it.

"Bless you," said John as he opened his eyes. "I sense my fever leaving." He shuddered and rolled his head toward Naamah. "If it's gone by the morn, I'll return to the temple."

"I know you're eager, but the temple can wait."

"But I've made my commitment."

Naamah leaned forward and caressed John's sweaty stubble-filled cheek. She kissed him and settled back. John smiled and shut his eyes.

He lay still, seemingly more at peace than he had been for some time. *Perhaps the cooling cloth is helping,* thought Naamah. In a quiet interlude, her eyes drifted about the room, pausing at the table where they offered thanks before eating. As they ate, they discussed their future all grounded in faith. A half-eaten corn ear was on the only plate at the table. Naamah lowered her eyes and thought, *Eating alone is so unfulfilling.*

Her eyes shifted to a darkened hollow next to John. Her head had lain there, and when it did, she would cuddle John while scents of the straw matting and their love making perfumed her blissful sleep. But of late, because of his chills and thrashing, she slept on the floor aside him. *Will I ever hold him again?*

Her melancholy increased as she remained transfixed on where she ached to be. *The pleasures of marriage are so fleeting.* She sighed as she closed her eyes. When she reopened them, hope flickered within her gloom. *Fleeting, but to be eternally enjoyed in His celestial kingdom.*

Images of them clad in white against a backdrop of puffy, radiantly lit clouds danced in her head. They were among Elder Maginn, Sister Harriett, and other saints who were awaiting them in paradise. Bliss filled her soul until her lower region gurgled. She winced as she massaged her side. Her side of the matting where once she and John had been one came back into view. *Am I destined to be barren, bringing no one into His kingdom?*

John thrashed, and the cloth slid off his forehead. He wrapped his arms around his torso and shivered. As she grabbed the cloth to refresh it, he opened his eyes and said, "Forgive me, Naamah." He stared, seemingly searching for words to complete his thought before closing his eyes.

She wrung out the cloth and placed it on his forehead. "Forgive you for what, my dear?"

John's eyes opened. "For bringing you to Nauvoo."

"I belong in Nauvoo. You were Heavenly Father's way of fulfilling what was meant to be."

John shuddered so hard his voice quivered as he said, "Life is hard in Nauvoo."

"Living the gospel eases life's burden, and in Nauvoo . . ."

"No," said John as he mustered strength to raise his head. He lowered it and his voice trailed off. "Nauvoo's changed, and without the Prophet . . ." John's vacant eyes remained on the ceiling. "And without the Prophet . . ." His shuddering ceased, and he released his arms from his torso. His eyes seemingly passed through the ceiling and grew curious. "And without the Prophet . . ." he murmured.

As John shut his eyes he heard, *"My brother, I never left you."* John's forehead creased into wonder. *Joseph?* he thought. As his delirious mind answered his tacit question, his facial muscles relaxed. A tranquility he had never experienced washed through his being.

Naamah thought about refreshing the cloth, but John seemed peaceful, and she didn't want to disturb him. She continued her silent vigil until the peace that had engulfed John came unto her. She eased back from her kneel and moved the bowl to curl on the floor. His gentle wheeze grew rhythmic and soothing. *Maybe his fever has broken,* she thought. And with each wheeze, her worries drifted farther from thought. Her body grew heavy as her adrenaline receded. Within moments, she was asleep.

A cock crowed, piercing through a dim gray shroud. Befuddled, Naamah lifted her head. The room was eerie, silent, absent John's rhythmic breathing. The cock crowed again, and Naamah rubbed her eyes. She uncurled and knelt beside John to resume her watch. She shivered since the night air had cooled the room and enriched its scents.

Still kneeling, she inhaled to enjoy a familiar hominess until an odd pungency aroused her. She sniffed several times trying to recognize it. Her heartbeat quickened once she recalled a similar stench while kneeling beside her mother as she lay dying. She wrung her hands and jerked forward to stir John. *Let him rest,* she thought as she pulled back. But a throbbing heart increased her worries to a panic. She lurched forward and caressed his face. Her hand shot off it as her eyes widened. He was colder than the room, a blue cold. She nudged his side, and he didn't stir.

She knelt back and collapsed her head into her hands. She sobbed for a few minutes before raising her head. Warm tears streaked her ashen face. She stared through watery eyes at John until it became too painful to endure. She looked up at the dark, gloomy ceiling.

As she wailed, she asked, "Heavenly Father, why?" She folded her hands and waited as utter blackness from above seemed to lower. She grew claustrophobic, and in a voice loud enough to penetrate the heavens, she asked thrice more, "Why?"

A deathly silence answered her until a cock crowed again. The ceiling seemingly ceased lowering as daylight spread throughout the room. Her panic eased as her head dropped into reluctant acceptance. Her eyes fell upon the matting where she often lay before shifting to the half-eaten corn cob. Her stomach gurgled as she raised her head. "Is this my destiny, to be alone?"

As she awaited an answer, Nauvoo's awakening broke the silence. A cock crowed, and birds chirped. She arched her head and seemingly looked through the ceiling. "If this be your command for me, then so be it."

Color sprinkled the grayness. Nauvoo's stirrings continued, growing to its distinctive morning bustle. For a brief moment silence returned, and a voice said, *"My sister, we will be amongst you."*

A cock crowed with a mellifluence never heard before. Several more followed with sounds as rich and sweet as honey.

"And I will be amongst you," and the voice paused for a final affirming crow, *"always."*

Chapter Twenty-nine

The phrase Naamah heard the morning John died remained to console her in the ensuing days. Aunt Susan, Cousin George, Sisters Amelia and Caroline, and the community at large gathered near. She was experiencing what she heard. "And we will be amongst you." Through the funeral and several days following she was among friends, which distracted her from remembering how dearly she missed John.

When she was alone, particularly at night, her longing was most acute. And by the following week, her kin and close friends had returned to their daily routines. A few days ago, just before daybreak, the "always" eluded her. But she found enough energy to arise and be among the faithful. Driven by guilt to honor John's promise to Elder Bates, she increased her tithe and discovered doing the Prophet's work was uplifting as ever. While conversing with the sisters, she realized several had lost a husband to a touch of ague. Sadly, being a widow was a rite of passage common for many of Nauvoo's women.

18 September 1845

Naamah lay awaiting the cock's crow and, as of late, with emotions surging through her soul. But this morning, demons didn't dance in her head. They were trumped by *"And I will be amongst you, always."* She grew lightheaded, a frequent condition given her sleepless nights. She rolled to her side and thought further. *I never bore witness to my Prophet and know not his voice. Was it He who spoke unto me?* Her eyes widened as she pondered. *Did it come from Him?* The question caused her to wonder if it was a revelation.

Her wonder eased to rapture, and she slept undisturbed by the cock's crow and Nauvoo's ensuing commotion. When sunlight streamed in, she scrambled to freshen herself and hurried to the temple. As regrets about oversleeping eased, she slowed to a stroll to muse further over her revelation, oblivious to the drama around her.

More wagons than usual creaked and thumped as they passed over the ruts. Women and children sat in them while dazed men followed behind, disheveled, grimy, and weary. A smattering of livestock meandered close; an occasional cowbell clanged.

Naamah veered to allow the oncoming wagons to pass. She waited, still deep in thought until the stench of smoke aroused her. Something was not right, and as her other senses came to the moment, she heard moans, sobs, and a lamb's bleat and saw the downtrodden. As a wagon neared, a woman with tattered clothing sat on its edge while two crying children clung to her. She was emotionless and unaware of her children. Naamah was engrossed until her pondering created images too horrific to endure. She turned away and thought, *Oh Lord, grant them peace.*

Once the wagons passed, she crossed Mullholland and proceeded to the temple. The sisters had arrived as scheduled, offering food and washing clothing for some. One doing the washing spotted Naamah and moved to her.

As she waddled near, she waved. "Good morning, Sister Naamah."

"And to you this sunny morn, Sister Emily." Naamah glanced at the distant wagons. "Although I sense not all is well."

"Alas, Brother Brigham's rescuing wagons still return," said Emily Partridge.

"From where?"

"From a small community of the faithful several miles from Nauvoo. Homes torched and Brethren murdered." Emily sidled close and shielded her mouth. "And it's been said some had their way with the women."

Naamah closed her eyes, and the horror she had sensed when seeing the woman with clinging children returned. She shook her head, hoping to clear her mind. But images of rape remained to haunt her.

"They're home now," said Emily. "Nauvoo shall protect them." She took Naamah's hand. "But I'm concerned for you. I heard of Brother Twiss's passing and want to offer my prayers to you." She embraced Naamah while rubbing her back until her stomach rippled.

Emily pulled back and rushed her hands to her face. "Forgive me, my child is active this morn." Once her stomach quieted, she said. "I know Brother Twiss awaits for you in eternity."

Naamah smiled her appreciation for Emily's thoughtfulness.

"In eternity with the Prophet." Emily sighed. "Ah, the Prophet." Her cheeks reddened as she caressed her stomach while lost in thought.

"Did you know him?"

Emily remained with her thoughts as she nodded.

"I never bore witness to him," said Naamah. "Yet I sensed he revealed himself unto me this morning."

Emily left her thoughts and turned to Naamah. "It's His way. After His death, He came unto me and comforted me. He comes to me often."

"I pray he does for me, too," said Naamah as she lowered her head.

"He will. If you're true to Him, He'll be true to you." Emily moved closer. "I understand as I was once like you. But Joseph revealed unto Brother Brigham that he should care for me for time, until we reunite in heaven."

Naamah wrinkled her brow. She stared at Emily before looking toward the ground.

Emily caressed Naamah's cheek and lifted her face. "The Prophet believes in the family principles of Abraham, Isaac, and others of the Old Testament. And Brother Brigham is so guided, too. Joseph said no woman can be perfect without a man to lead her, and no man can be saved without a woman by his side."

"But if I'm sealed for eternity?"

"I know your burden is heavy," said Emily as she took Naamah's hand again. "Joseph's principle passes all understanding, and once grief's dark curtain is rent, more will be revealed unto you."

As Emily returned to the other sisters, Naamah remained confused, unsure about "the principles of Abraham and Isaac". She had a revelation this morning; perhaps with time she would receive more, like Emily. And if Emily knew the Prophet well, He may have chosen her to reveal more of himself. *Maybe when my grief is rent, I'll understand.*

As she handed food to the workers, Amelia moved close. "Oversleep, dear?" As Naamah grimaced, Amelia touched her arm. "If I can ever help . . . We're sisters, you know."

"You've always been there for me as have all the Sisters." Naamah gestured to those doing the washing. "I was talking with Sister Emily Partridge, and she . . ."

"Oh ho, I've heard about her."

"Indeed. And her words caused me to wonder if they came from the Prophet." Naamah paused, and excitement came into her voice. "She knew him well."

Amelia chuckled. "I'll say. She was quite familiar." She shielded her face and whispered, "Sealed to him as a plural wife." Amelia dropped her hand and said with conviction, "And after Joseph departed, Elder Young inherited the kingdom." She flicked her head toward Sister Emily. "All of it."

"Who told you this?"

"'Tis rumor. But Sister Emily is in a family way, is she not?"

Naamah had heard rumors of plural wives and chose to ignore them. *"No woman can be perfect without a man to lead her."* Joseph's words to Emily returned, seeming prophetic. Amelia's smugness remained, and she considered repeating Joseph's words to her. But Amelia was single with no marriage prospects, and given her views on men, she most likely would remain a spinster. Speaking them now would be cruel.

"Well, isn't Sister Partridge in a family way?"

Naamah smiled. "Aren't we all part of God's family?"

*****

Naamah hadn't seen her aunt since John's funeral. She seemed weary then, and while Naamah longed to see her, she sensed giving her time to rest would be best. But as the days passed, her concern grew, and she decided to visit. As she passed the temple, its activity was like always until a sentry came into view. *Guarding the temple,* she thought. *Who would ever desecrate it?* But an answer came as she recalled recent events. *"The mobbers would destroy it in an instant or as soon as we leave."* She had envisioned the Angel Gabriel atop blowing his trumpet and calling the faithful. Now she wondered if he was sounding an alarm. She pictured herself among an erstwhile temple's smoldering rubble as Betsey's parting comments came in her nasal voice. *"Nauvoo -- heaven on earth? More like hell on earth."*

She neared a once-vacant area where the wagons she had seen earlier were grouped close, serving as temporary housing. Sisters moved among the wagons, helping the beset upon. The once pitiful faces now seemed more hopeful. She thought of the outpouring of comfort she had received, and now that outpouring was among the wagons. *No Betsey, it's not hell on earth at all.* She gave an exaggerated head nod.

Nearing the Jolley home, drawn curtains covered the dust filled windows. The only hopeful sign was a prism-like reflection off a window. *Maybe she's sleeping,* she thought, and she retraced a few steps. But she realized she was just rationalizing, so she knocked and waited. When she heard movement from within, she opened the door.

"Aunt Susan," she said in a lowered voice.

A throat cleared, and a gravelly voice followed. "Amy, come in. I've been longing to visit you." A bed creaked, and after a few moments, a noise like a body crashing was heard.

Naamah hastened into the dimly-lit back room. The invigorating outside air had been replaced with a stale odor, eerily familiar to what had hung above John. Aunt Susan turned to her side and propped herself under her forearm.

"How are you faring, my dear?" she asked.

Even in the faint light, Aunt Susan appeared different; saddened eyes, blotchy skin, and dried cracked lips. She caressed her aunt's clammy face that, like the room's stench, was similar to stroking John's face a few weeks ago. She remained hopeful, trying to ignore the worry building from within. "My grieving continues, but I'm faring well."

"You were too young, too newly married to lose Brother Twiss. And now alone, far from Peterborough."

"I'm amongst the faithful." Naamah ceased caressing to stroke her aunt's hair. "And most of all, I have you."

Susanna forced a smile and coughed while struggling off her cocked arm. She removed her bed covering and swung her legs to the floor. After a few moments, she rocked to propel herself off the bed. While standing, she swayed and sat. "I'll sit a tad. Catch my breath."

"And I'll sit near." Naamah left, found a weathered milking stool and brought it into the room. She placed it next to her aunt and sat.

Aunt Susan's head drooped, and a raspy wheeze accompanied each breath. Each hand gripped the bed frame as she raised her head. "Just a touch of the ague. I'm better today." Her head sagged for a moment before she stiffened it. "Truly, I am."

"Rest, just the same." As Susanna flashed an insincere smile, so unlike her, Naamah said, "You seem troubled?"

"Just lightheaded." She lowered her head while slowly swinging her legs. After a few moments, she looked at Naamah. "It's Eliza Ann -- her ague has worsened."

Naamah's chest tightened as she squeezed her eyes shut. *Oh Lord, not Eliza Ann.* She reopened her eyes and rubbed the moisture from them.

Susanna's head had sunk into her hands, and when she lifted it, her eyes were watery. "She got it from me." She shook her head.

"Always hugging her, cuddling her." She was forlorn when she said, "How selfish am I?"

Naamah arose and sat next to her aunt to cuddle her. "You mustn't blame yourself. Nauvoo is full of sickness." She pulled her aunt near and kissed her forehead.

"You mustn't," said Susanna, "I don't want to give it to you."

Naamah pulled more forcefully than before and placed a prolonged kiss on her forehead. "I didn't get it from John, and I won't get it from you." Her aunt ceased resisting and lowered her head on Naamah's shoulder while breathing slowly. She sensed her aunt drifting off, which eased Naamah's worries.

After a few minutes, Susanna gasped and jerked her head from Naamah's shoulder. She glanced around. "I must have dozed off." She looked at Naamah. "What brings you here?"

She didn't even know I was here, thought Naamah as she struggled to remain calm. She caressed her aunt's forearm. "To visit with you."

Susanna stroked Naamah's cheek.

"I'm alone now," said Naamah. "Let me stay and tend to you."

Susanna ceased stroking. "No dear. Brother Jolley is most attentive, and I'm better today, really I am."

"Then I'll stay until he returns."

Naamah offered to help her aunt with the baking, which she protested before agreeing. Naamah cooked since whenever Susanna arose, she needed to sit soon after. They chatted as Naamah moved between the rooms, a recurring scene from Naamah's youth when she was troubled and she helped her aunt with the chores while chatting. However, today the roles were reversed. Naamah paused in the main room while listening to her aunt cough and spit phlegm into a nearby spittoon. She closed her eyes. *She comforted me in my travails. God, let me comfort her now.*

About mid-day, Henry Jolley returned home. Naamah sensed he was relieved that she was there. He thanked her for coming before moving to the back room. Naamah followed soon after and paused outside the door, appreciating the attention her aunt was receiving. She nodded her head as she thought, *A woman truly needs a man to care for her.* She stepped into the room while removing her apron and gave Susanna a peck on her forehead.

"I'm better today, truly," said Susanna as she smiled.

For the first time today, her smile seemed genuine. "Of course, you are," said Naamah as she forced a smile. While looking at her aunt, she worried about what might be inevitable. *Heavenly Father, I beseech thee,* she thought.

*****

After Naamah left and after a brief nap, Susanna arose to help her husband in the main room. After a few steps, her dizziness returned. Reality set in. She wasn't better today, but worse. She returned to her recent recurring question that still had no answer. *Lord, what is your plan for me?* As Brother Jolley bustled in the main room, she wondered how he would get on without her. And lacking an answer, she thought of Naamah and prayed for her grieving to end. And while she tried to avoid it, her thoughts eventually drifted to Eliza Ann.

"Lord, if it must be one of us, let it be me."

Chapter Thirty

Springfield, Illinois

29 September 1845

Governor Ford paced in his office awaiting Major General John J. Hardin's report. He doubted he would hear anything encouraging, so he pondered alternatives. When the clock gonged on the hour, he stopped pacing while his eyes darted about the room until the gonging ended.

"Damn generals, always late. Like to keep civilians wondering. Their way of showing who's in charge." The Governor continued fuming until there was a knock, and General Hardin and an aide entered. Ford rubbed his hands and said, "How bad is it?"

"Worse than imagined." As the Governor's shoulders slumped, Hardin continued, "The County is armed, itching for a fight, and it ain't just whiskey talking."

"Do they know Young has promised to leave in the spring?"

"Ain't soon enough."

"Jesus, there's thousands of them. They just can't vanish."

"No matter. They don't believe what Young has told you."

"He said he won't plant his winter wheat."

"Maybe, but he continues building that temple. If they're leaving, why?"

The Governor shrugged.

"His legionnaires are in Nauvoo only, leaving them Mormons outside the city unprotected. Easy pickings for the mobbers. They intend to burn the surrounding towns and lay siege to Nauvoo."

"Sounds like a civil war."

"We're not far from it. The sooner they leave the better."

"Sooner than the spring? In the dead of winter? They'll die, just like they did when driven from Missouri."

"But it would appease the mobbers."

"Which, leaving or dying?"

"Both."

"Damn it, I've got enough blood on my hands from those Smiths boys and that ugliness in Carthage. I don't need more. You," and the Governor jabbed a finger at Hardin, "call out your militia. Let the rabble see we will protect these Mormons."

"Are you sure?"

A resolve came to the Governor's face as he gave a deliberate, affirmative nod.

"You're going against public sentiment."

"Hated minorities are never safe from the odium of a majority."

"They're not persecuted people," said Hardin. He didn't blink as he added, "All these disturbances, even the death of the Smith boys, arose from their depredations upon Hancock County's God-fearing citizens."

"We still need to protect them."

"Not sure my boys would join up for such a fight."

Their eyes remained locked for several moments until the Governor's head slumped. "All right then." He ran his hand through his hair before re-engaging eye contact. "Get more out of Young. Offer him land in California or on Vancouver Island. That ought to be far enough away."

"Might, but by and by . . ."

"Jesus, it's all I got." The Governor grimaced, upset at his outburst. His voice returned to normal. "I've asked Justice Stephen Douglas to help, and he's agreed. You boys head up there and get promises out of Young and whoever else. We've got to convince the mobbers these Mormons will leave, and for good."

The two exited, and the Governor paced anew, wondering how soon before Hancock County exploded into a civil war.

Nauvoo, Illinois

5 October 1845

It was the Sabbath, and Naamah walked with heightened anticipation. The temple was complete enough to host a general assembly. The sun glistened on the dew, remnants from the overnight frost, and the leaves, more yellow than green and with brown tinges on crinkled edges, foretold winter's advent. Today was the chilliest since Naamah had arrived six months earlier. She moved apace until a gaggle of geese distracted her.

They jockeyed while honking until a V emerged from the chaos. The commotion abated, and acting in unison with each knowing its position, the flock sliced through the sky. As they headed south across the Mississippi, she recalled another frosty morning -- her first pumpkin harvest beside her father.

"When frost covers the pumpkin, the geese know to fly south," her father said as he pointed skyward. *"Who leads them? Will they all leave?"* she asked. Her father shrugged and said, *"Can't say"* And when out of frustration she said, *"But why, Father?"* he smiled and said, *"It's simply God's way."*

Peterborough stayed in her thoughts as she ambled. *The trees must be bare by now. And the fireplace is finally lit.* She chuckled as she thought, *Father never lit it until after the first frost.* She drew her wrap close while continuing to reminisce until a voice disturbed her.

"Sister Naamah, may I walk with you?" said Amelia as she hurried up.

As she neared, Naamah said, "Doesn't this day remind you of Peterborough?"

"Peterborough?" Amelia wrinkled her brow. "I reckon." After several steps, she added, "I did receive news from

Peterborough, though. All is well with the Saints, and they've gathered contributions for our temple."

"How generous of them."

"I doubt they know we might be leaving Nauvoo."

"We won't be until the spring."

"Who told you?"

"Sister Emily. She overheard Elder Young."

"Oh her. Well, I reckon being near him has advantages."

Naamah thought further. "I reckon you're right."

"But if we're leaving, why do we still build?"

"It's simply God's way," said Naamah as she scrunched her neck. *I sound just like Father,* she thought. She gestured to the temple's entrance. "Perhaps more will be revealed unto us this day."

Inside and amazed by the temple's magnitude, Naamah moved with head up, feeling dwarfed. She stepped from the propelling crowd to turn slowly and take in more. Light streamed in to enchant her and create a warm ambiance. She inhaled, and her awe gave way to admiration. *Joseph's vision has finally come to pass.*

Four years earlier, Joseph broke ground for the temple. As Prophet, he decreed neither sacred endowments nor general conferences would occur until the temple was completed. While finishing details were still needed, the windows were in place, the flooring had been laid, and seating was adequate to accommodate the congregation.

Naamah sat next to Amelia and among sisters, many of whom were from Peterborough. As usual recently, Aunt Susan was not near, so Naamah scanned hoping to spot her. She ceased when Brigham arose and the clamor quieted.

He moved like a lion surveying his domain. When Naamah clutched Amelia's forearm, she twitched and turned to Naamah with a quizzical look. Naamah forced a meek smile and released her grip. A hush came.

Brigham bowed his head and uttered inaudible words before slowly raising it while tightening his podium grip. With a roar powerful enough to rattle the windows he said, "Lord, today we dedicate this house." He flung his arms toward the heavens, "We dedicate this monument of the Saints, and we dedicate ourselves unto thee." He paused as amen followed.

As he continued, Naamah was riveted. When he paused for a moment, she surveyed the sisters around her. They were captivated, too. She turned to the podium and thought, *Such a powerful man, and a mere step from the Prophet.* She glanced at Amelia and thought of her earlier comment. *Being near him, like Sister Emily, does have advantages,* she thought.

Brigham opened his arms and raised them skyward "On this Sabbath, I hereby decree the temple's motto for eternity to be," and he paused before roaring, "holiness unto the Lord."

As he strode from the podium, Naamah sensed her cheeks had flushed. She placed her right hand near her bosom, an instinctive effort to quell a fluttering heart. *Amen, Brother Brigham, amen.* She was unsure if she said it aloud or whether it arose out of her soul.

Others speakers followed, but lacking Brigham's vigor, Naamah's attention waned. Her eyes drifted, hoping to spot Aunt Susan. Her search became methodical as her hopes faded into worry. *I pray the killing frost kills her ague, too.*

Elder John Taylor, still with the musket ball in his left knee that he received during the martyrdom fifteen months earlier, limped toward the podium. He appeared sage-like with a thick mane of greying, unruly hair that extended into his sideburns to mask his ears. He clutched the podium, but unlike Elder Young, to steady himself. As he talked about the Saints completing the temple and leaving in the spring, Naamah thought, *I pray Aunt Susan will be among us.* She continued to wonder about the exodus until Taylor elevated his voice and stood erect.

With fists clenched and renewed vigor, Taylor said, "I shall rejoice on the day we are beyond the bounds of these so-called Christians." He patted the lump in his coat pocket and smiled broadly as his eyes opened farther, seemingly in delight. "For then, I will need not my six-shooter to fend against those blood suckers who tried in vain to drain life from me in that Carthage Jail."

"Amen," roared the crowd in unison.

*****

That night, Naamah lay with emotions swirling – so many questions, so few answers. The temple was finally built, and now the mobbers intended to drive them from it. *It's unjust, Lord,* she thought as she thrashed in anger. *I pray you put a pox upon them.*

But rage was uncommon to her, and she ceased thrashing. *"Vengeance is mine." sayeth the Lord. It's not for me.*

She reflected on the irony. Violence surrounded Nauvoo: Saints burned from their homes, children orphaned, and women raped. As the images kept coming, she shuddered. Wednesday last, four hundred state troopers marched into Nauvoo and took a Brother prisoner, only to release him before returning to their camp. *Will they keep coming?*

Gunshots crackling through the air interrupted her thoughts. When she had first heard gunfire, she was petrified. Now, Saints testing their guns whenever they feared their powder might not be dry was a nightly occurrence. She rolled to her side as Elder Taylor, patting his six-shooter, appeared in her mind. His smile no longer seemed joyful, but maniacal, vengeful. *For what he hath endured, he has due cause.*

Her fears kept building until she found an answer to ease them. *We must leave; there's no other way.* Soothed, her thoughts meandered until focusing on this morning's migrating geese. She smiled as her father's words came with a newfound appreciation. *"It's simply God's way."* She savored thoughts of that frosty October morn until she tripped across a question her father couldn't answer.

He shrugged when she asked, *"Will they all leave?"* And when she asked about the goose with the broken wing, he grimaced and said, *"She won't be leaving."* She remembered his embrace, and her pulling back to say, *"But her babies need her, Father."* He drew her into his arms and said, *"Now, now, so many questions. You know I'll always be here for you."*

Those words comforted her then, but within two months he had died. She felt abandoned and alone in the ensuing weeks. Only Aunt Susan could soothe her. The goose with a broken wing reappeared in her thoughts. *I fear Aunt Susan won't be leaving with us. What will I do without her?*

Absent an answer, she felt alone and isolated. *I so miss Peterborough.* Faces of former friends appeared, easing her sense of abandonment. And upon seeing one, a much-needed chuckle came. *I even miss you, Betsey.*

Chapter Thirty-one

19 October 1845

Two weeks had passed since Naamah first entered the temple. As she glanced around the interior, she was still in awe. She reflected on last week's hymn. The always mellifluent choir within the temple's confines had given "The Spirit of God like a Fire is Burning" a rich, reverberating sound. She hummed to a verse's melody.

"The visions and blessings of old are returning; and angels are coming to visit the earth."

She sighed, knowing her days of hearing the rendition again were limited. Earlier, Elder Parley Pratt had answered her question about building the temple and leaving, which she accepted. She thought of it again.

"God always requires sacrifice, and we leave the temple as monument unto Him and for others; for we must enlarge our numbers and extend our borders beyond a city, or a county, or the United States." She glanced to the choir loft, taking solace that others would follow and hear what she had already experienced.

Elder Young had taken charge and provided particulars for the exodus. His plan was thorough, like everything he undertook.

Naamah's worries eased until she realized the plan's first essential, a family of five adults, was problematic. She was a lone widow, so she commiserated with Amelia, Caroline, and other single women. They were anxious too. Many planned on joining with kin or friends to become a family. *Perhaps I'll join Aunt Susan or Cousin George*, she thought.

Last week her remaining crops suffered a killing frost. Most had been harvested, and she could manage and, if needed, could sell or rent her house. That thought would have been daunting, but Brigham had created a committee to oversee Nauvoo's real estate transactions. She smiled as she thought, *He's always there for us, attending to our needs.*

She thought of her husband, another man who tended to her. "If you ever be in need, our house will fetch its weight in gold," he said on his deathbed. She gazed seemingly through the ceiling and nodded. *Even from on high, you still care for me.*

The gathering concluded with the singing of "Hark, Listen to the Trumpeters". Naamah moved toward the exit, and as always, scanned for Aunt Susan. Spotting George ahead of her, she wended toward him, and once outside, she hurried. Slouched over, his gait lacked its usual vigor. She wondered if she had been mistaken. She called out his name, and he turned and shuffled back.

"Been a while, cousin," she said. "How have you been faring?'

"The ague has run me pretty low."

"And Aunt Susan? I've not seen her in a while."

George grimaced and shook his head.

"I pray this cold spell will help her. It's got to." George's eyes seemed to sadden further, and Naamah added, "Will she leave with Brother Jolley or with you?"

"Neither for now. We lack covered wagons. Can't speak for Brother Jolley, but for me, the cost is too dear."

"What will you do? Sister Fannie and Eliza Ann?"

"Not sure." He bowed his head. "I'm in deep prayer for them." He raised it, and his mood seemed to brighten. "God will answer when I need to know." He coughed and wiped the glistening sweat above his lip. He wrapped his arms to ease his shivering. "And you, Cousin?"

"I may join on with kin."

George shook his head. "Amy, I'm your only kin, and . . ."

"I meant other Peterborough families. If they'll have me." George seemed unconvinced, and now hearing her plan aloud, Naamah was dubious, too. "You're right, George. God will reveal himself in due time."

*****

Much in Naamah's life was in God's hands, but selling her house was not. As she strode to her realty committee meeting, she was re-energized, taking charge, and realizing John's legacy for her. She knew he was proud of her, and soon her financial woes would disappear.

Three white-haired men sat behind a table, hands folded in front of them. They seemed aloof, pious as they stared from an elevated platform. As Naamah explained her situation, they listened while remaining straight-faced. After a few minutes, she felt intimidated as they seemingly loomed over her. She rambled until her resolve returned.

"I'm obliged for your assistance," she said. "My late husband said the house is worth its weight in gold."

The man in the middle leaned forward, and his expression saddened as he said, "Sister Twiss, if it's worth a pound, we might fetch a shilling at best."

His words were sobering, and worse, she sensed she was a poor steward of John's legacy. "It's not stately, but cozy -- surely better than a tent. And it could be let to others."

"And to whom would you let it, Sister Twiss?"

As Naamah pondered, another man said, "When we leave, Nauvoo will abound with houses."

She glanced heavenward. *Dearest John, help me convince them.*

The man continued, "The gentiles desire farm land. And as for homes, the brick ones on the flats are the mobbers' fancy." He turned to a fellow member. "Pearls cast to swine like them. My heart is rendered ill as I imagine what they will do with them."

"Elder Woodruff's elegant home, recently completed, and now . . .," said another as he shook his head.

Naamah's disappointment remained as she left the meeting. She wondered if they had taken advantage of her, a woman and a widow. She knew if John had been there, the outcome would have been better.

During her nightly ritual with John as she lay in bed, he said, *"The Brethren will always care for the sisters,"* which assuaged her doubts about dismissive men ignoring her. As she lamented the house being worth a pittance, he said, *"Naamah, it's not your fault."* His unquestioning love was eternal, indeed. She slept, dreaming about being reunited with him.

The next morning she accepted her house as being worthless. Her financial issues remained, but she would manage until the exodus. As she waited for God to reveal his plan for her, she rationalized her inaction, believing she would leave with Aunt Susan. *She'd never abandon me.*

Autumn 1845

Nauvoo Cemetery

In late October when Aunt Susan died, Naamah was stunned. Her soul knew it was imminent, but she was still grieving John's passing and needed to believe Aunt Susan would be there for her. In less than two months, the most important people in her life were dead. Reality set in.

Standing graveside, she realized she had known Aunt Susan all her life, longer than she had known either of her parents. Her eyes passed by Amelia, Sister Fannie holding Eliza Ann, Brother Jolley, and one of George's friends. *Longer than anyone, except for George.*

She glanced at two markers next to the freshly dug grave, observing Oliver's birth and death dates. *I knew her longer than you.* She thought further and became envious. *And now she's with you, and I'm alone.*

George had aged considerably this past fortnight. The dark circles beneath his eyes accentuated their emptiness. Ashen, he perspired even in the cooling autumn air. He shuddered and drew his coat near. Naamah wondered what bothered him more, his ague or his mother's death.

She stared at the grave, a seeming abyss, symbolic of her emptiness. She had an eerily similar void ten years earlier: an autumn day, standing graveside with her sisters listening to Reverend Elliott's drone, grieving until Aunt Susan rustled through fallen leaves and clutched her hand while mouthing, *"Forgive me, I'm late."*

Naamah ceased rubbing her hands and allowed one to hang at her side. She inched it from her body while keeping her palm facing behind her. She squeezed her eyes to stem the tears, praying Aunt Susan would come alongside. A stir came, and her eyes reopened. Her heartbeat quickened, and upon hearing distinct steps within the thicket, she wondered, *Could it be?* Her anticipation built and exploded when two deer sprang from the undergrowth. They bounded before disappearing into the swale. She looked heavenward and smiled. *I know it's a sign from you, Aunt Susan.*

The crunching on fallen leaves continued as the deer moved east, toward Peterborough. She pondered while listening to the deer's exodus until it was inaudible. She glanced skyward. *Or was it a sign from God? Am I to return home?*

She contemplated her question while the men shoveled dirt over the rough-hewn casket. They tamped the grave, and George removed his hat and mumbled a few words. He wiped his brow with his handkerchief and replaced his hat.

Fannie, holding Eliza Ann, moved to him. He kissed the top of his daughter's head before embracing them. He shook as he cried while Fannie rubbed his back. He stepped back to brush his tears and re-embraced them, burying his head on Fannie's shoulder and muffling his sobs.

George's friend and Brother Jolley loaded the shovels onto the wagon and waited near the ox. After a few minutes, George gathered his resolve and trudged to them. He sat in the front between the men. Fannie and Eliza Ann sat on the back, sandwiched between Naamah and Amelia. The women dangled their legs from the flatbed. Brother Jolley snapped the reins, and the wagon jerked forward.

As Naamah moved her hand to touch Eliza Ann's face, she tried to grab it. Naamah moved it back and inched it closer, and as Eliza Ann swatted at it, Naamah snapped it back. Eliza Ann giggled. Naamah repeated the process several times, evoking the same response.

"She seems full of life today," said Naamah.

"Her fatigue this past month had been almighty. But her fever passed just after Susanna left us. So sudden I thought it odd, perhaps God had . . ." Fannie paused to grab Eliza Ann's swatting hand from her face. She said to her, "'Tis your Cousin Amy's game, tisn't mine."

Naamah and Fannie chuckled. "Ah me," said Fannie. "Blessed are the children." As Naamah reflected, Fannie continued. "God's way of telling us life goes on."

"Well, I wouldn't know," said Amelia. She drew her wrap close and looked at dust billowing from the wheels.

Amelia's snippy remark surprised Naamah. But thinking further, she realized Amelia had yet to understand the joy of children. The two of them were alike in that regard. *Perhaps someday,* she thought. But her someday lacked specifics, and she rubbed Eliza Ann's head before pecking her cheek. *I reckon I misunderstood Elder Young's marriage blessing for me.*

Fannie and Eliza Ann continued to enjoy one another while Naamah, overcome with melancholy, was silent like Amelia. Along the two-mile journey, the wagon lurched whenever it passed over ruts or hit a rock. Naamah rolled with the jerks, oblivious to them. The wagon stopped, and George came to the back.

"Much appreciate you coming, cousin," he said as he offered his helping hand.

Naamah left her gloom and looked around until she got her bearings. "Oh my, I'm home." She thought of her recent realty committee meeting. "At least for now."

George helped her off the flatbed, and she turned to Fannie. Eliza Ann was sleeping, and she resisted her urge to stroke the babe's face. *Fannie spoke truly,* she thought, *blessed are the children.*

She took a step before turning back. "Where's Sister Amelia?"

"Cousin, we left her at her house a while ago." George looked to Fannie who was captivated by Eliza Ann before returning his gaze to Naamah. "Don't you remember?"

"My mind's been elsewhere. I'm sure you're right."

George scratched his head as Naamah moved to her house and entered. George hopped onto the wagon while thinking about Naamah. *Rest will do her well.* He removed his handkerchief and wiped his face. *We've all borne a heavy burden this day.*

Chapter Thirty-two

George's assumption about his cousin was ill-founded. She rested, spending countless hours lying on her bedding, but it didn't do her well – in fact, she was worse. She thought often about Aunt Susan and Brother Twiss in eternity, seldom venturing out to mingle, even though her soul knew the path for reuniting with them was living the gospel daily. But those voices were not powerful enough to break her despair. She was nearly paralyzed, able to perform only the basics of sustenance and occasional grooming.

One sleepless night during an exchange with John, their gratifying nights as newlyweds were most vivid, part of her here and now. Her thoughts reached a climax, and she slept past the cock's crow, awakening in glaring light. Her bliss became remorse over pleasuring herself earlier in the shadows where Satan lurks. She worried if a miserable wretch like her would ever receive salvation. *Is my punishment to be barren for eternity?*

Nauvoo was abuzz, preparing for the exodus. The carpenters who once built the temple now were building twenty-five hundred wagons. Naamah remained unmindful, still lacking a plan to leave. Through her procrastinating lens, she had an eternity.

Deer hooves fleeing east came to her mind. Returning to Peterborough would be more certain than what lay across the

Mississippi. She could remain a faithful Latter-day Saint in Peterborough and be freed of Nauvoo's constant fears. Returning grew appealing until she thought of those in eternity. If she fled, she would be ashamed and unable to face John, Aunt Susan, and so many others who had endured, if indeed, Heavenly Father would let her enter his kingdom at all.

December

Naamah contemplated whether to arise or not. She glanced at the plates with partially eaten food on them and clothing strewn on a chair. The woodstove was cold, and the grease lamp needed re-wicking. A stench told her the double-folded linen over her chamber pot was insufficient.

Earlier, the cock had crowed as light crept into her cold darkness. Now, the room sparkled, yet December's chill lingered. She inched forward before crashing back onto her bedding. She closed her eyes to block out reality and gathered her covering closer, hoping for needed rest. Yet whenever she closed her eyes, the black void created an ideal backdrop for images of her despair; sleep seldom came.

She was fitful until she heard from outside, "Sister Naamah." She lay still, hoping the visitor would depart. "We know you're home and have come for a visit," said a voice that sounded like Amelia's.

Naamah held her breath and stiffened, praying to hear Amelia's departure. *Did Amelia say we? Who else is with her?*

The door scraped as it opened. "Sister Naamah."

Naamah threw her covering aside and arose as Amelia and Caroline entered. She tugged at her clothing and raked her fingers through her dirty, straggly hair. "Oh me, I've overslept this day." She took a few steps while looking around the room until pausing at the window. "And such a glorious day."

"'Tis," said Amelia as she crossed her arms.

Caroline stepped closer. "We've prayed for you. But nary have we laid eyes upon you. Are you in want?"

"I've been faring well."

Amelia scanned the cluttered room while shaking her head. "No one has laid eyes on you," she said. "We've missed you at the Sabbaths and at the quilting bees."

As Naamah fumbled with a dress button, Caroline touched her shoulder. "Sister, I'm a widow, too. I understand. And then to lose Aunt Susan, well . . ."

"We all understand," said Amelia as she unfolded her arms. "But if you're in want, you must be among us for comfort."

Naamah ceased her fumbling and looked away. "I've much to do here."

"No Sister," said Caroline as she grabbed Naamah's arm and turned her to be eye to eye. "*We* have much to do."

She released her grip and began gathering the clothing while Naamah watched, seemingly paralyzed. "Your rainwater barrel is full and has yet to ice over," said Caroline as she grabbed a wooden bucket and left.

Naamah turned to Amelia, who was scraping food into the waste bin. After stacking the plates, she gathered thin, dry wood near the stove. Naamah wrung her hands as Amelia built a pyramid inside the stove. Once completed, she turned to Naamah and said, "Matches? Or do we need to borrow fire from a neighbor?"

Without responding, Naamah moved her head about the room, seemingly unsure as to why.

Amelia sighed and rustled in the cupboard. "Aha, friction matches." She started the stove's fire, and once it popped, she arose from her crouch. "She's ablaze, and by and by, we'll have hot water."

Caroline returned, lugging the water bucket. The right side of her dress was damp from the sloshing. She plunked the bucket near the stove, exhaled, and turned to Amelia. "I'll wash, and if you'll clean the plates and tidy up, I'd be obliged."

"But first," said Amelia as she moved to the chamber pot, "we must dispose of this." As she grabbed the pot's sides she turned her head away.

Naamah seemingly came back to the moment. "Please, you mustn't." She took the pot from Amelia. Holding it as far away as possible, she went outside.

Caroline looked to Amelia and said, "I pray Sister Naamah will soon be among us."

After a while, Naamah returned without the pot. She avoided eye contact with either of them and said, "I dare say, my pot needed freshening."

"I dare say, too," said Amelia, and they laughed.

The two sisters had been successful in their mission. Naamah had returned to the here and now. They spent the morning doing the neglected household chores. As noon neared, Caroline left and returned within an hour, bringing food, a coil of wick, and a small embroidered container.

As they conversed while eating, Naamah realized how absent she had been. *Amelia was correct,* thought Naamah. *I must be among the sisters.* That thought triggered another when she was mourning John's death. *"And I will be amongst you always."* She grimaced while reflecting. *How soon did I forget His words?*

As their dining was concluding, Amelia arose to pour heated water into the basin. She grabbed a linen cloth and placed it and the basin in front of Naamah. "We will give you leave and privacy to bathe," said Amelia.

Caroline handed Naamah the wick coil. "It's dreary to spend a night without light, particularly with winter drawing nigh." She slid the embroidered container across the table. "And after you bathe, my rice powder for your cheeks."

Naamah studied the container, saying nothing.

"We'll return on the morrow and take you to the temple," said Amelia.

"The temple is now offering endowments," said Caroline. "Why Friday last, Elder Young and Elder Kimball worked until the cock crowed. There's much ado there."

"What shall I do?" asked Naamah.

"Help with the washing. Bring food for others," said Amelia. "Or begin your endowment for your marriage to Brother Twiss."

Naamah's head slumped.

"Forgive me. That was harsh," said Amelia.

"No, 'tis I who have been harsh, so consumed with my travails, I've forgotten what's important." She paused while looking doleful. She blinked her eyes, and her sadness left. "And I'll have little Reubie baptized so he can be with Aunt Susan, too."

Confused by little Reubie, Caroline and Amelia looked at each other.

Naamah glanced skyward. "He'll be with you soon." She turned to the sisters. "Oh, I have much to do." The room's light, which had been there since the cock stopped crowing, now brought warmth. "'Tis truly a glorious day."

She turned and noticed the embroidered container. "And the rice powder?"

"To not look a fright," said Amelia. "You never know who you might meet at the temple."

*****

Her two friends remained true and returned to take Naamah to the temple. As she neared, she realized Caroline had been correct – there was much ado. The faithful would soon depart, and not knowing to where or when another temple would be erected, they were determined to receive their endowment before leaving. With demand high, only endowments for the living were being performed. Naamah was disappointed, but understood her marriage endowment to Brother Twiss and Little Reubie's baptism by proxy would have to wait. In accordance with Church instruction a living person, acting as proxy, can be baptized on behalf of a deceased person. Baptism for the dead is based on the belief that baptism is required for entry into the Kingdom of God.

Ashamed by her absence, she avoided eye contact, spoke little, and did as directed. Those waiting their endowment were reverent, pensive, and upon receiving it, blissful and seemingly able to shoulder any earthly burden. As Naamah's guilt eased, she engaged more and found the sisters' joy infectious, brightening her mood. Her first day had been therapeutic, and she returned the following day.

23 December 1845

The gentiles had noticed increased temple activity, too. Their suspicions had grown to paranoia, and as Naamah headed to the temple, marshals, militia, and other strangers were more prevalent. Nauvoo's energy and independence seemed lacking. The faithful were wary, and conversations were often cryptic, in hushed tones, or discontinued whenever strangers drew near.

As she neared the temple entrance, two men several yards away moved toward her. She quickened her step and prayed their movement was a coincidence. But they veered toward her, and a burly man began to trot. She squeezed her eyes and hastened.

"Ma'am, halt," said her pursuer in a gasping voice.

She turned and waited. He was broad-shouldered, with his shirt oozing between his vest and britches. His belly shook as he trotted. "What's in the basket?" he asked as he neared.

"Baked goods for the hungry."

"Give it here," he said as he ripped it off her forearm.

As he fumbled through it, his companion neared, a lanky man with a polished badge on his chest. "Got a revolver in that thar basket, ma'am?" he asked.

Naamah shook her head.

"Maybe a knife is baked into one of these," said the burly man as he bit into a roll. "Here," he tossed a roll to his sidekick, "check for a knife." They chuckled as they wolfed.

Naamah quivered and gathered her arms close. She looked toward a few faithful gathered several yards away, who were observing, seemingly ready to help if she so indicated. She glanced at one and shook her head. They eased their watch, yet loitered near.

The burly man removed two more rolls and tossed one to his friend. "Move along, ma'am," he mumbled with his mouth half full.

"May I have my basket?"

"You said these were for the hungry." His smile broadened, exposing food clinging to his gums and teeth. "And we're hungry."

His lanky companion puffed his chest and leaned his badge toward Naamah. "We're Marshals, ma'am." He moved inches from her. His clothing reeked, which even a heavy scent of whiskey could not conceal. "Now, you git along, missy." His breath was as foul as his body odor.

Naamah turned and scurried until she was several steps from the temple entrance.

"That's it, missy. Go pray to yer whoremonger."

Those words ripped through her, and she felt as defamed as her Prophet. Snickering ensued, and she felt sullied, tawdry.

She rushed inside and leaned against the door. She closed her eyes while panting. Once her breathing steadied, she moved off the door. Standing between the vestibule and the magnificent Great Hall, she absorbed the ambiance until she was at ease.

She moved to the circular staircase and went down to the baptistery. She paused on the wooden landing to observe more magnificence. The hundred by forty foot basement had arched stone pillars supporting the floor above, which formed six rooms on either side. In the open area, a herringbone-patterned brick floor sloped toward the center for drainage. The fire red, cobbled flooring and the angel white walls created a dramatic contrast. Dominating the center was a sixteen by twelve foot limestone baptismal font supported by twelve life-size oxen crafted from pine. A staircase, centered between the oxen, rose seven feet to the font's rim.

She thought of her baptism outside and in the Nubanusit, simple compared to the grandeur she was beholding, which now reconfirmed her life-changing decision made while in Maginn's arms. She sighed and moved along the outside wall.

Only two unfamiliar sisters were hanging garments this day. The younger one, perhaps in her forties, approached and smiled.

"Sister Jemima Angell Young," she said. "You must be Sister Twiss."

Naamah furrowed her brow. "I am. How did you know?"

"Elder Young said you were most dedicated and would not fail to be here." She stepped back and eyed Naamah. "And just as he described, young, fair, ever smiling."

Naamah sensed she was blushing and hoped her rice powder would mask it.

Jemima cocked her head and said, "But where is your food basket?"

"Hooligans took it from me. I wish there were only Saints among us. Life would be easier."

"We will be one once we enter His celestial kingdom. Just Saints. No gentiles."

An aged woman hobbled near Jemima. "Sister Phoebe Angell," said Jemima as she gestured. She turned to Phoebe and said in a loud voice, "Mother, this is Sister Twiss."

"The one who bakes the rolls that Brigham spoke of," said Phoebe in a high-pitched, wavering voice.

"Yes, Mother." Jemima turned to Naamah and spoke while shielding her face. "Mother forgets at times and speaks too familiarly about Elder Young."

"Has she known him long?"

"Since Kirkland." Jemima smiled and said, "Elder Young's wife is her daughter and my older sister."

"I did not know." Embarrassed, Naamah turned from Jemima and glanced around. "Where are the others?"

"A few are in the Attic tending to matters. But many are busy, readying to leave."

Naamah grimaced and grew pensive.

"Why so doleful, Sister?"

"I've not given it a moment of thought, being a recent widow and all."

"Any family?"

"Only my cousin George, and I haven't yet . . ."

"Friends?"

"A few, but I've been out of sorts . . . I just don't know. And you, Sister?"

"Whatever Elder Young decides." She turned to her mother and said, "We're part of his family."

"He's always there for us," said Jemima's mother. "He's a saint."

"Well, Sister," said Jemima as she turned to Naamah, "you could remain behind." She sighed. "But with so many hooligans about, I just . . ."

"I have until spring."

"But spring draws nigh."

Naamah left them to gather the temple garments needing cleaning. Only men performed the holy rites, and thus Naamah could never realize their fulfillment. So she compensated by helping in small ways, and when Elder Young or others praised her dedication, she felt rewarded.

*****

Candle light settled upon Nauvoo as Naamah climbed the circular staircase to the Attic, carrying garments. She stored them in a curtain-partitioned room off the foyer. As she moved out of the room, Brigham and Elder Heber Kimball neared her.

Holding several garments in his hand, Heber said, "Could you tend to these, Sister?"

"Most surely, Elder Kimball."

Brigham smiled. "Just as I told you, Brother Heber. Sister Twiss gives herself unto the Lord's work each day."

Heber laid the clothing on a table and turned to Naamah. "I'll ask a few Brethren to remain until you're done."

"Our thoughts are with the Lord this day," said Brigham. "I was about to speak likewise. We are in perilous times and must tend to one another, particularly our widows."

Heber nodded. "And now, I'll fetch Brother Miller for you."

Naamah descended with the soiled garments to the first floor mezzanine and joined Sister Grace. They worked together until Grace's husband came to walk her home. Naamah finished hanging the few remaining garments alone.

She went down the stairs to the vestibule and stood in the Great Hall's entrance. Evening had come, and the candlelit temple had a mysterious glow. She was fearful, nervous, as she stepped into Hall. *Yea, though I walk through the shadow of death, I will fear no evil,* she thought. She paused in the flickering light and inhaled, allowing the familiar scent of burning oil to enrich her thoughts. She sensed the presence of her Prophet.

She looked skyward, slowly turning while growing lightheaded, uncertain if it was from the solemn atmosphere or from turning with her neck arched. She closed her eyes and thought of intimate times with Brother Twiss. Her bliss intensified until boots clacking the floor interrupted her. She scurried into the vestibule to meet a man at the stairwell.

"Elder Young sent me to escort you home." He made a slight head nod while holding his hat. "I'm Brother Thomas Eames."

"You're so kind," said Naamah.

Eames opened the large door and gestured for Naamah to precede him. She looked west as she exited into a darkened expanse before noticing a carriage several yards ahead. Several men moved in unison toward them, but stopped after several steps.

"We've enacted a curfew, and you're in violation," said one.

"Now git before we arrest yer," said a lanky man whose inflection resembled the marshal who had harassed her earlier.

Naamah and Brother Eames dashed from the group. While scurrying, Naamah asked, "Wasn't that Elder Young's carriage?"

"'Twas."

"Is he in peril?"

"No. Brother Miller will see to his safety."

Naamah ceased walking. "Brother Miller?"

"Sister, we mustn't tarry." Eames grabbed Naamah's arm and resumed his stride. She kept pace while still confused.

*****

What Naamah didn't know was the Springfield Court had issued an indictment against Brigham Young and eight other Apostles, charging them with instigating and harboring a counterfeiting operation in Nauvoo. Further, Brother Miller, similar in stature to the Brigham had donned his clothing and left the temple after Eames and Naamah had left. Once outside, Miller was arrested as he neared Brigham's carriage and taken to the Mansion House for further questioning. While there, other Saints continued the pretense that the marshals had Brigham in their custody. Only later, when Miller was taken to Carthage, did the marshals realize they hadn't captured Brigham. The deception gave sufficient time for Brigham, Brother Heber, and other high-ranking church officials to go into safe hiding.

Chapter Thirty-three

January 1846

The December indictments and rumors of troops readying in St. Louis to intercept the departing Saints caused Brigham Young to alter his plans. The exodus could not wait until the spring. The Saints had to prepare to leave in the dead of winter and on quick notice.

*****

Naamah's plans now had an urgency, and Cousin George was her sole hope. She had visited him a few days earlier and was surprised to learn his battalion would be leaving to protect the Saints as they headed west. Since Fannie and Eliza Ann would stay in Nauvoo, he had arranged with Brother Mills to tend to them until he returned or they could journey to him.

George's health had improved since Naamah last saw him, but she worried for what he would be enduring. "I'm doing as the Lord commands, building the Kingdom of God," he told her. He puffed his chest and added, "God will provide me with the strength to survive."

Naamah sensed an admiration for George's commitment in Fannie's smile. His wife of less than a year held Eliza Ann as George elaborated on the bitter cold he would face, sleeping on a frozen prairie, and possibly encountering the militia. Naamah saw fear in Fannie's eyes that belied her smile. She cuddled Eliza Ann close and kissed her often, avoiding eye contact with George. *A frozen prairie is no place for Eliza Ann,* thought Naamah. *It's God's wisdom that causes her to remain in Nauvoo.*

Later, after her visit, she wondered about God's plan for her. George was her only kin in Nauvoo and soon he would leave. She was far from Peterborough, from family, and isolated. Her fears were akin to those she perceived in Fannie's eyes. She curled into a fetal position and cuddled her bed covering much as Fannie had cuddled Eliza Ann, but her worries remained. She tossed her covers aside and rolled onto her back to ask, *Am I never to experience a child's joy?* Heavenly Father didn't respond. It didn't matter. Naamah had presumed His answer.

She rolled to her side and covered herself. She thought of Sister Jemima, her mother, and other widows. Each sister that flashed to mind was older and each had children. *I'm twenty-four, too young to be widowed, am I not?* Heavenly Father was silent, and she sensed His dismay with her irritation. *I reckon my ears are not open this night.*

Her helter-skelter thoughts continued until pausing at her wedding day. Soothing images came, and eventually, tears trickled. She didn't know if they were from the joy she had then or from sadness realizing now her joy was to be no more. As she sniffed, she recalled her marriage blessing. *"May you live long and bring many into His kingdom."*

She could not reconcile his blessing with her current situation. She revered Brigham and was loathe to dismiss his blessing as foolish, even though it seemed impossible to realize. Her dilemma remained as she tossed to her other side. She rolled onto her back and folded her hands, continuing to reflect.

Her dilemma still tormented her until she thought, *"Be still before the Lord and wait patiently for him."* A verse from a psalm her father recited whenever she grew irritated came to soothe her again. She was a mere child then, and she wondered why she had remembered it now. She sniffed and brushed her tears away. *Bless you, Heavenly Father, for opening my ears this night.*

****

With his exodus plans progressing, Brigham returned to the temple to attend to the surge in endowments. Naamah returned, too, and assisted in the Lord's work. Over the past several days, she and Brigham had been drawn closer together in serving the Lord. She was no longer awestruck, yet still fascinated whenever she was near him. He was the church leader, and a step removed from the Prophet, but also, he was Brother Brigham, one of the Brethren, living according to the gospel. It was this Brigham, Naamah was knowing more with each day.

Doing the Lord's work kept Naamah's mind occupied and not racing chaotically to resolve quandaries over which she had no control. Last night, she had slept on the temple's mezzanine floor in its northeast corner, feeling closer to God, as if she was in His hands. She slept peacefully, and when she awoke, she was revitalized despite a few achy muscles. She went home to eat and freshen herself before returning by mid-morning.

Upon her return, she went to where several sisters were busy. As she neared, Sister Jemima moved from the others. "Ah, Sister Naamah, I prayed you would come today."

"I'm here every day."

"Just what Sister Emma told me when I asked," said Jemima, gesturing to where she had just left. "You've been in my thoughts, and I've worried so." As Naamah tilted her head, Jemima said, "Did you meet with your kin?"

"Ah, George," said Naamah. "Yes, I did."

"And?"

"And he'll depart with his battalion."

Jemima stepped closer and embraced Naamah. "He's your only kin. You've endured much, and you're still of tender years." She stepped back and held each of Naamah's hand. "Many will soon leave. What will you do?'

"I know not." Naamah freed her hands from Jemima's clasp and looked to the floor. "I tarried in Peterborough, fearful to leave. And now I tarry again." She clasped hands and moved them under her chin. "I trust in Heavenly Father. He'll let me know. All will be well."

"When we were chastened from Kirkland and from Missouri," said Jemima, "He watched over us, too. And now . . ." Jemima paused for a moment to reflect. "And now, Mother prays this new Zion in the west will be everlasting."

"Amen Sister," said Naamah.

"And will you be in want while you tarry?" As Naamah shook her head, Jemima shielded her mouth and said, "Sister Emma said you slept in the temple." She moved nearer and whispered. "If you are in want of lodging, we could . . ."

"I was weary," said Naamah, "and intended to doze for a moment, and . . . well . . ." Jemima still seemed skeptical, and Naamah said, "Sister, I'm not in want."

"It does render my heart good to hear you say such."

An aged woman descended the stairs one step at a time while holding the railing. When she reached the landing, she paused and stared, seemingly confused. In January 1846, Phoebe Morton married her son-in-law Brigham Young.

"Isn't that your mother?" said Naamah.

Jemima spun around and hurried to her mother, Sister Phoebe. Naamah followed.

"Are you feeling well?" asked Jemima.

"I'm at peace," said Phoebe. She glanced up the stairs toward the Attic before staring at her daughter. "Your father is at peace, too. He understands it's for time only." She glanced at the floor and back to Jemima. "I pray Mary Ann understands."

Mary Ann? wondered Naamah. *Jemima's sister?*

Jemima glanced at Naamah and put her arm around her mother to lead her into the foyer. After a several deliberate steps, Jemima said to Naamah, "Forgive us. Mother needs some rest."

Naamah nodded and left while wondering. *Was Sister Phoebe referring to Mother Young, or another Mary Ann? Of course it was Mother Young.* Her conclusion caused her to speculate further. Some thoughts were unpleasant, and she ceased questioning. *As Mother always said, 'Thou mustn't listen to other conversations – 'tis the devil's work.'*

Twilight ensued, and the lit candles and oil-fired lamps created a mellowing atmosphere, which Naamah always enjoyed. As she ascended the circular stairway, she heard another person descending. She stepped onto the landing and waited. Sister Jemima who married her brother-in-law Brigham Young in January 1846 came into view.

"I thought you had left with your mother," said Naamah.

Startled, Jemima paused on a rung a few steps from Naamah. "No, I had an important matter to attend to." She fumbled with her dress. "A matter of importance to my mother, too."

"And has it been resolved?"

"Yes, satisfactorily so. I prayed on it, and . . ."

"Sister Jemima," said a voice from above. Jemima craned her neck to look up. "Thou mustn't tarry for idle chatter. Your mother awaits."

"Truly Elder Kimball," said Jemima. She looked to Naamah before scampering down the stairs. The temple door slammed and reverberated in the stairwell. Naamah stuck her head in the stairwell as Elder Kimball departed from the railing. *First, her mother comes from the Attic, now Jemima,* she wondered. *And both out of sorts.* She pondered until her mother's caution returned. *" 'Tis the devil's work.* " She moved into the first floor mezzanine and went about her chores.

After a few hour, she was finishing tidying an Attic room when Brigham approached. His gait was slow, clothing disheveled, and facial hair in need of trimming. His baggy eyes were more noticeable. Several months earlier on a platform in Peterborough, Naamah witnessed a virile, imposing man. Now, she saw a weary old man appearing more like a beloved father figure than the revered leader of God's earthly kingdom.

"Sister Twiss, you remain?" He looked about before turning back to Naamah. "Have all the others departed?"

"They had matters to attend to."

Brigham shuffled to a nearby chair in the foyer and collapsed into it. He sighed and said, "Been a good day for the Lord." He closed his eyes for several moments before reopening them. "Sister Twiss, you wouldn't perchance have anything to eat."

"I set a muffin aside, knowing you'd be hungry." She reached into her dress pocket, unfolded a cloth, and handed a muffin to Brigham. "A tad stale, I reckon."

"Shall we break bread together?" asked Brigham as he parted the muffin and handed a piece to Naamah. He gestured to a chair near him. "Sister, I'd be obliged if you would join me."

As they ate, Brigham didn't say a word. He seemed distant, either tired or pondering his numerous concerns. He finished his muffin and brushed a few crumbs from his whiskers.

"The winds blew cold this day," he said. "I told Brother Heber, 'It's the Lord's work. He parted the sea for Moses as he led his faithful, and he'll freeze the Mississippi so we can journey without need for ferries.' " He tugged on his suit lapels and curled his shoulders. "So cold it caused my mind to recollect my days as young boy." He closed his eyes and sighed. "I miss Vermont." When he opened them, he looked at Naamah and asked, "Do you miss your Peterborough?"

Naamah reflected for a few moments before saying, "I miss my kin." She thought more and chuckled. "But I don't miss the cold."

Brigham chuckled while nodding his concurrence. "Ah sweet Peterborough, which brought such bitterness. I had been troubled many days by thoughts of Brother Joseph, feeling some great calamity had fallen unto him." Brigham's eyes grew distant as he said, "And the Lord chose Peterborough to reveal it unto me."

Naamah lost her smile and lowered her head. Brigham eased off the chair and leaned closer. "Sister," he said in his commanding voice, which thus far had been absent, "worry not for Peterborough. She did not fell Brother Joseph. She merely confirmed the Lord's plan for him."

Naamah raised her head and smiled. As he inched closer, she had a whiff of his scent that had become familiar and unique to him – earthy like most mature man, yet softened and refreshed with temple aromas from doing the Lord's work and lacking the stench from strenuous outdoor labor.

"You see, fulfilling the Lord's plan for Brother Joseph is the sweetness of your Peterborough," said Brigham. He settled back against the chair rest. "Peterborough has served us well." His commanding tone remained as he continued, "We must know from whence we come, so the Lord can lead us to where he needs us. If thou knowest thy roots, thou will never become a lost lamb while in His earthly domain."

"And where does the Lord tell you to take us?"

"West. The mobbers, Ford's militia, only hasten what the Lord ordains. California, perhaps, but I know not for sure." He eased forward and touched Naamah's hand. "But as we journey, we'll be in the Lord's bosom. And he'll reveal unto us when we reach his new Zion." Brigham eased back and closed his eyes for a few moments.

If I trust in the Lord as Elder Young does, thought Naamah, *then He'll let me know when I should leave.* She found solace in knowing she'd be in the Lord's bosom whenever she left.

As Brigham arose, he slapped his knee, which resonated in the quiet foyer lit only by moonlight from the windows. "I've not seen Mother Young for nigh on a week," he said. "I must take leave or surely I'll fall into slumber right before thine eyes." He took a few steps before turning back. He furrowed his brow and said, "Forgive me, Sister, you are alone. Will thou join me in my carriage for safe passage home?"

"I will remain here. I've more to do."

"And where will you sleep?" Naamah didn't respond, and Brigham added, "Sister Jemima said you slept on the temple floor."

Naamah shied from Brigham's stare and nodded.

"Brother Heber has left, and I'm soon to take leave. You may use my resting spot. Come my child." He gestured, and Naamah followed.

"You're most dedicated in your service to the Lord, more than most I've known," said Brigham as they walked around the corner into partitioned areas.

Naamah was flattered, hearing compliments from one so close to the Prophet. Brigham continued lavishing praise, and she grew uneasy, wondering if there was a motive. When they reached the east end section, Brigham lifted a veil curtain and ushered her toward his bedding.

"It's straw," he said. "But more restful than the floor."

Naamah moved to a flannel-covered mound. She quivered as thoughts of being so close to Brigham in his makeshift bedroom swirled. They said nothing as they looked at one another before Brigham broke his gaze and moved away.

He paused and retraced his steps. Naamah's heart pounded, and her cheeks flushed. *Is there more this night?*

"We had many this day," he said. "And you Sister, have brought them into His earthly kingdom. Tomorrow, more will come unto us." He grabbed both her shoulders and pulled her near. "Will you be here for me?"

Naamah sensed her dress jiggling from her trembling knees. She swallowed and nodded.

He kissed the top of her head and eased her back while saying, "Bless you, Sister Twiss." He released his grip and left.

Naamah's head swirled from the far-ranging emotions that had just exploded her mind. She closed her eyes, hoping not to swoon as she thought. His grabbing of her shoulders and easing her closer frightened her. The peck on her head shocked her. But when she inferred the peck to be a kiss, and coupled with being the closest ever to him, a passion inflamed her soul. When he stepped back, she knew he was going to his wife. She felt dirty, like a tramp, until an aged man with shuffling feet changed her emotions again. His actions were merely gratitude, similar to her father's after saying their nightly prayers – a kiss on her head, well wishes, and a shuffle away.

She lay on the straw mound that Brigham had occupied for several nights. Her emotions from her close encounter with him ceased jumping among fear, shock, passion, soiled, and gratitude to an easy flow. Her wooziness subsided, and she rolled to her side. Brigham's scent was about the flannel, and became omnipresent as her breathing quickened. Her emotions swirled again, moving between passion and tawdriness.

She rolled back onto her side, and the intensity left as she thought of their earlier conversation about joyous Peterborough times and doing the Lord's work. Her breathing was deep, relaxed, and her eyes grew heavier thinking about Brigham and the Lord's work. Her thoughts massaged her, and she was nearly asleep.

Suddenly, her eyes flew open, and she bolted up. Her mind had lodged on a bit of conversation, which came in Brigham's voice. *"Sister, you've brought many into His earthly kingdom."* Those words were the same as his marriage blessing for her. She crashed back onto the straw mound. With eyes wide open, she asked Heavenly Father, "Is this what you have chosen for me?"

She did not receive an answer. Her mind raced for a few minutes until pausing to wonder, *Is this why John was taken so quickly from me?* She shook her head. *Thou wouldn't be so cruel.* She questioned if her inference of Heavenly Father's plan for her was truly His or just her addled mind. She thought of doing the Lord's work before returning to the moment. *Am I to never to know another man?* She was doleful, resigned, when she thought, *I'll be barren for eternity, won't I?*

*****

Early the next morning, Naamah returned home to bake for the temple sisters. Last night's emotional whirlwind remained, yet less intense as sunshine and a new day brought reasoning. She was far from Brigham's bed, yet his fragrance was still distinct among the yeasty aroma in her home. She thought it odd at first; she had to be mistaken. But it lingered, at times hovering, and lacking a plausible explanation, she wondered. *Is God trying to reveal his plan?* She shook her head. *I'm silly as a goose this day*, she thought and continued with her chores.

When she arrived at the temple, the sisters were already busy. Several stopped their chores to congregate and await Naamah's baked goods. While they ate and chatted, Brigham approached Naamah and the sisters. Last night, he left a weary man, went to his wife whom he hadn't seen for some time, and returned earlier than Naamah to continue the Lord's work. As her heart fluttered and body warmed, she thought, *He's truly the most dedicated.* She grew more anxious with each of his approaching steps. When he reached her, he asked, "Were you granted a peaceful rest last night?"

His question reawakened last night's passions, which seemed as vivid now as they had been in candlelight. Reflecting, her night had been anything but peaceful, but she sighed and nodded a yes.

"Splendid," he said as he gestured toward the queue of Saints awaiting their endowment. "We've much to do." He flashed his eyes skyward and shook his clenched fists. "It doth render the soul good to do the Lord's work."

Throughout the day, Brigham moved about the temple attending to ever-demanding matters. On occasions when he neared Naamah, she hoped he would engage with her again. But he didn't; he didn't even notice her, and she felt neglected. Her funk remained until she realized the significance of his work. *You're acting like a selfish child,* she thought. *What's your bother this day?*

It was late, and many had left when Naamah trudged upstairs with cleaned temple garments. She placed them in the storage area and returned for more. She was several steps down the stairs when Brigham said, "Sister Twiss can you join me?"

She looked through the railing toward him. "I've more garments to gather."

"The Lord's work is done this night." Brigham beckoned, "Come," and went back into a room.

She thought while retracing her steps, *What could he want?* Her anticipation rose to a near climax when she pulled back the veil and entered the room. Heber Kimball and Brigham were near a flickering oil lamp, standing and conversing quietly. They ceased once Naamah entered.

"You know Brother Heber Kimball," said Brigham.

Naamah had seen him often of late and knew his prominence. She made a brief nod.

"Sister, if you would." Brigham gestured to a chair. He turned to Heber and said, "Could you be so kind?"

Heber moved away and lifted the curtain. "If you need me, I'll . . ."

"I know," said Brigham.

Sitting in a chair, she was alone with Brigham in a hallowed setting reserved for Church clergy. She fumbled with her dress bunched on her lap and swallowed as he drew close and hovered.

He stepped back and gestured to a table with papers and an ink bottle. "This day more have entered His kingdom." He turned to Naamah, and with fists clenched like a mighty warrior, said, "My soul is aroused like never before." He exhaled and stepped back. "You've been with me for nigh on a fortnight. Are you aroused, too?"

Naamah didn't speak; her flushed cheeks were sufficient for Brigham. As he neared, she tingled, grew weak, and lost strength to even knead her dress. She eased back in the chair and rested her hands on her thighs. When he took her hand, she jolted off the back rest. Her hand trembled until his meaty grip held it steady. He raised their clasp and placed his other hand on it. "We've more to do together, as we spend our time on earth, do we not?"

Naamah's head shook much like her hand had trembled earlier, unsure if she was responding or succumbing to stress. Her forehead creased, wondering where the conversation was leading.

"May I call you Sister Naamah?" Brigham assumed her quivering was yes. He eased down onto one knee in front of her. "Naamah, I desire to be sealed to you. Will you accede to my desire?"

Naamah fell back against the chair, breaking their clasped hands. She wedged her clammy hands between her inner thighs as her eyes moved haphazardly around. She had heard the plural marriage rumors and dismissed them at first. But as talk persisted, she accepted it begrudgingly until eventually she reconciled it to the Prophet's teachings, never believing she would be faced with it. Her eyes ceased dancing and locked onto Brigham's. They were steely, determined, and awaiting a response.

"Well, I . . .," Naamah squeezed her thighs so tight, her muscles nearly cramped. She struggled to match the Brigham's determined eyes. She straightened in her chair and said, "Elder Young, you are sealed to another."

He grimaced and arose from his knee. "Mother Young and I are sealed for eternity. But she, like I, believes in Brother Joseph's principle." He tugged his vest and twitched a shoulder. "Last night I told her of a young woman, dedicated to serving the Lord, who was alone and in need. I told her of my desire to care for you. We talked longer, and she recalled a Sister Naamah who had paid a visit summer last. She spoke highly of you."

Naamah was surprised that Mother Young remembered her and flattered that she spoke favorably about her. She thought further about Brother Joseph's principle, which was contrary to all she ever believed. *Mother Young has known Brother Joseph since the beginning,* she thought. *Does she see a deeper meaning that I'm too young to see?*

Brigham's resolve intensified when he said, "Mother Young desires what I desire. Will you accede unto me?"

Naamah gulped and ceased thinking about the principle. She clutched her dress. "Brother Twiss's passing was so soon, and then my Aunt Susan . . ."

"You're widowed, like many sisters." He took a step closer. "I desire you for time. You and Brother Twiss are sealed for eternity. When our time ends, you will return to him in God's celestial heaven."

Her marriage with Brother Twiss had yet to receive the temple endowment. Theirs would have to wait. *Heavenly Father, are we truly sealed for eternity?* As she waited a response, she wondered what John would say too. Without answers, her doubts increased. "Elder Young, I . . . well, it's all so sudden."

Brigham lowered his head and stepped away while stroking his chin. As he stepped farther from her, his physical dominance lessened. Naamah ceased clutching her dress and exhaled. Brigham ceased stoking his chin and turned to her.

"Brother Joseph oft said no woman should be without a man, particularly widows awaiting their reunion in eternity." His eyes narrowed. "You're on your own, and soon your lone remaining kin will depart with his battalion."

How does he know of Cousin George? I've spoken only to Sister Jemima about him. Her forehead creased. *Why did she tell Brigham?*

Brigham drew nearer. "Will you leave Nauvoo alone?"

She ceased pondering about Jemima. She hadn't made any preparations, and she grew doleful, knowing her procrastination had caused her predicament.

Brigham closed in and hovered. "My soul tells me you are in want of a plan. Understandable of course, being a woman and all." He lifted her chin to be eye to eye with her. "My soul could not rest knowing you remained alone in Nauvoo."

As Naamah looked into his eyes, she sensed a heartfelt love coming from his soul. Her sensations were similar to those she felt when she first bore witness to him in Peterborough, eighteen months earlier. *Heavenly Father, is it meant to be?* She waited for His answer while savoring an affection between them. *A love for a lifetime,* she thought. His proposal to be sealed for time seemed more appealing. *Heavenly Father, are you guiding me to him?*

Brigham knitted his brow and said, "If you remain alone in Nauvoo, I fear mobbers will render unto you an almighty harm."

His brow remained knitted as his eyes narrowed, darkening Naamah's view into his soul. The sincerity she had just sensed now seemed like a cloaked threat. As his eyes narrowed further, she felt coerced. *Heavenly Father, are you still with me?*

Brigham ceased glaring. "I want you to join me," he said. He stood patiently, waiting for Naamah's answer.

He no longer appeared intimidating. His eyes seemed sincere and hopeful she would say yes. Silence continued, looming between them. The hope she sensed in his eyes was drifting toward doubt.

"Oh, my heart so desires you," she said before collapsing her head into her hands. "But . . . it's . . ." She shook her head to free confusion from it. "Heavenly Father, I so . . ." Her voice trailed off as Brigham held her head against his chest.

"I know, my child," he said while pressing against the back of her head.

His hand strength shocked Naamah at first. Held firm against his chest, her head and thoughts swayed in and out as he breathed and combined with his heartbeat to grow rhythmic. The candle's flickering merged with his undulating chest to dance in unison. Her mind was at peace, similar to when her father held her head on his chest when she was young, troubled, and especially in candle light when demons frightened her the most. She shut her eyes and oozed an exhale. She could have savored the sensations for an eternity, but Brigham released his hand and stepped back.

"Spend the night in prayer with Heavenly Father," he said. "For certain, He will guide you unto me."

Naamah was confused, as if she had woken from a dream, not unlike when she awoke after intimacy with Brother Twiss. She wrung her hands before slowly arising from the chair. Her mind was still muddled when she reached the curtain.

"Sister Naamah," said Brigham, and she turned back. Standing near the lamplight, he appeared surreal when he said, "I desire you not for eternity, but for time." As he moved farther from the light, his face became shadowy, and ever-changing with the flickering, except for the harsh glare surrounding his eyes. He appeared sinister when he said, "Merely for time, but your time draws nigh, my child."

Naamah lowered her head and turned away.

"Tell Brother Kimball I have no further need of him this night."

She turned back. Brigham had moved so far from the light, he appeared more a silhouette than a living being. "I will, Elder Young," she said.

Naamah raised the curtain and moved outside it. She paused, unable to rid her mind of the ghostly image she left in the room.

Brother Heber moved down the corridor and stopped before reaching Naamah. "I thought you might be Brother Brigham," said Heber.

"He said he has no further need of you this night."

"Oh, a pity." Heber took a few steps away before turning back. "And are you faring well this night, Sister Twiss?"

Naamah made a slight nod and moved away from the curtain.

"You seem troubled."

"No, just almighty tired." Upon reaching Heber she added, "In need of rest, I reckon."

As she moved past him, he grabbed her arm and tugged her closer. "I reckon prayerful thought will help." Heber smiled and released her hand. He moved to the curtain and went into the room she had just left.

She headed down the stairs to where the other sisters had been folding garments. She neared Sister Madeline Jones who, like most of Naamah's temple companions, was in her forties. Startled, Madeline spun around. "Mercy, I thought I was the only one here."

"Has Sister Jemima left?"

"A while ago, don't you remember?" Madeline stared, puzzled as she waited for Naamah's response. When she didn't, Madelaine said, "You seem peaked, my dear. Why don't you leave these for me?"

"Elder Young says there'll be no more endowments this night. I'm sure you and Brother Jones have much to do, preparing to leave and all."

Madeline neared and clutched Naamah's hand. "I know of your dedication. But promise me you'll not sleep here tonight. Return home for rest."

"But it's cold, and walking outside . . ."

"A walk in vigorous air is good for mind and body."

Naamah's head lowered. "Unlike you, no one waits for me." As a forlorn Madeline looked at her, Naamah said, "I'm closer to Heavenly Father when I'm here."

"So be it." Madeline headed toward the foyer. At the stairwell, she turned back. Naamah folded the garments, oblivious that she was being watched. Madeline pursed her lips and left.

When Naamah finished, she brought the clothing to the Attic. As she stored the last one, she smoothed out the wrinkles and pressed on it tenderly. *All set for Elder Young,* she thought.

Mumbling came from behind a curtain, and she moved toward it until her mother's counsel came. *"'Tis the devil's work to listen to other conversations."*

She pivoted and tiptoed away. As she stepped on the riser, it creaked. She looked back while her heart raced. After a few moments she proceeded with slow, deliberate steps. When a light flickered in the stairwell, she stopped and pressed against the wall. She heard footsteps approaching from above.

"Ah, no doubt a sister readying for tomorrow's work," said a voice that sounded like Heber's.

When the footsteps retreated, she exhaled and continued to the first floor mezzanine. She moved east along the inside railing, pausing mid-way to look below at The Great Hall. On her right were the Aaronic Priesthood pulpits reserved for young males, many her age or younger. To her left were the Melchizedek Priesthood pulpits reserved for the Church elders and where young males aspired to be. While leaning on the railing, she gazed and thought, *Their path is clear, and mine* . . . She closed her eyes and breathed deeply, unable to complete her thought.

She reached the northeast corner and sat braced between the temple walls. "Heavenly Father, you revealed a path for me, and I left Peterborough. But soon I lost my John; I lost my Aunt Susan." She stared at the floor and mumbled, "And I became lost, too." She languished in thoughts of her dreary November before lifting her head. "But you found me, and I found joy in serving you." She steadied her head between the walls and reflected for several moments. "Is this my chosen path?"

She drew her legs to her chest and laid her head against them. She breathed deeply while hoping for an answer. She thought of Brigham's proposal. He could be the foundation to reassemble the shattered pieces of her life and hold them together. So obvious, so perfect, yet she thought, *Am I merely being desperate?*

She shook her head and raised it from her knees. Looking skyward and with Brigham in mind, she said, "When I first beheld you, I saw Joseph in you and in Joseph, your almighty power, my Lord. Why Peterborough, of all the places you could have gone, Brigham?" She gazed out a window and thought further. "And why did I first bear witness to my Prophet so soon after the martyrdom in your soul?"

She rested her head on her knees, waiting an answer. Through hours of prayer, she realized God didn't answer questions when the answer was within one's soul. She lifted her head and nodded. "If it's meant to be, why do I tarry?" She grimaced as her thoughts provided a possible answer. *I tarried in Peterborough, and now with the exodus upon us, I tarry again.* "Why do I always doubt you?"

It wasn't Heavenly Father's voice Naamah heard, but Aunt Susan's. *"Even Jesus had doubts the night before he was turned over to Pontius Pilate."*

Her aunt's voice caused her to smile, and she thought of other sage counsel Aunt Susan had given her. "It's meant to be, isn't it?"

Aunt Susan nodded before morphing into Naamah's mother.

"Mother, is it to be?"

She nodded just as Aunt Susan had done.

"I miss you both so dearly," said Naamah.

She reflected on the motherly love she had received through the years. Images flashed, as vivid now as when they had occurred. She was in a dream, relishing each pleasing vision, until Mother Young appeared. Her dreaming ceased, and she deliberated, *Why Mother Young now?*

As a possible answer evolved, her spine tingled. *Of course,* she thought, *my future mother.* She smiled until she realized her relationship with Mother Young had added complications. She believed Brigham when he said Mother Young had accepted Joseph's Principle. But now Naamah harbored doubts that tinged her soul with guilt.

"Why did you reveal so troubling a principle to Joseph?" she asked of Heavenly Father. He didn't answer, and even within the depths of her soul, she could not fathom one either. "If Mother Young understands, will I understand one day, too?"

Doubting an answer would come, she thought of her visit with Mother Young. She was warm, welcoming, and just as a mother should be. As images of that visit flashed, one stayed and preyed on her mind, a crestfallen Mother Young hearing Sister Lucy Decker nursing little Brigham Heber behind a closed bedroom door. She remembered Mother Young flinching as she heard Lucy say, *"Oh Brigham, you give me such pleasure."* Now, Naamah flinched, too.

"Does Mother Young still harbor doubts?"

Heavenly Father didn't respond to Naamah's question. She drifted to Mother Young's kin, Phoebe her mother, and Jemima her sister, who would be similar to a grandmother and an aunt in Naamah's extended family. That thought was pleasing until she wondered again why Jemima had told Brigham about George. Had Jemima betrayed her?

As Naamah pondered, her mind unearthed a nearly forgotten conversation with Aunt Susan. Just after reciting a Psalm, an enthused Naamah said, *"King David was a great man."* *"True,"* said Aunt Susan, *"but even great men have failings."* Susan then related the story of David and Bathsheba. What remained foremost with Naamah was David for lustful purposes sent Bathsheba's husband Uriah into battle, where he died.

Heavenly Father, why do I remember this now? Naamah scrunched her neck as a possible answer blackened her mind. *Is Elder Young King David? Is Cousin George, who is my only hope, Uriah?* She grew fearful she would hear yes. She collapsed her head on her knees to ask, *Are Elder Young's desires solely lustful?*

She rolled her head back and forth, attempting to drive away evil questions that had no answers. She raised her head and gazed upon the temple's sanctity. "'Tis Satan's work that causes doubts," she said. Her voice raised when she said, "How did you get in here?" She arched her back and held her head up. "Not in here," she said. "You get behind me, Satan."

As her last exclamation reverberated, Satan was chastened from her mind. Brigham was not David, and she was not Bathsheba. Brigham and she were both sealed for eternity to others. "My dearest John, you do understand?"

It wasn't her husband who answered her question but Aunt Susan, just after she had told Naamah she would marry Brother

Jolley. *"We marry to survive as best we can until the end of time before we reunite with our other."* And that followed with Aunt Susan's response to Naamah's snide question about her mother and Eli marrying. *"Don't be harsh on your mother, dear. Loneliness is a terrible way to live."*

John had yet to answer, but Aunt Susan's responses helped. She thought of her mother before she married Eli. They were on Jarmany Hill, and she had laid flowers at her father's gravestone. She asked her grandfather Reuben, *"When we're all in heaven, will you sit next to Grandma Allis or the widow Ruth Piper?"* She remembered her mother scolding her, but struggled to recall her grandfather's response.

Suddenly, a chill rushed through her spine with a force that she had never felt before. She looked skyward and said to John, "Grandfather said he would sit next to Grandma Allis." Her head collapsed onto her knees. "He's with Grandma Allis." She rolled her head back and forth and while crying said, "He's with Grandma Allis. He's with her."

She lifted her head and dried her eyes. She sniffed and looked heavenward. "And my dear, dear, dearest John, I say unto you as God is my witness, I will sit next to you. I will sit with you for eternity, Brother John Twiss."

Her husband's image was as vivid as ever when he said, *"You have more to do for the Lord before joining me. When your work is complete, I'll have a seat in Heaven next to me waiting for you."*

"A seat in heaven next to me." She had exchanged those words with her grandfather so often, she heard his voice in John's response. She wondered as tears blurred her vision, *Why did I hear my grandfather's voice, and not my husband's?* She sniffed and brushed her tears. She inhaled and answered her question. *Because Heavenly Father reveals himself in many ways.*

She was exalted when she said to Heavenly Father, "I know you have called me." She pondered ways she might serve before lowering her head and mumbling, "But I'm a woman." She tried reconciling God's calling to her gender but couldn't. She thought of the Priesthood pulpits aligned in a clear path, but for males only. She was envious and rued such a feeling. Her lament ebbed, and she raised her head. "Is it through Elder Young that I can best serve you?"

Sitting in a structure erected to the glory of God, she scanned its majesty. A triad appeared, Brigham, Joseph, and Heavenly Father as one, more vividly than she had envisioned earlier in Peterborough, and now she was part of it. She nodded and said, "Truly, you offer me a higher calling."

A voice she had never heard before came so pure, so true, it could only have been God's. *"I have chosen you to bring many into my heavenly kingdom."* She slumped against the wall, relieved her mental ordeal had found resolution.

After several minutes, she mustered enough energy to arise. She straightened her dress, fluffing the portion clinging to her legs. She moved toward the stairwell while brushing a few remaining tears. *I must look a fright,* she thought. She paused and leaned on the railing to gaze at the Great Hall. She now saw a path for her, too. Overwhelmed, she glanced back to where she had just her been, her private sanctuary. She longed to retreat as she thought, *Life would be far easier, if I say no.* She sighed and gazed at the pulpits again. She took several deliberate breaths and moved apace along the corridor and up the stairs to the Attic.

She stepped into the Attic's foyer and paused to catch her breath. Once her heart stopped racing, she moved to where she had left Brigham. As she moved from the foyer, the light dimmed, and voices could be heard. At the curtain, mumblings were distinctive. They were discussing Church matters, and Naamah thought of leaving. She dithered before giving a resolved exhale, and with hands quivering, she raised the curtain and entered.

Brigham rose out of his chair, seemingly out of sorts, so unlike him. She rued her impulsiveness, out of character for her, too. As Brigham looked to a surprised Heber, Naamah resisted her urge to flee back to her sanctuary. They both looked back to her and waited. She had rehearsed the words she would say as she traveled up the stairs. Now, they seemed a jumble and stuck in her throat. She inhaled and puffed out her bosoms while straightening her posture.

"Elder Young, after prayer-filled thought, I humbly submit to accede to your desire."

Stunned, Brigham looked to an equally stunned Heber. Naamah's legs trembled. She prayed her dress hid them. She clutched her hands to ease their quivering while waiting a seeming eternity for Brigham to respond. The silence was tormenting, and unable to control her nerves any further, she blurted out, "Elder Young, I so desire. . ."

"Sister Twiss," said Brigham as he opened his arms in a gesture she had witnessed often when he welcomed the faithful from the pulpit, "come unto me, my child."

She rushed to him and put her arms around his back to pull him closer. Her bosoms flattened into his manly chest. She sensed their hearts beating as one. And as Brigham put his arms across her shoulders and drew her closer, they formed a perfect union. She was at peace and could have relished the moment for an eternity.

Brigham released his arms to pat her head. When he kissed it, Naamah released her embrace. He moved beside her and took her hand. "Brother Heber had been thinking of departing, but tarried instead." He turned to her and said, "The Lord's work, I suspect." He nodded to Heber. "Shall we?"

As they recited their wedding rites, Naamah's mind drifted to her first marriage several months earlier. Her emotions were entirely different then. Tonight seemed surreal, and she was troubled until she realized the reason. She was and would be sealed to Brother Twiss for eternity. Her sealing this night was for time, and to work with the highest earthly Church authority in service to the Lord. Overcome by the responsibility she was undertaking, she quivered anew. She squeezed Brigham's hand as images of Brother Twiss, Aunt Susan, and others she knew awaiting her came to mind. *A noble calling. I pray you are most proud of me.*

As Brigham dropped her hand, she came back to the moment. He turned and kissed her lips, which startled her. He embraced her and caressed her face while saying, "I will care for you and all your earthly desires." He kissed the top of her head and broke their embrace.

Heber came near, grabbed her hand, and kissed it. "Welcome, Sister Naamah Twiss Young."

Naamah inferred his welcome as an official acceptance into the Church's inner circle, underscoring her new responsibilities. Hearing her new surname seemed odd, and she repeated it in her mind. Brigham stood beside Heber, both with smiles of satisfaction. Their silent stares remained, and Naamah broke eye contact and said, "The garments have been stored and are ready for tomorrow."

"Then our work this night is concluded," said Brigham. "May I escort you to your home?"

"Well, I reckon . . ." Naamah paused, unsure if there was more to his offer. "No bother, my home is but a few blocks away."

"But if I insist?"

Naamah sensed Brigham's desires heightening. "I'm peaked, and a fright," she said as she brushed her cheeks.

Brigham's and Heber's smiles hadn't changed, yet they seemed less pleased, less satisfied; they appeared lecherous.

Naamah rubbed her hands. "Elder Young, my earthly desire this night is for a peaceful rest. We have much to do tomorrow."

Brigham said as he nodded, "And for many morrows to come."

Chapter Thirty-four

Except for occasional visits from Brigham, Naamah's routine was unchanged. She arose and ate a morning meal before going to the temple where she worked past sundown and returned home. While her schedule was similar, her mindset was not. Now she was responding to her higher calling, and when working alongside others, she knew she was experiencing a glory they had yet to achieve. She was often chosen whenever Brigham had important tasks for the sisters – she was special. And when she worked with him, she sensed she was a step closer to the Prophet.

As the chosen Church leader, Brigham oversaw all matters, including the imminent hegira, an overwhelming task in itself. *His work is almighty important; no wonder one woman cannot satisfy all his needs,* thought Naamah. That realization awoke a still-lingering dilemma -- Joseph's principle of plural marriage. *Does his principle give more women the occasion to achieve greater glory through one man?* Her soul tingled as she pondered, *Did you just reveal your answer, Heavenly Father?*

*****

On February 4, Charles Shumway led wagons across the Mississippi and established a temporary camp in Iowa. The exodus had begun. He and the others who followed would wait until Brigham Young could leave since he still remained in Nauvoo administering endowments.

Several days had passed since Shumway left, and Naamah returned home earlier than usual. She lit a fire and was about to prepare her supper when she heard a familiar voice.

"Sister Naamah, are you home?"

"Most certainly." She hurried to open the door and gave Sister Amelia an extended hug. "It's been far too long," she said as she took Amelia's coat and hung it on peg. She gestured to the table. "Come, sit and I will make us supper."

"No. I can stay but a minute."

As they sat across from one another, Naamah said, "And what's the pleasure of your visit?"

Amelia fumbled with a cloth napkin on the table. "I've not seen you in nigh on a few fortnights. Nobody from Peterborough has."

"I've been almighty busy."

"As have we all." Amelia stopped fumbling and straightened her posture. "I just saw your Cousin George, and he said he's leaving with his battalion."

"I know. I pray for him, and for Fannie and Eliza Ann."

"So you knew." Amelia grimaced and snorted. "Well, I was concerned, fearing you'd be alone."

Naamah smiled. "I appreciate your concern, but I'm in good care. And what are your plans?"

"The widower Brother Evans has but two boys and an aged mother. He's asked me to go with him. You know to help with the woman's work." As Naamah's eyes widened, Amelia said, "It's nothing untoward, just a sister helping a brother."

"Untoward?" said Naamah as she waved her hands dismissively. "I'd say not. Brother Evans is an honorable man. Land sakes, we've known him for some while."

"Most certainly. But there are some, well you know," Amelia straightened her posture, "who gossip like magpies." She leaned from the chair to ask, "And when will you leave?"

"Not sure."

"Who will you be leaving with?"

"Not sure."

Amelia collapsed against the chair back. "Doesn't sound like a plan at all." She glared, wanting a response.

"I have a confession to make," said Naamah as she folded her hands and placed them on the table. "When you and Sister Caroline were last here, I was out of sorts."

Amelia raised an eyebrow. "Yes, we remember."

"If not for you, I'd still be lost. But you brought me to the temple, and I found my calling, my salvation."

"Calling?" Amelia wrinkled her brow. "You sound like a Catholic girl before she enters the nunnery."

"Catholic? Hardly. But I sense the Lord near wherever I'm serving Him."

"Pshaw. Many sisters serve the Lord and feel as you do. Hardly a calling."

Naamah stared at the napkin. "I wish Heavenly Father could inspire me with words to express what my soul feels." She looked at Amelia while longing to find a way to tell her.

Amelia took Naamah's hand. "You've always been faithful, more so than most. Perhaps God has given you the words but hasn't given me the ears."

"Bless you," said Naamah.

Amelia released her grasp and sat back. "Will you leave with someone you've met at the temple?" As Naamah nodded, Amelia inched forward. "Who?"

"Elder Young."

"Oh gracious." Amelia scanned around, searching for words to say.

"I've worked with him often these past few months."

"As have others."

"True, but we've worked late into the evening. We've become close."

"How close?"

"I don't rightly know." Naamah grabbed the napkin and fumbled with it. "Close enough that he wants to tend to me."

Amelia leaned forward and lowered her voice. "You've been in Nauvoo long enough to hear what some say. You're not . . ."

"Mercy no." Naamah ceased fumbling and pushed the napkin aside. "Now you sound like a gossipy magpie."

Amelia squirmed and waggled her shoulders before sitting back.

"Our joy comes in serving the Lord."

"I'm sure it does. Well," said Amelia as she arose, "I came because I feared you'd be stranded here." She removed her coat from the peg and put it on. It gathered awkwardly in the shoulders, and she twisted to straighten it. "But you have fared well. Well indeed."

"Amelia," said Naamah as Amelia reached the door. When she turned back, Naamah said, "Bless you for your concern. You're truly a Sister."

Amelia stared at her longtime friend, who at times could be naïve. "I pray your joy continues to be in serving the Lord." She stepped out and retreated. "But be careful, my Sister," and she left.

******

While eating supper, Naamah reflected on Amelia's visit. She had been absent from Peterborough friends because her dedication to Brigham had drawn her into new relationships. Oddly, in only two months, she felt estranged from those with whom she once had close relations.

She retired to bed while continuing to reflect. She couldn't steel herself to tell Amelia that she had been sealed to Brigham for time. Joseph's principle was still difficult for her to reconcile, and for Amelia, it would be impossible. She snorted as she thought, *And she can be a gossipy magpie, too. She'd tell everyone from Peterborough.* Naamah nodded, convinced of her decision.

She rolled to cuddle her blanket. Not long ago, she had lain with Brother Twiss on the same bedding enjoying an intimacy she would never forget. Now, remarried so soon, her nights were lonesome. On a few occasions, Brigham came to see if her earthly desires were being fulfilled. He was the ultimate church authority, and viewing him as a romantic partner was challenging. Now, cuddling her bedding, she was unsure if she wanted more visits from Brigham or if she was disappointed with their infrequency.

She rolled onto her back and pondered. As a warmth entered her nether regions, she squeezed her thighs. She closed her eyes, and when an erotic image of her and Brigham appeared, they flew open. Her heartbeat quickened, and she crossed her arms over her bosoms. Her breathing was uneven.

Sister Lucy Decker nursing Brigham Heber appeared in her mind. Her right hand cupped her bosom to ease a racing heart. She savored the feeling until Sister Emily Partridge appeared clutching her expectant stomach. Naamah caressed her abdomen and bosom in unison as her breathing accelerated.

"Be careful, my Sister." Amelia's parting words came, and Naamah's hands collapsed to her side. While on her back, palms

facing up, she thought, *Am I destined to be barren?* She had asked the question before and never received an answer. Frustration grew as she wondered. *Will I be chosen like Sister Lucy, like Sister Emily?*

She pondered as the fire within her re-ignited. Brigham appeared clad in a full-length white robe. His white mane, flowing like his robe, disappeared into his white beard. A halo circled his head, accentuating the creases chiseled into his face. He held a rod fashioned from Jesse's tree and offered it to Naamah. An unexpected boldness came unto her as she thought, *Am I destined to bring one from your loins?* She became lightheaded as Brigham morphed into her childhood visions of God. *Heavenly Father will I be chosen like the Virgin Mary?*

As she waited an answer, her heartbeat returned to normalcy. Her cheeks and nether region cooled. Now comparing herself to the Virgin Mary seemed blasphemous. Her blissful arousal seemed sullied, impure. And her quandary remained – was she sealed to the highest Church authority, or to a father figure, or to a loving husband, or all of it?

*****

On the morning of February 15, Naamah crammed a dress into her carpet bag. She grabbed another dress from a chair and raised it for closer inspection. She grimaced and tossed the threadbare dress aside. She doused the fire and took a last look at the table, chairs, bedding, and kitchen utensils she would be leaving behind. She pursed her lips, and as the embers hissed, she shuddered.

With a sigh, she grabbed her flannel covering and draped it over her shoulders, picked up the carpet bag, and left.

She walked on frozen ground against a biting wind to the temple, where she paused on the rise. Ice formed the river's edges and extended toward open water, dark and forbidding near shadowy nooks, glistening and inviting in the sunshine. Ice chunks frozen to debris were held in place while others flowed freely, ominous obstacles for crossing wagons.

She turned back to her house. Brother Twiss was ecstatic when he had first showed it to her, shortly before it became their home: a place for fellowship, for intimacy, and too soon after, for dying -- and in eternity, a legacy worth its weight in gold. Now, his legacy would be easy prey for looters who would surely follow. She snorted, wondering why she had bothered to douse the fire. She wiggled her numbing toes and lowered her bag to pull the drooping flannel tight to her shoulders.

She gazed at the temple that dwarfed her while reflecting. Her salvation these past few months now seemed distant. She wondered if it would remain a beacon for others or be ransacked. She dipped and picked up her bag. *Lord, surely not this magnificent structure.*

She headed to the flatlands where wagons had queued to ferry across. As she reached level ground, the exodus preparations were ubiquitous. Beside one ill-constructed wooden house was a flatbed hitched to emaciated, graying oxen. Two befuddled children clad in tattered clothing shivered while blowing on their hands. When their panicky father barked at them, they scurried to load meager provisions onto the wagon. Nearby, a forlorn mother swayed a babe in her arms. The family seemed ill-prepared for what they would endure. Naamah reflected on her inadequate planning before Brigham rescued her. *There but for the grace of God go I.*

She shook her head and continued, turning onto Parley where wagons were aligned, facing west. Several blocks ahead, a crowd gathered near Brigham Young's lead wagon. A young man approached her and stared at her carpet bag. "Are you leaving with Elder Young?"

"Yes, I'm Sister Naamah."

"And you're alone?"

Alone, thought Naamah. She glanced at the temple and envisioned her abandoned home not far from it. Brigham had ceased his temple activities to prepare his extended family for the departure. She hadn't seen him since receiving her departure instructions from him.

"Sister, are you alone?"

"I reckon I am."

"A few lone sisters are in this wagon." He extended his hand to lead her. He took her carpet bag and tossed it into the wagon. He slid a box near with his foot.

Naamah gathered her flannel and stepped onto the box, then onto a hanging step, and into the back. A cold leather bag crackled as she squirmed among the grain sacks and baggage. She blew on her hands.

The woman in her forties nearest to her smiled. "I'm Sister Mary Eliza, widow of Elder John Greene. I'm new to Elder Young's family." She had been sealed for time to Brigham Young on 31 January 1846.

"I'm Sister Naamah," and she paused, wondering if she should say she was new to the family. "Widow of Brother John Twiss."

"A widow? You seem so young, so pure."

A sister sitting farther away in dim light said, "We are of similar age. I, like Sister Naamah, am widowed, too." She was cradling a baby and looked familiar.

"Aren't you Sister Emily?" Naamah asked.

Emily smiled and nodded.

"And your child has been born."

"October last. Edward Partridge, named after his grandfather." Emily unbundled the blanket and leaned her son toward Naamah.

"Such a joy."

"He surely is," said Mary Eliza. "Having a young child will ease our journey."

"I pray you're right," said Emily as she grew forlorn. "I so recall our ordeal as we were chased from Missouri. Homeless wanderers in a bleak, cold winter with scant food and clothing." She grew reflective, visualizing her earlier suffering until realizing its irony. "And now I flee back to where I left to begin anew."

She clutched her son close. While gazing upon him, she said, "It's a wonder we survived." She stared at Naamah. "Many, too many, found an early grave." She turned to Mary Eliza. "Now do you see? No one is ever too young to be a widow." She gazed at her child and seemingly became lost. Emily's account of the 1838 Missouri Mormon War sobered the wagon's mood.

Naamah wrapped her flannel around her. She pulled it to her frozen nose as she thought of the young man who asked her if she was alone. Brigham was in the lead wagon with Mother Young and his immediate family. Other family members, no doubt Sisters Phoebe and Jemima, were in wagons close behind his, and others behind them. She was distant, bringing up the rear. The infant's squalling broke into Naamah's melancholy.

Emily cooed while nestling her son. Her soft sounds brought a smile to Naamah until she realized how far from Brigham she was, tangibly distant like Emily, yet she had his son. She grew jealous and pulled her covering closer as she shivered.

Naamah dozed for an hour or so, and when she awoke, the wagon was next in line to ferry the Mississippi. The gales swept across the river into the covered wagon, causing a subzero wind tunnel. As she peered out, the overcast sky was blue-gray, and with nightfall coming, ominous looking. Less than a year ago, she had steeled her courage and left Peterborough, filled with hope of reuniting with Brother Twiss and others. Now, looking west, her hope was as blue and cold as what lay ahead of her.

She threw her wrap off and inched to the back. She craned her neck for a last look at the temple. *My home, and how quickly I leave thee.* Light splotches twinkled in a few temple windows, yet it appeared cold and lifeless. *If you are a beacon reveal yourself.*

As she remained transfixed, the wagon jerked forward. A light near the Attic brightened. Unsure if it was her imagination, she glanced away to refocus before returning to the light. The Attic light grew brighter, seemingly engulfing the top story. Awestruck, she couldn't turn away. Her hand trembled as she asked, *Heavenly Father, are you with me?* She waited, wondering if the answer was in her soul.

She blinked her eyes, and the light grew dim. She turned away and inched closer to her flannel covering. Emily's son sucked with enthusiasm, and Mary Eliza gushed while gazing at mother and child. Naamah glanced toward the sound before staring at wagon's dingy covering. She felt detached from the others until she heard a voice from her recent past.

"And I will be amongst you."

Naamah smiled, and while staring ahead, whispered, "Always." As Emily and Mary Eliza looked toward her, Naamah had a smile that brightened the wagon's mood, lasting for an eternity.

Chapter Thirty-five

Epilogue

Naamah's cheery outlook did indeed last an eternity, in part, to endure her arduous trek before finally reaching the Salt Lake basin. Her ordeal over the next few years was similar to the travails of over ten thousand pioneers who left Nauvoo. She spent a year in Winter Quarters, near present day Omaha, eventually reuniting with Cousin George, his wife, and child. She left for Utah the following year with her sister wives. She devoted her life to temple work, endowing her marriage to Brother Twiss, working for the redemption of the dead, and fulfilling Aunt Susan's request to have little Reubie and her other non-believing sons baptized. The Taggart family is now reunited in His eternal kingdom.

In her later years, "Aunt Twiss" was in charge of the Lion's House, doing most of the cooking for Brigham's extended family. Her oft-asked question, "Am I destined to be barren?" was answered in due course. She remained childless. In 1909, at the age of eighty-seven, she died in Salt Lake City. She now resides in His celestial kingdom sealed for eternity to Brother John Twiss. There, this petite, fair-complexioned, genial, devotee of the Gospel as revealed unto Joseph Smith has an eternal smile shining upon all believers.

Cousin George endured an arduous trek, too. He left Nauvoo with his battalion two days after Naamah and traveled more than forty-four hundred miles on foot into the desert southwest and California, enduring tremendous hardship, suffering from thirst, starvation, and sickness before reuniting with his wife and daughter in Winter Quarters. In October 1852, George, Fannie, Eliza Ann, and three other children reached Utah. In 1856, he took a plural wife, Clarissa Rogers, and they would add twelve more children to their family. George died in 1893 at the age of seventy-six, leaving a legacy that his many descendants honor this day. He worked as carpenter and wheelwright, building grist mills and working on the Salt Lake Temple.

The Nauvoo Temple, which Naamah believed would be an eternal beacon unto the world, was gutted by a mobber set fire in October 1848. Two years later, a tornado flattened two of the standing walls, and by 1857, it was completely razed. Joseph Smith's beacon of hope was now open land on a promontory overlooking the Mississippi, seemingly lost to the ages. But in 1999, The Church announced they would rebuild the temple on its original footprint. Two years later, it was dedicated, and today, especially at nightfall, it is a beacon that can be witnessed for miles around.

Lastly, Naamah's sister Betsey and her husband Horace Eaton would have a daughter, Arianna, in 1846, and a son two years later. In 1867, Arianna married Benjamin Young in Lowell, Massachusetts. They would have a son the following year, and in 1881, a daughter, Grace Belle, both born in Fitchburg, Massachusetts. In 1907, Grace married Francis Nault in Fitchburg, and gave birth to two daughters late in life, one of whom died in infancy. Their lone surviving daughter, Elizabeth Frances, 'Betty', would in 1944 marry Alfred Woollacott, Jr, son of the then-Mayor of Fitchburg, just before he left for overseas duty.

On 30 October 1946, Alfred Sr., while campaigning for his fifth and final term as Fitchburg's Mayor was handed a note saying his first grandson had been born. He announced to the gathering, "Alfred III has just been born."

Alfred III married Jill Chandler in 1973, and they would have four children. He retired in 2002 from a career at KPMG, an international accounting firm, and began dabbling in family history, which soon became an obsession. He had heard that a relative had become a plural wife to Brigham Young. He researched further to prove that Naamah Kendall Jenkins (Carter) (Twiss) Young was his great-great-grand aunt and became intrigued with the events occurring in Peterborough and Nauvoo in the 1840s, which would form the basis of this book.

 *My Four Legged Stool*

Appendix

While "The Believers" is fiction, it is tightly woven to facts and interpretation of facts, with few fictional characters. To assist the reader with differentiating between the two and to provide resources for those who want further insight, the following is arranged by chapter.

Chapter One

Jarmany Hill descriptions are based on several visits. A narrative of the author's first visit and Jarmany Hill images can be found at: http://www.myfourleggedstool.com/september-2009-sharon-new-hampshire.html.

Woollacott, III, Alfred, "John Law of Acton, Massachusetts, and Reuben Law of Acton, Massachusetts and Sharon, New Hampshire" *MASSOG Vol 35 nos. 1 and 2* (Spring and Summer editions) (2011) available at: http://www.myfourleggedstool.com/john-law-of-acton-massachusetts.html and http://www.myfourleggedstool.com/reuben-law-of-acton-massachusetts-and-sharon-new-hampshire.html; Reuben Law's image is available at the second link.

Billings Carter's gravestone image of can be found at: http://sharonnh.org/cemeteries/.

King, H. Thorn, Jr. *Sliptown – The History of Sharon, New Hampshire 1731 – 1941* (Rutland, Vermont, Charles E. Tuttle Company, 1945), 131. "Billings Carter was running a mill. By some accident he fell into the water; pneumonia resulted, and he died."

Woollacott, "John Law . . . and Reuben Law", 62. "James and his wife knew much sorrow as six of their nine children died in their infancy. In the summer of 1849, James, his wife, daughter Rachel, and son Isaac died of dysentery."

---, 58. "He … married (1) … ALLIS PIPER born in Concord, Massachusetts, on 13 February 1759 … and died in Sharon on 5 February 1821, having borne thirteen children. On 5 September 1827 Reuben, said to be of Sharon, New Hampshire, married (2) at Acton 5 September 1827 RUTH (REED) PIPER, widow of Captain Daniel Piper, son of Joseph and Elizabeth Piper and nephew of Allis."

---. 65. "Naamah quite likely was named after her father's next eldest sister, who died 10 February 1821, about a month before her birth."

Young, Naamah Kendall Jenkins Carter Twiss, *Temple Record Book, 1640-1909,* "Naamah Kendall Carter b. 20/5/1789 in Wilmington, MA The sister of Naamah's father, Billings Carter, married Benjamin Jenkins and d. 10/2/1821". Microfilm available at: https://familysearch.org/search/catalog/165968?availability=Family%20History%20Library,

Chapter Two

Findagrave.com memorial # 134254400. Image at Findagrave: https://www.findagrave.com/cgi-bin/fg.cgi?page=gr&GSln=upton&GSbyrel=all&GSdyrel=all&GSst=32&GScntry=4&GSob=n&GRid=134254400&df=all&. The author visited Elizabeth (Law) (Carter) Upton gravesite in Peterborough during 2015.

"Mormons Once Flourished Here" *Peterborough Transcript,* (June 24, 1965): "He [Elder Maginn] held his meetings in a hall in the Goodridge block on Main St. Riley Goodridge, the man who built the only recently demolished tavern ..."

Barney, Ronald O., "'A Man That You Could Not Help Likeing [sic]': Joseph Smith and Nauvoo Portrayed in a Letter by Susannah and George W. Taggart", BYU Studies 40, no. 2 (2001), 165 – 166. The article has George Washington Taggart's image, available at: http://www.jstor.org/stable/43042848?seq=1#page_scan_tab_contents.

What Christian denomination Reuben Law's children were raised is unknown.

"New Hampshire Marriages to 1937", available online at Familysearch.org. Eli Upton married (3) Jaffrey, NH 22 September 1836 Eleanor White, a year after Naamah's mother's death.

"New Hampshire, Marriages, 1720-1920", available on line at Familysearch.org. Eli Upton married (1) Jaffrey 16 May 1809 Abigail Snow, born 1790, died Peterborough 19 May 1830.

Findagrave.com memorial # 29327519 lists six children born to Eli and Abigail (Snow) Upton at: https://www.findagrave.com/cgi-bin/fg.cgi?page=gr&GRid=%2029327519. Whether any of these six children, and/or Naamah and her five siblings, and/or two stepsisters from the marriage of Eli and Elizabeth (Law) Carter lived with Eli in 1841 is unknown.

Chapter Three

Barney, "A Man That You Could Not Help Likeing [sic]", Robinson, Eileen Taggart (Spencer-James-Clarissa) "George Washington Taggart – A Biography and Tribute" (April 1998). Each discussed the conflict within the Taggart household. Available at: http://www.taggartfamily.org/GWT%20by%20Eileen%20Robinson.html.

Woollacott, "John Law . . . Reuben Law", 63. The six sons of Washington and Susanna (Law) Taggart are listed.

Whether the entire Taggart family was living together at this time is unknown.

Robinson, "George Washington Taggart", 2. "George worked at carpentry (planing and milling), sawing timber, repairing wagons, carding and spinning wool."

--, 2. "In December 1841, at the age of twenty-five, George … asked a Mormon missionary by the name of Elder Eli P. Maginn, to baptize him …"

--, 2. "George's parents, Washington and Susannah, and his brother Oliver also joined the LDS Church, but the new religion divided the family as George's remaining brothers, Albert, Samuel and Henry, did not join."

Chapter Four

"Mormons Once Flourished Here" "Mormonism had arrived in Peterborough about three years before (June 27,1844) in the dynamic person of Elder Eli P. Maginn, whose fascinating speaking attracted audiences from far and near."

"Peterborough in 1842", Peterborough Historical Society Collections, 195. The whole number who have been admitted into the Church of Latter Day [sic] Saints, as given by Jesse C. Little, an Elder in the Church is 116 – 48 males and 68 females. A Horace Eaton is listed. Further research indicated two Horace Eatons existed, and the one listed by Jesse C. Little is probably not the Horace Eaton Betsey would ultimately marry.

Young, *Temple Record Book*. "Naamah . . . Baptized into the Church of Jesus Christ of Latter Day [sic] Saints 3rd April 1842. Was Baptized and Confirmed by Eli P. Maginn."

The Book of Mormon, 3 Nephi: 18-25. Maginn's quotes follow those verses.

When Brother Twiss and Naamah first met and when he left for Nauvoo is unknown.

Chapter Five

"Mormons Once Flourished Here" "Elder Maginn, who quoted from the Bible constantly, and was always alert to take on any clergyman or layman in a religious discussion was shunned by the churches."

Robinson, "George Washington Taggart", 3. "Harriet seems to be the only member of her family who joined the LDS Church."

Chapter Six

Whether the Taggarts left together, whether they left at separate times, and where the three non-believing sons were residing in 1843 are unknown.

Barney, "A Man That You Could Not Help Likeing", 167. "Washington, Susannah, and Oliver moved to Nauvoo a short time prior to George and his wife Harriett Bruce Taggart, who arrived there in June 1843, . . .", which conflicts with Robinson, "George Washington Taggart", 3. "One month after their marriage (June 1843), George and Harriet along with his parents and brother Oliver, left family, friends, and their home to move to Nauvoo, Illinois to gather with the main body of the LDS Church."

Chapter Seven

Brennan, James F. "Extracts from Joseph Smith's History", correspondence. "Under date of June 12th 1843, Joseph Smith journalizes as follows; "About forty Saints arrive (at Nauvoo, Ill) from Peterborough, New Hampshire." "Millennial Star" 21:203

Robinson, "George Washington Taggart", 3. "George married Harriet Atkins Bruce (born March 20, 1821) on May 7, 1843. Having been baptized two months after George on February 20, 1842, by the same Elder Maginn, Harriet seems to be the only member of her family who joined the LDS Church."

Chapter Nine

Jeffress, Melinda Evans, "Mapping Historical Nauvoo" *Brigham Young Studies Vol 3, nos. 1 and 2* (1991).

Nauvoo Land and Records, George Washington Taggart File 23386 list property in Nauvoo; Block 29 Lot 2.

Barney, "A Man That You Could Not Help Likeing", 171. From George Taggart's letter to his brothers, "Our Father bought an acre lot within the precincts of the citty [sic] and paid twenty dollars."

Bushman, Richard Lyman *Joseph Smith – Rough Rolling Stone*, (Alfred A Knopf, New York, 2005), 494 – 495. Discusses the Partridge sisters, the strife between Emma and Joseph Smith, and plural marriage generally during May/June 1843.

Robinson, "George Washington Taggart", 2. "George was a talented musician capable of making violins, guitars, fifes, and other instruments. He wrote at least one ballad."

Chapter Ten

Bushman, *Joseph Smith,* 504 – 506. "Joseph was two hundred miles north of Nauvoo in mid-June 1843 when he learned that Missouri was pursuing him again . . . A Missouri Sheriff and an Illinois constable were on their way to arrest Joseph . . . When the message [about Joseph's capture] got to Nauvoo on Sunday, June 25, 1843, Hyrum called a meeting . . . Upwards of 300 volunteered to ride, and 175 set out that night. When the two contingents [who had rescued Joseph] met, Joseph greeted Emma and Hyrum, mounted his favorite horse, old Charley, and marched slowly into town. . . .the band played, "Hail Columbia". Cheering citizens lined the streets while guns and cannons were fired."

Chapter Eleven

Givens, George W. *In Old Nauvoo –Everyday Life in The City of Joseph* (Salt Lake City, Deseret Books, 1990), 112 – 130. Chapter 10 "Sickness and Death", 116

--, 68 – 73. Chapter 6 "Purse and Post"

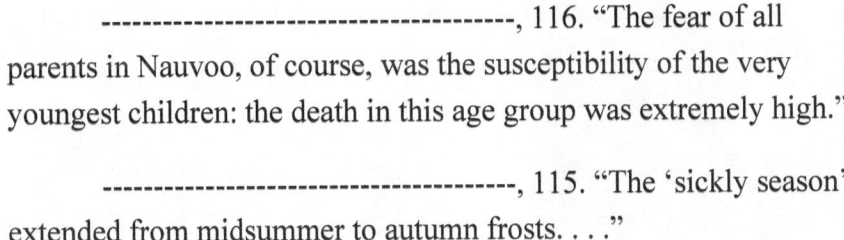

--, 116. "The fear of all parents in Nauvoo, of course, was the susceptibility of the very youngest children: the death in this age group was extremely high."

--, 115. "The 'sickly season' extended from midsummer to autumn frosts. . . ."

Robinson, "George Washington Taggart", 1 – 2. "Of his earlier Taggart ancestors, George wrote: 'It is supposed that they were of Scotch origin and were among the old Scotch Protestant stock that first emigrated from Ireland to the New England shores . . . My kindred . . . were of the middle class that in those days would be termed small farmers, neither rich nor poor, but very moral in their course of life and honest in their dealings, but making no professions of religion."

King, *Sliptown,* 46. "Wearing snowshoes, he [Reuben Law] walked the distance from Acton, Massachusetts, bringing his possessions and supplies with him on his hand sled. The story is, he made his first night's camp there, high on a rock which he believed to be refuge from animals that might prowl; and that there he decided to remain. The place was afterward to become his north field. The temporary shelter gave place to more permanent quarters; he cleared the land for a small cabin. Spring found him bringing his family to a new home after a winter of patience and hard work"

Givens, *In Old Nauvoo*, 116. "Quinine . . . was known by Nauvoo doctors, but unfortunately the supply was often adulterated and expensive, a single ounce costing as much as a good cow."

----------------------------, 117. "A classic medieval "cure", bloodletting, was practiced on all age groups . . ."

----------------------------, 119. "Nauvoo had its share of qualified physicians. . . Others practicing in Nauvoo . . . H. Tate . . ."

Chapter Thirteen

Findagrave.com memorial #14657736. The author visited Old Nauvoo Burial Grounds in July 2016. An image of a grave stone recently placed by descendants of Washington Taggart is available at: www.findagrave.com/cgi-bin/fg.cgi?page=gr&GSln=Taggart&GSfn=washington+&GSbyrel=all&GSdy=1843&GSdyrel=in&GSst=16&GScntry=4&GSob=n&GRid=14657736&df=all&.

Robinson, "George Washington Taggart", 2. "Oliver died the first day of September five o'clock in the afternoon and your father about the same time the next day."

Givens, *In Old Nauvoo*, 71. A list of the value of each coin used in Nauvoo is shown in this page.

----------------------------, 75. ". . . postage rates varied considerably, from six cents for mail traveling up to thirty miles to twenty-five cents for mail travailing more than four hundred miles. Two pages doubled the postage rate and three pages tripled it. . ."

----------------------------, 126 "A coffin was usually made of pine . . . Although usually stained or painted black, it was occasionally covered with black cloth. . . "

Chapter Fourteen

Where Albert and Samuel Taggart were living in October 1843 is unknown.

Barney, "A Man That You Could Not Help Likeing", 170. Susannah's entire letter is presented on this page.

Chapter Fifteen

Barney, "A Man That You Could Not Help Likeing", 174, footnote 5. "His [Maginn] brief but productive career came to close on April 27, 1844, in Lowell, Massachusetts, where he died at age twenty-six from consumption (tuberculosis)."

Chapter Sixteen

The author observed a re-enactor portraying Joseph Smith delivering part of Joseph's King Follett Discourse in Nauvoo, July 2016. His opening line was: "May the Lord strengthen my lungs and stay the winds." The full text of King Follett's discourse is available at The Church of Jesus Christ of the Latter-Day Saints at: www.lds.org/ensign/1971/04/the-king-follett-sermon?lang=eng.

Beam, Alex, *American Crucifixion – The Murder of Joseph Smith and the Fate of the Mormon Church* (Public Affairs, New

York, 2014), 28. "In April 1844, he [Smith] preached the most famous sermon of his life, what some regard as one of the most famous sermons ever preached in America. As if on a whim, Joseph turned nearly 2,000 years of Christian belief on its head at a funeral service for his loyal colleague King Follett. . . . He spoke for two hours, shouting against a heavy wind. The following day, he lost his voice."

Bushman, *Joseph Smith,* 538. "Joseph ultimately faced his accusers [about plural wives]. At a Sunday meeting on May 26, before the entire congregation, he answered the specific charges about spiritual wives and malfeasance levied against him in Nauvoo municipal court. . . . About eight o'clock on the morning of Monday, May 27, Joseph, though not yet arrested, left for Carthage, to have the grand jury indictments investigated."

"Joseph Smith's Boasting and Polygamy Denial Sermon" on May 26, 1844. History of the Church Vol. 6, p. 408-412, and Millennial Star 42:23, 672-674. Available at: http://www.utlm.org/onlineresources/sermons_talks_interviews/smit hboastingandpolygamydenial.htm.

Chapter Seventeen

Nauvoo Land and Records, George Washington Taggart File 23386 list property Nauvoo; Block 29 Lot 2 and Hyrum Smith: Block 8 Lot 2. It is unknown if both lots were George's or if one was his and another his father's. Also unknown is where Susanna lived after her husband's and son Oliver's deaths.

Special Collections - *Early Mormonism Collection 2*, "Nauvoo Expositor (part 1)", by William Law, (June 7, 1844), available at: http://www.solomonspalding.com/docs/exposit1.htm.

Beam, *American Crucifixion*, 110 – 116. "The editorial team assembling the *Expositor* inside the Laws' printing office on Mulholland Street, just a few hundred feet from the Nauvoo Temple site, was a motley crew. . . . Copies of the *Expositor* flew out the doors of the Laws' print shop."

------------------------------------, 116 – 122. " . . . Joseph Smith quickly decided that Nauvoo didn't need an independent newspaper."

Bushman, *Joseph Smith*, 540. "The fine legal points were lost in the subsequent chaos. The city council met for six and a half hours on Monday, June 10 . . . They seemed to realize they were taking a huge risk when they finally passed an ordinance concerning libels, but they concluded that the action was necessary and legally justified."

Chapter Eighteen

Bushman, *Joseph Smith*, 540 – 541. "In the "considerable excitement" the day after, the dissenters stormed about saying, 'the Temple shall be thrown down, Joseph['s] house burned & the printing office torn down,' possibly thinking of an anti-Mormon invasion, Francis Highbee predicted 'in 10 days there will not be a Mormon left in Nauvoo.' "

Beam, *American Crucifixion*, 124. "When Francis Higbee swore out a complaint accusing Joseph of inciting a riot to destroy the *Expositor,* the Carthage court sent Constable David Bettisworth to Nauvoo to arrest Smith."

Bushman, *Joseph Smith,* 543. "The closing of the *Expositor* was a perfect excuse. The long campaign [by sharp and his *Warsaw Signal*] against Joseph and the Mormons made their 'extermination from civilized society' the logical course of action."

Beam, *American Crucifixion*, 135 – 136. "Thomas Ford was the accidental governor of Illinois. . . .Thomas Ford was not Stephen Douglas. He was a tortured soul. Though only forty-one years old when elected governor, 'he appeared like a man weary of human nature and of life.' "

------------------------------------, 143. "Joseph issued instructions to the city police and to Jonathan Dunham, the major general commanding the Nauvoo Legion: guard the waterfront and station pickets along the roads leading into the city."

------------------------------------, 143 – 145. "On the following day, June 18, Joseph donned his gold-braided, buff-and-blue brigadier general's uniform and summoned the Nauvoo legion to a full-dress review in front of his home. . . . The sword that Joseph unsheathed would never be sullied with a drop of blood. And he would never address the Saints again."

Bushman, *Joseph Smith,* 544. "Then he [Joseph] put the city under martial law and marched the troops up Main Street. Through the week, armed Mormons moved in from the outlying settlements to prepare for battle. Reports of armed attack on Mormon farms arrived almost daily. Joseph deployed the troops throughout the city to prevent invasions by water or land."

Chapter Nineteen

Bushman, *Joseph Smith,* 546. "Late Saturday night [the 22nd], he [Joseph Smith] crossed the swollen Mississippi River. Joseph remained on the Iowa side less than twelve hours."

Beam, *American Crucifixion,* 152. "While the four men [Joseph, Hyrum and two others] were battling the currents and flotsam of the wild Mississippi, word of Joseph's flight flashed through Nauvoo . . . With rumors swirling of an imminent invasion from Carthage, the leaderless Saints panicked."

-----------------------------------, 151. Chapter 9 Surrender "BANK OF THE RIVER MISSISSIPPI, SUNDAY, 2 p.m. TO: His Excellency Governor Ford: SIR: I now offer to come to you at Carthage on the morrow, as early as shall be convenient for your posse to escort us into headquarter, provided we can have a fair trial, not be abuse . . . --Excerpt from Joseph Smith's letter to Thomas Ford, June 23, 1844"

Chapter Twenty

Some descriptions used in this chapter were from a Carthage Jail visit in July 2016 and the emotional testimony from a young missionary as she relived the events that occurred on 27 June 1844.

Beam, *American Crucifixion*, 157. ". . . the Carthage Greys caught sight of the mounted entourage [Smith and his co-defendants] and immediately started whooping and jeering."

----------------------------------, 160. "In the afternoon, the Smiths . . . met the man who would decide their fate: Robert F. Smith, justice of the peace and captain of the restive Greys. . ."

----------------------------------, 161. "He [Justice Smith] agreed to free all the defendants on bail, which he set at an extremely high $500 apiece . . . Earlier in the day, two of Smith's enemies. . . had filed pleas accusing Joseph and Hyrum of treason for placing Nauvoo under martial law."

Bushman, *Joseph Smith*, 547. "Ford told Joseph that he planned to . . . search the town for the counterfeiting equipment the Mormons were suspected of operating."

----------------------------, 547. "Ford practiced a little political theater, marching Joseph and Hyrum between the lines of troops."

Beam, *American Crucifixion*, 169. "Thursday, June 27, 1844, in Carthage Illinois, dawned rainy, humid, hot, and glum."

Bushman, *Joseph Smith*, 547 -548. ". . . He [Ford] decided to go to Nauvoo with a small number of men to search for counterfeiting gear."

----------------------------, 548 – 549. "The Greys had been the most hostile of the armed men gathered in Carthage . . . When the

Greys assured him [Ford] they would not act without his permission, he believed them. As he told the story later, he did not think they would endanger the governor's life by killing the Prophet while he was in Nauvoo exposed to the Mormons' wrath."

Beam, *American Crucifixion,* 176. ". . . Inside the Carthage Jail, the prisoners ate their lunches; Joseph, Hyrum, and Willard Richards ate upstairs in the Stigalls' [the jailer] family room, while John Taylor and Stephen Markham dined on the ground floor."

Bushman, *Joseph Smith,* 549. ". . . in Carthage, the friendly jailer had moved the prisoners. . ."

----------------------------, 549. "Hyrum read extracts from Josephus."

Beam, *American Crucifixion,* 177. "The stone jail was oppressively hot in the late afternoon. Even with all the bedroom windows opened, and stripped to their shirts and breeches, the Mormons were sweltering."

Bushman, *Joseph Smith,* 549. "John Taylor sang A Poor Wayfaring Man of Grief." Whether all fourteen verses were sung is unknown.

Beam, *American Crucifixion,* 178. "Fourteen-year-old William Hamilton of the Carthage Greys . . . was the first to spot the irregulars approaching the woods along the Warsaw road. . . . Thirty minutes later, around 4:30 p.m., he [Hamilton] saw about 125 men emerging from the woods in single file . . . The men [Warsaw militia irregulars] had smeared their faces with mud and with gunpowder, and some wore their jerseys or coats turned inside out."

Bushman, *Joseph Smith,* 549. "Ford heard rumors of assassination plots all the way to Nauvoo. Perhaps growing anxious, he . . . stayed long enough to address the citizens. . . . He climbed on the platform of the unfinished building across the street [from the Mansion House]. . . . . He advised the Saints to lay aside their arms . . ."

Beam, *American Crucifixion,* 184. "Then Ford threatened the Mormons in the starkest possible terms . . . At 5:30 p.m., Ford and his entourage toured the unfinished Nauvoo Temple and made caustic remarks about the twelve life-size carved wooden oxen that supported the massive laver, or baptismal font."

Beam, *American Crucifixion,* 179 – 182. "While the greys fussed with their muskets . . . the irregulars had already reached the jail . . . The inflamed Warsaw militia . . . stormed up the staircase . . . Richards and Hyrum Smith braced themselves against the door . . . The second shot fired entered Hyrum's skull . . . His [Hyrum] lifeless body lay in the middle of the floor, blood pouring from his wounds. . . . Joseph pulled out his six-shooter and started firing . . . Falling to the floor the blood-spattered Taylor rolled under the bed. . . . Desperately hoping for safety, Joseph Smith followed Taylor to the window, planning to jump. . . . A mobber . . . shot him in the back . . . and shots from the ground struck Joseph . . . Smith tumbled out the window . . . Voorhis [a mobber] taunted the half-dead body of Joseph Smith, 'Now go see your spiritual wives in hell!' Voorhis stood aside and watched a handful of his comrades fire several more rounds into Joseph's lifeless body."

Bushman, *Joseph Smith,* 550. "Richards raised his head above the sill far enough to see that Joseph was dead and then turned to help John Taylor. Taylor's watch had stopped at sixteen minutes past five."

Manuscript History of Brigham Young, 1801-1844, ed. Elden Jay Watson (Salt Lake City, Smith Secretarial Service, 1968). "June 18 went to Salem. Saw my daughter Vilate. ... June 22 Went to Lowell. 23 Preached in Lowell." Available at: http://www.boap.org/LDS/Early-Saints/MSHBY.html.

Jensen, Andrew, "Extracts from the History of Brigham Young" a letter from L.D. S. historian, Andrew Jensen to James F Brennan, (July 21, 1920). "Thursday, June 27, 1844. Spent the day in Boston with brother Woodruff, who accompanied me to the railway station as I was about to take cars to Salem. In the evening, while sitting in the depot waiting, I felt a heavy depression of spirit, and so melancholy I could not converse with any degree of pleasure."

Chapter Twenty-one

Robinson, "George Washington Taggart", 2. "George was one of those that went to meet and return with the bodies of Joseph and Hyrum as they traveled the twenty miles from Carthage to Nauvoo."

--, 5. "According to George's son James: "I have heard him [GWT] tell of going with those that went to Carthage for the two bodies of Prophet Joseph Smith and Hyrum Smith to bring them to Nauvoo, and I have heard him play the tunes he helped to play in the band that were played when they marched into Nauvoo with the bodies. This would cause us to picture in our minds the awful event of the martyrdom."

Beam, *American Crucifixion,* 191. "An Indian blanket covered one of the coffins, and straw and prairie brush was heaped over a second, to prevent decomposition and to ward off flies. . . As the wagon approached Joseph's mansion in the town center, huge crowds lined the street. As many as 8,000 . . ."

----------------------------------, 194. "The next day found Nauvoo in mourning. . . . On a clear, hot and sunny Saturday, starting at 8:00 a.m., 10,000 Saints found their way to the mansion and filed past the open coffins. . . . The scene was not for the faint of heart."

Holzapfel Richard Neitzel, Holzapfel Jeni Broberg *Women of Nauvoo (*Salt Lake City, Bookcraft, 1992), 130. "The martyrs' mother could not be consoled; Sarah M. Kimball held her hand for a long time before the grieving woman spoke. "How could they kill my boys! O how could they kill them when *they were so precious!* I am sure they would not harm anybody in the world . . ."

Chapter Twenty–two

Robinson, "George Washington Taggart", 5. "Surely George was influenced by the example of Brigham Young, someone George knew personally . . ."

Walker, Ronald W., "Six Days in August: Brigham Young and the Succession". "Traveling with Orson Pratt, Young went on

Church business to out-of-the-way Peterborough, New Hampshire, a few miles north of the Massachusetts border. His sermon there suggested that he might be coming to grips with some of these awful rumors. "The death of one or a dozen could not destroy the priesthood," he told the local Saints, "nor hinder the work of the Lord from spreading throughout all nations."

Manuscript History of Brigham Young, 1801-1844. "July 12 spent the day in Peterboro with the brethren. July 13 Attended conference and preached to the Saints."

-- "July 16th Brigham Young receives the word of Joseph Smith's death while at Brother Beament's House in Peterboro."

Whether Brother Twiss was in Nauvoo at this time or if he ever wrote to Naamah is unknown.

Walker, "Six Days in August". "The ambiguity ended on July 16. Young and Pratt were leaning back in their chairs at Brother Bement's house in Peterborough when a letter arrived from Nauvoo telling of the killings. Later in the day, Elder Woodruff's letter with the same news arrived. "I felt then as I never felt before," Young later said. There were no tears but an awful, paralyzing headache. "My head felt as tho my head [would] crack." His thoughts went everywhere. Had Joseph and Hyrum taken the keys or the authority of the Church with them? At last, his despair lifted "like a clap," he said. The answer came to him like revelation: "The keys of the kingdom [are] here." He brought his hand to his knee to make the point. ... The day after hearing of the Smith brothers' deaths, Young hurried from Peterborough to Boston. That night he shared a room with Elder Woodruff at Sister Voice's home. Young slept in the bed while Woodruff, who was grieving the Prophet's death, slept in a large chair and did his best to shield his convulsive tears. Young's grief, in contrast, was clear-eyed and determined."

Chapter Twenty-three

Walker, "Six Days in August:" The details of the events during the succession crisis are contained in this article, from which the written narrative in this chapter has been derived.

Smith, William "Mormonism: A Letter from William Smith, Brother of Joseph the Prophet", (New York Tribune, 1857-05-19) "However, Samuel died suddenly on July 30, 1844, just a month after Joseph and Hyrum were killed. The last of the surviving Smith brothers, William, initially claimed the right to succeed his brothers only as Presiding Patriarch. Much later, after breaking with several Latter Day Saint factions, he exercised his own claim to the presidency of the church, with little result. William alleged that his brother Samuel was poisoned at the behest of Brigham Young."

Launius, Roger, "Joseph Smith III: Pragmatic Prophet". "Several church leaders later claimed that on August 27, 1834, and April 22, 1839, Joseph Smith indicated his eldest son, Joseph Smith III, would be his successor. At the time of Smith's death, Joseph Smith III was eleven years old."

Avery, Valery Tippetts, "From Mission to Madness: The Last Son of the Mormon Prophet". "Similarly, in April 1844, Joseph Smith had reportedly prophesied his unborn child would be a son who was to be named 'David' and would eventually become 'president and king of Israel'."

Chapter Twenty-four

Church History: In the Fulness of Times Student Manual, (2003), 297–307, Chapter Twenty-Four: Nauvoo under Apostolic Leadership. "The Twelve met in council the day after they were sustained as the presiding authority of the Church. In that meeting and in several others in succeeding weeks, they began to set in order the organization and affairs of the Church. . . . Wilford Woodruff was sent to England to preside over the Church in Europe, and Parley P. Pratt was called to New York . . . Lyman Wight went to Texas, in accordance with a previous assignment from Joseph Smith, to locate potential sites for settlements. John Taylor was reassigned to edit the *Times and Seasons,* while Willard Richards continued as Church historian and recorder. Church organization in the United States and Canada was expanded. . . . In Nauvoo and surrounding settlements, teachers in the Aaronic Priesthood were urged to visit the homes of the Saints regularly . . ."

Arrington, Leonard J., *Brigham Young American Moses* Chicago (Illinois University of Illinois Press, Urbana and Chicago, 1985), 122. "The Mormons' enemies demanded both the repeal of the charter and the disbandment of the Nauvoo legion. When the Illinois legislature revoked the charter, on January 24, 1845, the Mormons were left without police protection or a civil government."

Whether Naamah and Brother Twiss ever exchanged letters is unknown.

Woollacott, "John Law ... and Reuben Law", 65. "Susan Marie Carter, born Sharon 19 Aug. 1825; died Peterborough 26 Feb.

1910 age 84 years 6 months 7 days; married Thomas S. Nichols [29 March 1846]"

--, 64 – 65. The six children of Billings and Elizabeth (Law) Carter are listed.

Robinson, "George Washington Taggart", 4 – 5. "On August 21, 1844, Henry wrote to Albert: "We rec'd your letter yesterday and I was glad to hear that you was well and that [you] was again to start for Nauvoo so soon . . . If you go to Nauvoo, I want you to fetch Mother back with you and I want you to write as soon as you get there and let us know how you prosper. You must be careful and not let them put a knife into you." On March 5, 1845, George wrote to Albert: "We were very much gratified to hear that you were yet in existence, and so near at hand. My health is now pretty good, Mother also and my little daughter Eliza Ann are in comfortable health, although they have both been sick 3 months each the past winter. "My wife [Harriet] has ceased to live. She now lies in the grave by the side of Father and Oliver. She died Feb 19th, after a lingering illness of 6 months. I think my lot has been one of sorrow and tribulation since I come to Nauvoo but I do not feel like complaining for sorrow and perplexity is the common lot of mankind here in this life. I am glad that you are intending to come to Nauvoo for I want to see you very much. As you intend coming up in the month of April, don't fail to be here by the 6th, for there is to be a general Conference to commence on the 6th, and if you will be here at that time, it will be the greatest treat that you ever had."

Whether Albert journeyed with Naamah is unknown.

Chapter Twenty-five

Nauvoo Land and Records, John Saunderson [sic] Twist [sic] File 24669 list property Wells; Block 26 Lot 2 W/2 part. Early Mormon Records page 283. This block is three blocks east of the temple on Mulholland.

The descriptions in this chapter are based in part on the author's July 2016 Nauvoo visit. Maps and images of Old Nauvoo are available at: http://www.historicnauvoo.net/.

Nauvoo Land and Records, Henry Jolley File 16732 "Married Francis Manning 23 Jan 1806, Pitt, North Carolina USA, married Susannah Law 4 May 1845 Hancock, Illinois"

Chapter Twenty-six

Young, *Temple Record Book*. "John Sanderson Twiss birth: 21 June 1820 Rindge, Cheshire, N.H. marriages: Naamah K. J. Carter of Peterboro, N. H. 30 May 1845 Nauvoo, Hancock, Ill, by whom: Brigham Young, witness: Ormus Bates, William Cutler, Death: 10 Sept 1845 Nauvoo, Hancock, Ill."

Where John and Naamah were married is unknown.

Robinson, "George Washington Taggart", 5. "There is evidence that George worked on the Nauvoo Temple, sometimes taking his young daughter Eliza Ann with him. He'd make a bed in a wheelbarrow and care for her the best he could while he worked."

Chapter Twenty-seven

Crockwell, James H., *Pictures and Biographies of Brigham Young and His Wives (*Salt Lake City, F. W. Gardiner Co., 1896), 15-16. "MARY ANN ANGELL. The second wife of Brigham Young, daughter of James and Phoebe Morton Angell. She was born June 8th, 1803 . . . Every one of President Young's wives loved Mother Young, as Mary Ann was fondly termed. . ."

--, 17-18. "LUCY DECKER Lucy Decker, Brigham Young's third wife . . . She bore seven children, as follows: Heber, born June 19th, 1845 . . ."

--, 22-23. "EMILY DOW PARTRIDGE . . . After the Prophet Joseph's death, Sister Emily was sealed to Brigham Young, September, 1844 . . . She is the mother of seven children, who rank in age as follows; Edward P., born October 30th, 1845 . . . "

Chapter Twenty-eight

Robinson, "George Washington Taggart", 6. "On July 12, 1845, George married Fannie Parks of Livonia, New York and Fannie adopted seventeen-month-old Eliza Ann as her own child. Fannie wrote in her autobiography: "While I was in Nauvoo, I became acquainted with George Washington Taggart, and . . . was married to him by Father John Smith, the prophet's uncle."

Young, *Temple Record Book.* "John Sanderson Twiss . . .
Death: 10 Sept 1845 Nauvoo, Hancock, Ill."

Chapter Twenty-nine

Arrington, *Brigham Young,* 124 – 125. "Brigham reported on
September 15 [1845] that forty-four buildings had been destroyed . .
. The terrified Saints . . . fled to Nauvoo, and 134 teams and wagons
were sent . . . to aid in the evacuation. . . . and some Mormon men
were murdered and their wives and daughters raped."

Crockwell, *Brigham Young and His Wives,* 22-23 "EMILY
DOW PARTRIDGE . . . After having resided with them [Joseph and
Emma] about a year, the principal of plural, or celestial marriage
was made known to them, and Emma Smith, wife of the Prophet
Joseph Smith, selected Emily and Eliza [Emily's sister] as wives in
the celestial, or plural order of marriage, and gave them to her
husband, Joseph Smith."

Nauvoo Land and Records, Henry Jolley File 16732
Property: Block 18, lot 3, tenant. Block 2, Lot 3, tenant. Both blocks
are north of Temple and near where Naamah was living.

Whether Susanna was living with Brother Jolley or with
George's family is unknown.

Chapter Thirty

Arrington, *Brigham Young*, 124 -125. "He [Brigham] advised the Saints to prepare for a siege: . . . Governor Ford felt there was little he could do in the face of overwhelming public sentiment against the Mormons. . . Brigham and the Twelve were joined by a committee sent by the governor, consisting of Judge Stephen A. Douglas; Major General John J. Hardin, commander of the Illinois State Militia; and two others. By noon of October 1 the following agreement had been reached: . . . "

--------------------------------, 125 "The October 1845 general conference was held, for the first time, in the nearly completed temple."

Crockett, David R., "The Nauvoo Temple: 'A Monument of the Saints'", 1. "In August 1840, Joseph Smith announced to the Church members in Nauvoo that the time had again come to build a temple. On 19 January 1841, he recorded a revelation from the Lord commanding the Saints to 'build a house to my name'."

---, 4. "On 5 October 1845, general conference was held in the temple. The windows were in, temporary floors laid, pulpits constructed, and seats brought in. Brigham Young dedicated the partially completed temple 'as a monument of the Saints'."

Church History: Chapter Twenty-Four. " . . . Brigham Young opened the services of the day by a dedicatory prayer, presenting the Temple, thus far completed, as a monument of the saints' liberality, fidelity, and faith, concluding: 'Lord, we dedicate this house and ourselves, to thee.' The day was occupied most agreeably in hearing instructions and teachings . . . and whose motto is: 'HOLINESS TO THE LORD'. "

History of the Church, 7:247. "Sunday, October 5, 1845 Nauvoo, Illinois: There was a severe frost overnight. The leaves were turning yellow on this very historic day in Nauvoo when the first public meeting was held in the Nauvoo Temple."

"Norton Jacob Autobiography", 15. "Norton Jacob recorded that Elder Taylor stated that he would feel to rejoice when he had got beyond the bounds of the Christians for he would not then have to carry his six-shooter in his pocket all the time as he had since the blood suckers tried to suck his blood in Carthage Jail."

Chapter Thirty-one

History of the Church, 7:457, 66. "Monday, October 6, 1845 . . . In the afternoon, Elder Parley P. Pratt addressed the Saints. He discussed why the Saints were building houses and a temple even though they planned to leave the city. 'The people of God always were required to make sacrifices, and if we have a sacrifice to make, [I am] in favor of its being something worthy of the people of God.' Nauvoo would be left as a monument to the people. 'The people must enlarge in numbers and extend their borders; they cannot always live in one city, nor in one county. . . . In short, this people are fast approaching that point which ancient prophets have long since pointed out as the destiny of the saints of the last days.'"

History of the Church, 7:470, 81. "Wednesday, October 8, 1845 . . . At 2 p.m., the conference reconvened. The choir sang, "The Spirit of God Like a Fire is Burning." . . . Elder George A. Smith expressed concern that too many guns were being fired and powder wasted. You cannot wake up in the night, but you hear them cracking away. You can hardly walk the streets, but sometimes a bullet will whistle over your head. Men say they are afraid their guns won't go off, it is wet; then I am in favor of getting something to draw (the charge from) them; I hope there will be no more firing."

Hartley, William G., "The Pioneer Trek: Nauvoo to Winter Quarters". "Instructions for the trek asked people to bring enough food per wagon for five adults or the equivalent, which means that, adding children, each wagon on average probably had six people assigned to it. With six per wagon, 2,500 wagons would assist about 15,000 people. Some doubling up of friends, relatives, or single adults was expected. By 23 November 1845, reports indicated that 3,285 families were organized for the trek—800 more families than wagons."

Proctor, Scot and Maurine, "The Expulsion from Nauvoo" (excerpted from The Gathering: Mormon Pioneers on the Trail to Zion July 23, 2015). " . . . Speculators knew that property was in abundance in Nauvoo and that buyers were few. The Saints, forced to sell, were selling cheap, and since little money was in circulation, they took most of their pay in trade. 'As a stranger passes through,' the reporter observed, he will find himself frequently beset, mostly by women and children, with inquiries, 'Do you wish to purchase a house and lot? Do you wish to buy a farm?' Then the stranger would 'be pressed and entreated to go and examine, and all the advantages [and] cheapness' of the property would 'be fully explained.' . . . Heber C. Kimball was one of the fortunate whose lovely brick home brought six hundred dollars, mostly in goods, but as time wore on buyers were rare. . . . 'In the city, houses and lots are selling at from two to five and ten hundred dollars, which must have cost the owners double that sum. They are willing to sell for cash, or oxen or cattle, or to exchange for such articles of merchandise as they can barter or carry away with them'."

Woollacott, "John Law ... and Reuben Law", 62. "SUSANNA LAW, born Sharon 10 Oct. 1786; baptized Acton 4 Feb. 1787; died Nauvoo, Ill., 21 Oct. 1845."

Chapter Thirty-two

Arrington, *Brigham Young,* 126. "Late in November 1845, special rooms in the temple's attic story were plastered and painted and borrowed carpets laid. Brigham and Heber placed the curtains their wives had made in the windows. On November 30 there was a dedication, and ten days later, the first group of Saints passed through the endowment ceremony . . . . Thereafter, 'temple work', the performance of ordinances for the living and the dead, proceeded night and day, without interruption. Brigham noted . . . he had been giving himself 'entirely to the work of the Lord in the Temple. Almost night and night I have spent . . . but seldom ever allowing myself . . . of going home once a week. . . . By then [February before the exodus] the ordinances had been administered to more than five thousand people'."

--------------------------------, 126 – 127. "The first [threat] was an indictment against Brigham Young and eight other apostles . . . Government officials tried to serve the warrants, but failed when William Miller put on Brigham's overcoat and cap and left the temple where the apostles were gathered and stepped into the president's carriage. The waiting marshals arrested Miller and took him to Carthage before they discovered that they had only a 'bogus

Brigham'. The other threat, probably unfounded but accepted as genuine at the time, was the warning by Governor Ford and others that federal troops in St. Louis were planning to intercept the Mormons and destroy them."

Chapter Thirty-three

Johnson, Jeffery Ogden, "Determining and Defining 'Wife': The Brigham Young Household", *Dialogue: A Journal of Mormon Thought Vol 20, No. 3* (Fall 1987), 57 – 61. "In the five week period 7 January to 6 February 1846, Brigham Young was married to nineteen women . . . Fourteen of his nineteen wives had been married before and seven were significantly older, including Phoebe Morton Angel, the mother of Mary Ann Angel [Brigham's second wife] (then fifty-nine), and Abigail Marks Works (then sixty-nine), the mother of his first wife, Miriam Works."

Johnson, "Determining and Defining 'Wife' ", 65 -69. "Table 1 Wives of Brigham Young . . . [wife #] 3. 1842 June 14 Lucy Ann Decker, 1822 – 90 [other husband] (1) William Seeley . . . [wife #] 7. 1844 Sept. Emily Dow Partridge, 1822 – 99 (1) Joseph Smith . . . 27. 1846 . . . Jan 28, [wife #] 28. Jemima Angel, 1803 – 69 (1) Valentine Young . . . [wife #] 29. . . . 1846 Jan. 28 Phebe Morton, 1776 – 1854 . . . [wife #] 31. 1846 Jan. 31 Mary Eliza Nelson 1812 – 85 (1) John P. Greene (3) Bruce I. Philips . . . [wife #] 39 1846 Feb. 6 Naamah Carter, 1821 – 1909 (1) John S. Twiss."

Robinson, "George Washington Taggart", 7 – 9, "George Taggart left on February 17th in the Company commanded by John Scott. . . About the 1st of June, George and all but five or six of his companions headed for Mt. Pisgah, arriving about the 10th. 'Scotts Company stoped [sic] here 8 or 10 days in which time I received a letter from My Wife stateing [sic] that She expected to start from Nauvoo about 1st of July with Brother B Mills with worn [sic] I had Made a contract to this effect before I left Nauvoo,'. . . "

Johnson, "Determining and Defining 'Wife' ", 61. "Brigham Young wrote in his diary on 12 January 1846, "I gave myself up entirely to the work of the Lord in the temple almost night & day. I have spent [sic] not taking more than 4 hours upon an average out of 24 to sleep & but seldom ever allowing myself the the [sic] time & opportunity of going home once in a week . . ."

Young, *Temple Record Book*. "N.K.J.C. [Naamah Kendall Jenkins Carter] Twiss Sealed to Pres. Brigham Young 6th January 1846 in Nauvoo, Ill. By Heber C. Kimball".

The date of Naamah's marriage to Brigham Young is uncertain. Her temple book has 6th of January while other sources have the 26th of January and 6th of February.

Chapter Thirty-four

Arrington, *Brigham Young,* 127. ". . . The first group . . . crossed the Mississippi on February 4. In succeeding days several hundred left and assembled in temporary camps in Iowa. Brigham, who had remained behind to help administer endowments to Saints who begged him to do it, crossed with his wagons the evening of February 15 . . . Brigham's contingent consisted of fifteen wagons, and fifty members of his family. . . On February 24 the temperature dropped to twelve degrees below zero, freezing over the Mississippi and permitting great caravans to cross on the ice."

It is unknown if Naamah left on February 15th with Elder Young.

Young, Emily (Dow) (Partridge) (Smith), "Autobiography of Emily D. P. Young" (Woman's Exponent 13, 1884). "Far West, Caldwell County, Missouri, January, 1839 . . . We were set down on the banks of the Mississippi River, opposite Quincy, and were again houseless and homeless, wandering in the cold and bleak winter weather, with scanty food and clothing. We pitched our tents and waited for an opportunity to cross the river. There were several families of Saints there when we arrived, and they were continually coming, so the bank of the river was dotted with tents, now the only home of the again exiled Saints. The wagons bringing families were unloaded and taken back for more of the Saints. When we crossed the river it was partly on the ice and partly in the ferry boat. The shore on the Quincy side of the river was lined with the inhabitants of that place, to witness the crossing over of the Mormon outcasts even the exiled Saints in midwinter. Perhaps many thought they were a strange people, or some kind of animals; not human beings like themselves, subject to sorrow and pain, cold and hunger and distress. In all our wanderings and being driven, we have had to go out in the cold winter months, and the suffering of the people must have been very great. Children could not sense the awful reality of the situation as older ones did, on whose shoulders the burden rested. I sometimes look back upon those scenes with horror, and wonder how the Saints did continue to endure, time after time, such heartless cruelties. But many could not endure, and so found an early grave."

Chapter Thirty-five

Arrington, *Brigham Young,* 330 – 331. "Lucy, who was an excellent cook, presided over the Lion House kitchen from the time it was built in 1856 until 1860 when she moved into the Beehive to entertain the official guests. The childless 'Aunt' Twiss then took over the Lion House kitchen and directed it until after Brigham's death. . . At family dinners, usually at five-thirty, Brigham sat at the head of the table, Eliza Snow at his right, Twiss at his left, and each family, as a unit, with assigned places around a long table."

Crockwell, *Brigham Young and His Wives*, 28. ". . . Sister Twiss was married to Brigham Young for time January 26, 1846. She moved . . . to Salt Lake Valley, in 1848, where she still resides. Sister Naamah has done great work for the redemption of the dead . . . She is also treasurer for the Relief Society of the eighteenth ward, in which she resides, and is honored and respected by all who know her. She is rather small in stature, of fair complexion, kind and affectionate, genial in disposition, and devoted to the principals of the Gospel as revealed through Joseph Smith . . ."

Robinson, "George Washington Taggart", 10 – 29. "So at the age of twenty-nine, George Washington Taggart enlisted in Company B in the Mormon Battalion, one of five hundred men who set out between July 16 and July 22, 1846 to commence an unparalleled march of two thousand miles on foot through the barren deserts and across the mountains of the Southwest to California. George enlisted as a Musician, a Fifer, playing a fife he made himself. . . The battalion members would suffer greatly from sickness, thirst, starvation, mistreatment, even death, but as promised by Brigham Young, 'would not have any fighting to do.' . . . George hoped to take his family to the 'Great Valley of the Salt Lake' in the Spring of 1849 or 1850. They left in July 1852: George, Fannie, Eliza Ann, and three more children, Harriet Maria, George Henry, and Charles Wallace. They reached the valley on October 17, 1852 almost five years to the day from when George arrived there for the first time . . . He worked as a carpenter, joiner, and millwright assisting in the building of a number of grist mill . . . He also worked on the Salt Lake Temple. At the age of forty, George entered into plural marriage with Clarissa in December of 1856. Together they had twelve children including two sets of twins. . . George Washington Taggart died on June 3, 1893, at the age of seventy-six."

Church History, "The Nauvoo Temple: Destruction and Rebirth", available at: https://history.lds.org/article/museum-treasures-nauvoo-temple-in-ruins-lithograph?lang=eng. "Then, on October 9, 1848, fire destroyed the temple. The History of Hancock County describes the scene: 'About 3 o'clock (in the morning) fire was discovered in the cupola. It had made but little headway when first seen, but spread rapidly, and in a very short period the lofty spire was a mass of flame, shooting high in the air, and illuminating a wide extent of country. It was seen for miles away. The citizens gathered around, but nothing could be done to save the structure. It was entirely of wood except the walls, and nothing could have stopped the progress of the flames. In two hours, and before the sun dawned upon the earth, the proud structure, reared at so much cost— an anomaly in architecture, and a monument of religious zeal—stood with four blackened and smoking walls only remaining.' In 1849 the Icarians, a French communal group, purchased the charred superstructure in hopes of renovating it for use as a school. After the tornado in 1850 rendered the walls unsalvageable, they abandoned their project.... at the April 1999 general conference, President

Gordon B. Hinckley made the dramatic announcement that the Nauvoo Temple would be rebuilt."

 My Four Legged Stool

www.ingramcontent.com/pod-product-compliance
Lightning Source LLC
Chambersburg PA
CBHW030249270626
47156CB00021B/296